Swiss Cheese

Ziyad Elgaid

Edition 1 published in 2022

Independently published
Copyright © 2022 Ziyad Elgaid

Paperback ISBN : 979-8-35281-767-4

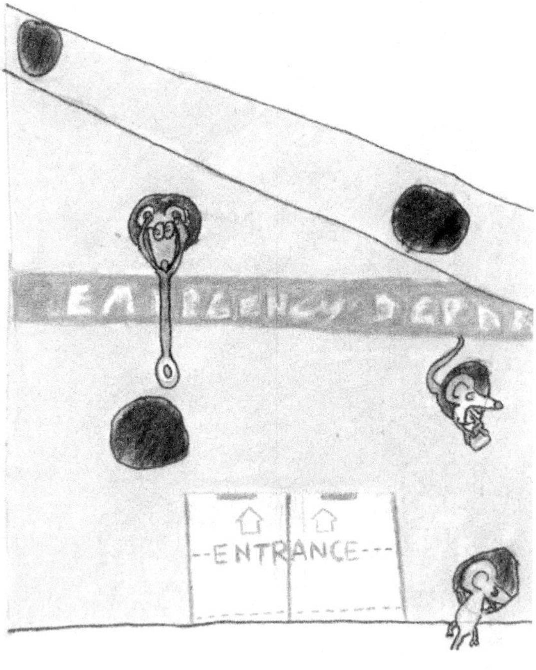
ENTRANCE

The Swiss cheese model: The Swiss cheese model of accident causation, is a model used in risk analysis and risk management, including aviation safety, engineering, healthcare, emergency service organisations and as the principle behind layered security, as used in computer security and defence in depth[1]. In the Swiss Cheese Model, an organisation's defences against failure are modelled as a series of barriers, represented as slices of the cheese. The holes in the cheese slices, represent individual weaknesses in individual parts of the system and are continually varying in size and position in all slices[2]. In summary the lining up of several individual errors leads to a systemic failure.

1

https://en.wikipedia.org/wiki/Swiss_cheese_model

2

https://www.skybrary.aero/index.php/James_Reason_HF_Model

"There is nothing holier than **Swiss Cheese**"
- Some might say.

Many thanks to all those who I have met and all those who supported me throughout my life and who have given me inspiration through the years. Each person's story contributing to this book and to the person I am.

Special thanks to those who without their support I couldn't have written this.
The Hun Bun
Landlord Nurse
The Hairy Araf

Prologue

He was finding it harder and harder with each passing year to stay awake during the meetings. It didn't help that the summer sun beamed through the window and made his head feel like a frying pan. Although every time he did stay awake, he was harassed by a burning feeling in his chest, guilt or indigestion, both had been there for years. The indigestion only started getting worse over the last few months. Logically he knew the meetings did make a small difference but emotionally he was checked out. He always wondered if this was burnout or if it was just his personality. Over the years One thing had changed for sure, he wasn't the same person he was when he was 25, despite what science said about the brain stopping its frontal lobe (personality area) at that age.

"Let's talk about the streamlining of budgets and our new referral pathway for vascular and cardiothoracic surgery."

He should and would probably care if another service was removed from his hospital.

"Yeah I believe the Royal will take on the service and we have a pathway where you bleep[3] their team for advice and send patients across if they require their input. Remember they are also planning an emergency clinic with slots that can be referred to."

He goes to speak up but then realises that anything he did complain about would amount to him saying; - *I am angry another service has been cut.*
15 years ago, he might have said something. However nowadays he never rocked the runaground boat.

A few half hours passed by, and a few more dull voices answered each other - *Who'd have thought change could sound so monotonous.*

"Good now it's all agreed, we can call this meeting to a close."

Everyone stood up, he watched them before slowly following behind, like a passenger wanting to leave the flight which had become too claustrophobic. He sighed and closed his eyes before looking up at a coming shadow.

---

[3] Bleep – to page someone

The shadow was called Dr Bethany Anderson. She always wore high heels, a small pencil skirt and a blouse with a pattern, to add a little vulnerability to her appearance. She was a go-getter, and had never been hindered by anyone, not even her husband who was a "stay at home" trophy GP. The second less known Dr Anderson.

"Hey Abdul, old dog,"

He winced at the term *old dog*, he had a feeling it was more aggressive than endearing, although he was certain she would say different if ever put on trial.

"Hey Dr Anderson, productive meeting by the sounds of it."

"You were there *old dog*, don't need to say by the sound of it, although I'm glad they took on board the emergency clinic idea, I feel you got to listen to us a lot, who bloody keep it running right!"

"Yeah probably, but that would imply we know best."
"So sarcastic Abdul as always. It gives you a bit of character at least, compared to the

bozos running this place." She laughed at her own joke, but with so much confidence it's hard for him at least, not to smile.

She looks at him again, staring at his head, a little intently, "first grey and now balding, surely the wife has something to say, or are you just that funny."

He thought her next line would always be "anyone can laugh someone to bed" and "that was the power of comedy, communicating or manipulation;" - or whatever you called those talents. He called it - getting people to do what you want. Not that he could act as a saint as he has done the same.

"She tolerates me, my cooking helps, you know me, I don't abide by gender stereotypes."

"How PC of you!" She laughed again and he reluctantly joined in, despite willing his body not to. She got him.
"Look Abdul, I think you need to help the department out. I got us some new Fy1s[4]

---

[4] Fy1 - Foundation year 1 doctors, the first year after graduating medical school. Usually a broad, non-specialized, training scheme

starting here, you know us DGH[5]'s we don't get many spare doctors and I believe getting them here young is how we get them loving our specialty, before they know any better. So I think and have decided you should be the lead. I mean we are looking for you to contribute something to the department that wasn't from fifteen years ago."

He smiled again, sighed, nodded and realised with all this he must look like a tired monk. He had long had the appearance of one anyway. "Yeah, I guess I could be, I feel sorry for them."

"Sorry for a bunch of riff raff who are here to provide a service and fall in love with us. It's a dream. Like I said they also won't know any better! Plus, to be taught by a pioneer of emergency medicine and simulation. When I was young, I would respect that. I mean, I did respect that."

---

[5] DGH - District General Hospital - a hospital providing secondary care only with no official partnered Medical School. Usually smaller in nature in comparison to teaching and tertiary centre hospitals

"When we were young you mean, well, no, of course I'll get myself prepared." He stumbled in response.

She laughed at his statement, probably to make him feel at ease or because she was a nice person. Paranoia had slowly started to creep into his life, now that made him smile. He always imagined he would be the crazy paranoid demented fool no one could handle in his elderly age.

She clopped off and he couldn't help looking. He was after all a terrible man and that's what terrible men do when confronted with powerful women. After his moment of weakness, he walked onwards.

As he arrived at his office, he looked at his plaque. Which now was covered in dust and no longer gleamed like it used to do in the neon lighting at the department.

He read it internally:
Mr. Abdul AbuRahman Assem, FRCEM[6], MRCP[7], PHD, MRCS[8], Directorate of

---

[6] FRCEM - fellowship of Royal college of emergency medicine (title given after finishing the exams and training to be a specialist in

Education and simulation at Darthington River District General Hospital.

---

emergency medicine)
[7] MRCP - membership royal college of physicians (title after sitting the physician board exams)
[8] MRCS - membership royal college of surgeons title after sitting the board exams (this title allows you to have Mr instead of Dr)

Chapter 1: Marmite sandwiches

She always made marmite sandwiches. It was her ritual. It took seconds and she loved them, something she was sure the advertisers were glad to hear. Given she was vegan the spreadable fillings were the way forward.

It was always a talking point to let her be *the butt of the jokes*. She self-identified herself as a passive communicator and didn't mind it. Those who talked too much, in her mind, didn't actually have that much to add. It was arrogant to think, but she knew she was right.

This was her first time living on her own and the morning wake up was easy, with everything ready and no issues in the kitchen. She had her coco pops - okay maybe not the "mature" student meal, but good for carbohydrate and sugar release. She had a cup of breakfast or builders' tea and walked in the summer with no breeze.

The full summer sun beat down, slowly crisping her fair skin. She liked it but it got too hot in august, far too hot. She hoped a cooler breeze would come to help her and her easily friable skin out. She didn't want to be lobster red on her first day.

Today, the first day of a real job after nine years at university doing two degrees and being a so-called "mature student". She felt like she did as a young girl, starting high school.
She compared herself to a cheddar cheese. Ready to be sliced on top of the crackers which was the emergency department of Darthington hospital. Not forgetting the chutney of patients which would arrive and be cured by her now nine years of knowledge.

The thing is she knew her stuff, she wanted to be different from medical school. She wished to be no longer placid, still thoughtful, but not always *the butt of jokes*, sometimes the front butt of jokes (or vagina of jokes given her feministic view). On the other hand, it's hard to change past 25, especially after the frontal lobe has fully developed.

She'd already met a few of her colleagues at the welcome event and also some of her Seniors, her SHOs[9]. Everyone seemed

---

[9] SHO - Senior house officer an old term for

pleasant and she had a good feeling about a smaller hospital away from any of the big smoke, away from ego and arrogance. She liked them. No one had been inappropriate. No one had put her down and everyone was "happy to help".

Although upon arrival she had doubts about the word "small" being used to describe the hospital. She saw the long building that kept going and going.

The main entrance in the middle of a criss-cross of corridors splitting the department like fans at a football game. She looked up at the signs with different colours and looked down to see that she was meant to follow her team's colour. *Come on you reds-* she joked to herself.

An elderly man walked around her and looked. He smiled, "hello young pretty one, d'ya need help?"
It irked her that she had to be defined as a pretty one, not smart or intelligent. She felt a small vein pop up on her forehead, waiting a second it subsided, looking up and smiling at

---

anyone who had finished their pre-registration year, anyone after finishing the fy1 up till specialist registrar

15

the volunteer, "no worries I got it, red's my favourite colour."
She walked with a mixture of nervousness but upbeat confidence. She never thought that the combination would ever be a possibility.

Along the red line road, she passed by what she assumed would be her many colleagues to come. People dressed in blue with theatre hats indicating they did *the fixing*. Those dressed in smart shirts and chinos with a lanyard and stethoscope indicated they did *the thinking*. Those in tweed or just jeans and colourful shirts showing they did *the accepting*. Finally, the thousands of different coloured scrub-like uniforms (the non-doctors) showing they did the actual hard work.

The doors almost swung in her face, she managed to dodge them. She looked up to see the department was down behind the swinging doors. It felt real, she could hear all the beeping. It felt like casualty or ER but even more real than television because, her included - no one was as attractive as George Clooney.

"Hey eyes up here," a voice bellowed from in front of her. It was a chap dressed in an odd way. She looked upwards to see what could only be described as a genetically chosen face through years of breeding, with the top in society. A little horsey but not too horsey. He wore a pinstripe suit and ted baker shirt which screamed. "I'm better than you and I look good whilst doing it."

Although she did note a slight nervousness in his overall George Osborne stance.

"I don't want to have to report you to HR for that, do I!" He boisterously bellowed.

"Umm, no probably not, I guess," she was a bit taken aback by his mix of nervous stance and confident voice.

"Richard Twain, new to the emergency department. Y'know an ED doc, charmed." He laughed which made her wonder if he knew that he was a satire of himself.

"Isabella McCullen, I'm one of the new Fy1's here, I guess it's nice to meet you?"

"Brilliant, we gotta stick together don't we. Proper siege mentality against the oldies telling us off."

This was his confirmation to her that he was another Fy1. Although the fact he didn't say that outright said a lot about him. In summary, what it said to her was that he was a twat.

"So, I think we were meant to meet a consultant to get our final words before we go and sort out everything they can't," he bellowed again.

Wincing, she wondered if he had an inside voice.

She stared at him then looked away. He seemed to be a little shifty. She wondered what he was thinking about, probably the next line to bellow out to try and exert himself more in the conversation. An aggressive communicator, no doubt. Just before he was about to lurch jaw forward, another body blocked his direct eye contact from her. Guess god was up there, and he didn't just listen to people who sacrificed goats.

Both of them stared at what was in front of them. It was a 20 something brunette, with green eyes. Although to describe her beyond that was difficult as she wore the blue scrubs which gave her the same body shape as everyone else who did. The only other identifier was the lanyard with aggressive block capitals describing her role, **"foundation year 1"** it shouted from her neck. Beneath the loud lanyard was a small ID badge which if you stared at long enough read- *Rachel Amis, Foundation Doctor Emergency directorate.*

"Hey guys, nice to meet. This looks fun." She smiled and the room suddenly felt easier. She watched Rachel continue to speak, feeling the colour become green from red or orange. Rachel was an effective communicator.

"So just because I've figured it out by staring enough, you guys are Richard and Isabella. Now that's far too long for us to say so I imagine Rich, and Izzy are acceptable? If not, I can sometimes go *prim and proper!*" Rachel used both her Liverpudlian accent and fake posh English accent.
It made it easy for Izzy to smile, which weirdly made her feel unsure. She responded with the juxtaposition in her… "Yeah friends always call me Izzy. So go for it."
Richard took a moment before saying, "Rich is what mommy calls me, but I guess I can let it slide. I am Freudian after all".

The tone was lowered, and she now knew exactly what to watch out for. Which at least made her grateful for his straightforwardness.

"Also, not to be bossy, but let me show you the changing rooms. We get to wear scrubs. Isn't that exciting?" Rachel politely exclaimed. Which was an impressive feat.

She nodded and followed her with Richard in tow. Now to remember the corridors in a department is the first task of being a newbie and then the codes to the doors. This is where the wheat gets separated from the chaff in the hospital. Who's the most useful person, the one with the information of the door codes; everyone knew knowledge was power.

They arrived as Rachel said out loud, giving information to everyone. She almost disliked the naivety in which Rachel presented herself. "1066y for the boys and 8008x for us ladies." There was an expectant pause as Rachel waited for her and Richard to write down the numbers. She unfurled her small notebook which was plastered with some drug company name on it and slowly wrote it down. She glanced quickly over to Richard and realised he would obviously remember the battle of Hastings, like every "*proper Englishman*" did.

"So, shall I meet you guys out here when you're ready and then we can mosey as a full-blown team to the consultant's office." Rachel kept the nice flow going.

They nodded and into the locker room she headed, feeling like she was back at high school as captain of the tennis team. After all she wouldn't be a medic now without being captain of something.

The lighting flickered as she stepped in. She awaited any voice. Once the silence had been obvious, she was able to let her mind relax. No need for conversation, she'll have plenty of that during her first day.

The lighting flickered once more before the intense glow revealed to her the two showers; row of toilets and just beyond that lockers in different states of condition. Some destroyed, some used, some with bronze placards and some with a sticky label reading very non-descriptive Anne, Anna, or Annie. She wondered if she would get a locker. She would probably go for a coloured label at least, her being original and all. She smiled before reaching the scrubs shelves, all stacked with different sizes. Well, any size medium and above. That was for tops, trousers only seemed to exist in large in this changing room. This showed two things to her:
1. Everyone must have a healthy waistline in ED.
2. She was going to have to improvise sizes and convince her body to keep the scrubs on.

She dressed in the medium top which was pinned at the top with hair clips to keep some decency for her collar bones. The trousers hiked up like Simon Cowell and tightened with a bowline knot to keep them up no matter wind or rain.
She looked at the mirror and realised without her blonde hair she felt indistinguishable to Rachel. Which was comforting to her.

She stepped into the corridor and was greeted by her two colleagues.

Richard had dressed in scrubs a little too tight and she wondered if they should have swapped sizes. However, Rachel willed them along, towards the loud bleeps they went and hurried along past lots of smiling workers who, whilst looking nice, seemed preoccupied with the pieces of paper they all held. Different colours of paper to indicate that they were doing something special and different to everyone else.

Arriving now the sign in front of the three was difficult to read as it had long lost any shine to it. She noticed that all three of them were squinting.

Mr Abdul AbuRahman Assem, FRCEM, MRCP, PHD, MRCS, Directorate of Education and simulation at Darthington River District General Hospital. She imagined their minds read in unison.

It sounded scary and very proper, and she became more and more aware that this was her first day and she was small and insignificant. She felt her placidness crush her a little, her shoulders felt heavier.

One breath hold and exhalation later and they were inside. Stood like insects in front of this so-called director, consultant and many letters owning man. Whilst the words didn't match his looks, she noted that the dusty and dullness of the placard itself did.

"Hello, welcome, hey," He nodded whilst repeating three different greetings.

His nod revealed his greying balding hair. She wondered if, as he got wiser, did his hair go greyer, because if that's the case, she should listen to his every word.
She looked around; it was nice to see that the collective room anxiety had begun to suffocate all of them.

"So Fy1, or House officer, (HO)[10] or whatever pre-registration is called now. It is a new job to come to this Emergency Department. So, I'm here to be the... steamroller to make roads smoother."
She noted his analogy was meant to comfort, but steam roller had its own terrifying connotations.

He looked at all three of them and she could feel his raised eyebrow in an almost comforting way. The eyebrow and steamroller caused her neck to stiffen in emotional whiplash.

"Now I think we need an introduction and the hot drinks preferences. You have to wait for the next night out for alcoholic preferences." He smiled a tired smile back at her. The bags under his eyes showing up a little more along with his crow's feet. The room felt like it was now under a much softer lighting.

"I'm Isabella, Fy1, and I like tea with some milk but strong, no sugar, never coffee!" she

---

[10] House officer HO - old name for Foundation year 1 doctor (the pre-registration year) the first year as a doctor after university.

blurted, feeling her placid self-take the reins submitting to the tired smile.

She watched him shift the gaze to Richard. He also couldn't help but reply in the same way she had done. Although in her opinion he could have used his inside voice.
"Richard Twain, Fy1 sir, at your, err, com, no... service. Coffee and milk please!"

Finally, she watched the consultant gaze shift one last time and the smiles of both Rachel and his met, no placidly this time.
"Rachel and I'll have whatever you're in mood for, mostly coffee though with sugar if that's allowed."

She watched his eyes dart between them with a smile which grew extenuating further how tired he looked.

"Sounds good, let's show you the staff room and see if I can fulfil those orders."

*

They followed like privates to a general. In step, in time, their slavery to the hierarchy most likely driving this. She realised that the word consultant made her act like this, ever since she started at medical school. They were these weird non-human creatures, who had all the answers. They never faltered and they had the superpower of not worrying about anything. It also felt that if you dared anger them then Dante's inferno would appear in front of you. It made her wonder, what happens when you transform into a consultant and what would lead her to be that all knowing other worldly spirit. She imagined the cocoon of years of training which would eclipse her. Would she be a moth or butterfly?

Her stomach rumbled, or maybe she would just be a hungry hungry caterpillar.

Her thoughts brought abruptly back to reality as Dr Abdul raising an eyebrow and looking at her rumbling stomach said - "don't worry we have biscuits and pot noodles here".

Smiles all round as the door opened to a brightly lit room, so brightly lit it shone like heaven's doors in comparison to the corridor they had stepped out of.

She noticed the *all mod cons* staff room. White Plastering with a Russell Hobbs microwave and kettle. The toaster bore that branding too. The TV was mounted above quietly trying to remind people a world existed outside the hospital.

She watched the drinks being made and handed out one by one with an efficiency that only someone of vast experience could pull off. She noted his memory must be great because each drink came out exactly as asked for. All three of them held their mugs sheepishly and before he began talking, he offered her the biscuit tin, more sheepishly so much more she felt like a lamb, she reached out and grabbed a biscuit. With her crunching away, the lecture began.

"So welcome to the emergency department, my name is Dr Aseem or Abdul. Never Mr. I am here to support you through this adventure, although there will be hoops to navigate, the first being the start of placement meetings. I'm meant to leave that to you, empowering proactiveness is what you need as a doctor, or so they say. I imagine us old schoolers are meant to preach; speak when spoken to, so that we don't lose any of our power." He chuckled, the joke becoming obvious with his laughter. She imagined his laughter taking physical form holding a "laughter" neon sign to his audience.

"Now you guys are supernumerary. You may be wondering what that means. Well, it means you are here to learn. You are **not** to be used to plug gaps, although you'll feel that pressure from people like me, but today I want you guys to pick up one patient and follow them. Come to me once you're done. You have got to experience what our patients go through. To me It's the most important thing."

There was no tired smile this time, to her he seemed 15 years younger with that last line. It was a brief change as he continued to talk, his demeanour reverted.

"Now enjoy the drinks and snacks and come through to Majors once you're ready, I'll find some patients for you."

He stepped out leaving them, the new lambs to walk or I guess drink in the hospital for the very first time on their own.

She noted the usual chatter over the hot drinks, almost like it was a plenty of fish bio, tinder, bumble or whatever dating apps people liked.

The questions answered below:

Where they grew up.
Where they studied, their medical interests and
Why Darthington.

As they had finished their drinks, she stepped out in front of the pack heading towards majors summarising her two colleagues behind her.

For Rachel Amis:
1. Born in a commuter village outside Liverpool she rode horses as a girl and loved it. Dad was a doctor and she wanted to be one too although a few times she almost fell off the bandwagon
2. Studied at Liverpool medical school, which was a fun experience of partying, learning and also screwing around with a few people as well as pissing them off.
3. Darthington was further from home and also what she could get two years in compared to other programs. She didn't know what she wanted to do at all, but she was
smiling and ready for everything.

For Richard Twain:
1. A London boy through and through, went to one of the private boys' schools, medicine was easy as his career guidance told him. His dad is proud as everyone else in his life who told him he was amazing.
2. Studied at Nottingham, which was well wicked, great parties.

3. His mate who he lives with is at Darthington and it's near the big city. Also, there was a good club in a factory with hot girls. The cherry, as he reminded them, was he had heard lots of young single nurses.

And finally, despite her best efforts to be more than a summary, to create a complex character she had failed, giving them and reducing herself to 3 simple points.

1. She had grown up in Warwickshire on the border between Wales and England. She had also ridden and became a doctor just because her sister seemed to enjoy it.
2. Studying in London made her realise it was diverse with lots of opportunities, but also filled with egos.
3. Leading to why Darthington, it's nice, small, near home and less egofofied (a word that could only really be looked up in the McCullen's dictionary of random amalgamated letters).

She wondered how compatible their personalities were and what values each held dear and what would be tested today by the Majors environment. They arrived and suddenly her slow thoughts crashed into the fast pace of what was going on in front of her.

30

People running around all in scrubs of different colours. Beeping going on from each bay. Complaints from everyone running left, right and centre and **the** word repeated in a chorus over and over again. Like some chanting crowd for their favourite striker. "Breach, breach, breach, breach!"

She felt her heart race. Had she been spiked by coffee in her tea, but before she could wonder anymore a piece of yellow paper was handed to her. It had many words, including patient details but the big header read "ED Clerking". The person handing the letter was the *tired smile* which seemed to slow down the pace for a moment.
"Here you go, a chap with a racing heart and chest pain. Go, see and report back."
As *the smile* disappeared, the pace returned to its pounding rhythm.

She looked at the patient details:

Jonathan Creek
54 years old,
Lymington lane, Darthington
DT2 3rr

A brief summary had been written in the strange language she had spent 5-year learning (doctor speak).
Racing heart, chest tightness on mobilising up incline, currently symptoms free ECG NAD[11].

She looked up from the paper as a nurse stood above her. The nurse's eyes told her she was definitely more senior than her, the **doctor**. It was the lack of anxiety which revealed all. Although the nurse appeared too cocksure to be really senior.
The nurse spoke up with joyful laughter, "Looks like you got a good old creek, boozer, pie eater. Probably just missed his larger piece of pie or saw United lose another game."

She felt like she wasn't actively part of the conversation even though the nurse was maintaining conversational eye contact. They were looking at her. She gave a laugh but by that time they had vanished. She stared again at cubicle 4 written next to his summary and looked ahead to meet her first patient.

As she approached the curtains that hid her first patient, she looked to the next nurse she would meet who appeared coyly from behind

---

[11] NAD – No abnormality detected.

the very strongly lit cubicle. She swore it was Celia black, she could hear the accent in her head, asking if she was ready for who was behind curtain one. She blinked and Celia disappeared, but the red headed nurse seemed un-amused by her open mouth and vacant look combination.

"I said, are you ready to see him? By the way his veins look terrible so can you please bleed him yeah? Thanks!"

She was then left again without a moment to join in with the conversations she was meant to be a part of.

She drew back the curtain and stepped in.
It went by like a first date, the patient going through his life story and like many of her first dates, she felt she had no control over the conversation which preceded her.

"Y'alright, they do make you doc's young these days, but at least pretty."

She was about to interject with her opinions about his phrasing but alas he continued.

"You see I was walking about today when I felt my heart racing and then some tightness as I started to walk up the hill. All pretty much vanished when I took a break. I'm much better now, well, apart from that last nurse being quite old if you don't mind me saying. Look I can't be blamed for her jealousy over your prettiness."

She wanted to say something, was it to ask about his vague use of tightness, or maybe to ask if he was better now why was here or maybe say something to finally stop his objectification of her and the nurse, but once again the conversation continued without her.

"You see, my dad had a dodgy ticker, and he had these problems. Then one day no more, but that was long ago, back in those bad days am I right?"
A non-rhetorical question, a chance for her to interject.
"Although I guess people did get to see their GP a lot quicker back then, coins and silver linings, right?"
A mixed metaphor, but now was the time. She felt her heart race as her lips pursed, she was going to do it. She was going to be part of a conversation with a patient.
"So, tell me a little about the tightness, what did it feel like?" - she managed to edge in quickly whilst biting her pen lid showing the patient she was thinking.

"Well, it felt like an elephant or my cousin Stevie on me. Just really crushing, but it was gone at the top of that hill."

"I'm glad," her empathy needed work, she soldered on despite this not wanting to miss her shot, "and what about your heart racing?"

"Yeah, that was at the same time, but it was gone pretty soon after."

"So, you say soon, but how long?"

"I couldn't tell you doc!"

"Was it seconds, minutes... Longer?" she replied hastily, already feeling her pen lid disintegrating under her incisors.

"Not longer than minutes, don't think so doc."

Internally she felt her temple veins bulging once again, "So I'll write minutes", through a forced smile.

"You're the doc, doc."

She scribbled as she heard repeat again about his heart and how he couldn't see the GP.

She ended up probably being flippant in her response to his blathering, "Can I examine you?"

In her interruption she had lost all her medical student skill of sitting quietly and being talked to. It was probably all the noise around her as well as the bleeping. She guessed this was what it was really like being a doctor.

He nodded and kept talking as she felt his pulses and she did have to get her librarian out with a big finger shush, to listen to his chest before checking his stomach and legs.
He of course managed to let his beer belly gurgle when he joked to her, "I wish my heart were down there, it'd have a load of protection".

"So, what now doc? A few tablets and home?" He sounded almost like he was begging.
"Let me go and look at all the information and discuss your case and we can take it from there." She tried to once again get back to her old self and let empathy be the double reed to her voice as the words left in a woodwind-like hum.
"What about the blood tests?" he smiled.
"What about the blood test...?" she replied like an echoing cave.
"They said I'd get some and I wanna go home so you'll be back quickly?"
"I won't be long, I promise", and as she hurried out of the curtain, she hadn't consciously noticed the fake promises she was already giving. It was one thing to joke about

the similarities of first dates, but to actually act like someone on a bad first date was something else.

Walking through the department, or the battlefield as others would describe it; children's party would be her choice of words. She dodged, ducked and weaved the eyes and conversations directed around and at her. She finally reached Dr Abdul, who stood at the desk like a gargoyle watching his department at work.

"Umm," her placidity had returned after a bout of suppression.
She stood waiting for the response, but the stone gargoyle didn't move.
She continued the mms and umms, until she was humming the melody of *Fur Elise*, that is when she realised that Dr Abdul was looking at her and it appeared he had been the one waiting.

"Mmmm Mr Creek I've just seen." She Yoda-ed (another one for the personal dictionary).
"Yes, what do you think?" The gargoyle spoke to her like the guardian it was.

She felt a flow of words fall out of her mouth, it was a summary, disjointed, but good

enough and surprisingly long for the minimal information she had gathered.
"Good so what do you think is going on?" Dr Abdul probed.

She didn't want to gasp or let her jaw open. She was barely getting her head around gathering information, let alone interpreting and now he wanted diagnosis and a plan. Who did he think she was, a **doctor**!
"Umm ischemic heart troubles", she floundered and knew it was the wrong way to say his heart is struggling, the medical term was …eh… umm… **Angina!**[12]
"Angina is what we like to call it", she felt at ease hearing Dr Abdul say it through a smile.

There was another pause, whilst she felt the pressure of Dr Abdul waiting. It was surprising how he produced so many slow moments in her mind despite the chaos going on around them.

"So, what is the management, Dr McCullen? You can say you don't know; the computer

---

[12] Angina - Latin for choke, however now used synonymously with angina pectoris which stands for chest pain on exertion due to ischemic heart disease.

sits to the left of me and often is smarter than me". He gestured to his left.

She looked up, blank. Her mind was blank despite having revised this again, again and again.
She sheepishly walked over to the computer and got the guidelines up under cardiology. A few clicks and she was able to read it all out.
"So, a Troponin[13] and if that's okay then depending when the chest pain was, possibly home?"
"I imagine that was an answer not a question?" He continued probing. Her brain hurt with each poke of his Socratic probe.
"Ye," She just about managed the two-letter response.
"I guess so, but why do you think we are doing it?" He left a pause for her.
"To rule out ACS![14]" She confidently said, reading it off the screen.
"Is this Acute coronary syndrome?"

---

[13] Troponin - a chemical released by the heart during a heart attack used in medicine to see if chest pain can be linked to a heart attack.
[14] ACS - Acute coronary syndrome an umbrella term for the different types of heart attacks

She looked back looking again at the guideline and was confused at the line of questioning, she could feel the mystical powers of a consultant to see through it all and imagined he saw a whole different world.

She was impressed at the educator and healer who stood before her; she felt a flight of fancy around his tired eyes before looking at his greying bald head ripped her out of it.

"Umm yes it sounds like ACS, from the history I took." She tried her best at a confident response.

He gave her a quick look before speaking, "Everything you are doing is right. I'll let you handle it, but I want you to think that this isn't the only way to manage it and if you come up with anything we can definitely discuss it." He smiled again at her, this time she could feel the intensity in his eyes. There was something more behind them, but before she could interpret Rich arrived bellowing once again.

"I think you're gonna like this one sir!"

She slinked off before she lost her ear drums.

Back to her first date, well now the second date or was this the drinks after dinner on the first, and why would she agree to drinks when she was already uninterested.

She entered through the curtains.

"Back for the blood I bet." He grinned.
She waited for the vampire joke to come out of her or him but for once silence, she unfortunately ended up disturbing it, "Yes I'll get right to it."

The blood taking goes well, the tubes fill up with the red juice and she feels her accomplishments loud and clear. She rushes to pod them and gets excited about the results. She finally smiled and for a small time was letting the chaos happen around her.

20 minutes pass and she is on the computer hitting refresh for the results. She had marked them urgent, but they still hadn't come back. Maybe she was too optimistic, but she stood down and waited a few more minutes before refreshing once again.

More time passed and she kept hitting refresh, wanting to be the first one to act on the results.
Refresh.
Refresh.
Another refresh.

She decided to walk around the department. Before long, after witnessing much of the

same at every corner of her walk, she finds her fingers on the mouse and keyboard
Refresh.
Refresh.

Still nothing.

Surely another walk around the department wouldn't hurt, but once again she ends back no different than when she left.
Refresh she hit again, it'd been an hour, when has an hour ever been urgent.
It was also interesting how no one had told her off or told her to get back to work. She didn't envision the notoriously busy emergency department would allow her an hour of hitting refresh and walking about.
However, there wasn't much time for her to think about the contradiction now as suddenly the results were plastered on the screen.
It was negative and her date could go home, the relief of escape or maybe that he was alright gave her a bit of a buzz. With that same buzz she read the guideline again before going to tell the man.

"You can go home but we just need to make sure you see the cardiologist as an outpatient and we'll give you this spray, a few tablets and oh a leaflet also."

He didn't look any different nor did he seem happy it wasn't a heart attack.

"Is that okay?" She asked him, which felt like the opposite of what she should be doing.

"Yeah, doc told-ya it was nuffin, but even so that's a lot of stuff yar giving me, will I be okay?"

"Of course, everything you need to know is in that leaflet." She gestured to it, replacing herself with the piece of paper.

"Well, the leaflet isn't you but I'm glad you think I'm alright doc. Can I leave?" He replied with sincerity and no humour for the first time.

"Of course, bye now." She replied quickly, maybe too quick, probably accidentally dismissively, however despite her mind being aware now on reflection it was too late as she had already played those notes to the quite vulnerable man in front of her.

"Thanks so much." He was now shaking her hand and she appreciated the real physical contact from this man, her first patient," You've been brilliant!"

She saw him walk out, he seemed to be slow but steady. She worried that if she let him out of her sight before he left the department, he might suddenly have a proper heart attack. So, she watched him leave the double doors before she took another breath.

She sat down on a chair and looked at the clock. It was 13:00 and she had seen one patient and hadn't had her marmite sandwich. There was a rumble, which sounded like a ringing phone. Answering it, she realised it was her tummy, she opted to fix that next before people beyond the surrounding bays started to hear it.

She stepped out and into the *all mod cons* staff room. There she ate her marmite sandwich. She let her thoughts turn to how great it was to reassure that patient, she then reflected back on her day judging all the people she had met. Dr Abdul was her favourite, then Rachel, then the patient, then maybe Rich. He might be below the red headed nurse who had talked **at** her.

Before long the marmite sandwich was gone, and she was back on the floor looking for purpose. She was momentarily stopped by a woman in a pencil skirt but a very disarming patterned top.

"Hello, you're one of the new Fy1s, Isabella, is it?" The woman looked at her with cautiously inviting eyes.

"Umm, Yes I guess so, yeah that's me. What's the matter? What happened?"

She immediately went placid, panic being the main emotion leading her to this state. Like the feeling you get when a police officer stops you, you presume your own guilt.

"Nothing's matter, nice to meet you, I am Dr Anderson. I just wanted to say good clerking, only feedback is probably tell one of us consultants before you discharge them home yeah." Dr Anderson laughed and for some reason she found herself joining in too. She didn't want to, but she felt she had to.

"Also watch for that old dog Abdul. He has his way with talking about why we do things and multiple answers, I think you did the only right answer, so you don't need to put a question mark next to your diagnosis,"

The smile and laughter ping-ponged between them, "You did everything right though"! Dr Anderson re-iterated.

"Thanks" was all she could muster before being left to think about her conflicted feeling about being told to do something different but also that she did everything right. She felt disarmed, listened to but also slightly patronised, and it confused her.

*

It was day three of being a doctor and she sat in the *all mod cons office*. Her marmite sandwich was, as always, delicious and satisfying. Next to her was Rich who had grown slightly on her and ranked above the redheaded nurse now. He was talking about how funny his patient was and what sports they used to play. He cared and that's why he was tolerable. Although he did keep trying to flirt which she didn't know how to address.

Rachel sat smiling with the nice leftovers of a pasta dish she gobbled up whilst Richard talked and drank weird coloured mixture that had health benefits he swore by.

It was weird that they were already talking about patients like they knew what they were doing and gossiping about colleagues like the best of friends, like Steve Martin, Chevy Chase, and Martin Short, the **three amigos**. Although she doubted one was flirting with the rest of them.

As she took another bite of her marmite sandwich, she was filled with the lovely taste of yeast extract-a by-product of beer brewing don't you know her mind smugly proclaimed to her the pub quiz knowledge- as well as hope about the future.

Chapter 2: A Pint of lager and a pot of valiant

One rep, another rep and a look into the mirror. He liked the routine in the morning and always looked good after it. He wanted to look good, always, it's what made him be better at what he did.
He looked again at the mirror, "Richy boy your flex is definitely on!"

He slowly finished up with some time on the treadmill, increasing the intensity when a lovely girl of about 20 something with blonde hair and a gifted sports bra set up on the treadmill next to him. He used the mirror to note when she glanced at him, he smiled and she smiled, it was enough to make him feel good about himself.

This routine to help him keep going had worked for his first month on the job. He was a big shot doctor now and he was finding it a lot harder than he had imagined. After all, medical school was a breeze or super fun. This job was tiring, exhausting and for once in his life he would come home and not want to talk to people.

He walked past some of the lassies going towards spin classes. "Y'alright", he bellowed, putting another smile on, distracting himself from his line of thinking. They rolled their eyes, but one giggled, which was enough once again to give himself the boost.

He got changed back to his joggers. He saw the others around him wearing work clothes, it annoyed him slightly that he couldn't wear his work clothes because he wore pyjamas at work. Looking like everyone else irked him because he wanted to be different. Despite not wanting to admit he knew he wasn't.

The mornings after the gym became more and more predictable. Out of the door making a joke about how he needed to get laid to his flat mate who laughed and agreed. He'd skip along past the small park near his flat, making sure not to get his trainers too wet or muddy. He then would cross the road dodging the cars skilfully; he was a city boy after all. Walk past the same dog walker and then a few students who all seemed to be having far too fun for kids going to school.

He then arrived at the main entrance, and the colours grew dimmer; he walked in and followed the red line, to the double doors of his current life. He then would smile and walk through with his strut saying hello to everyone he walked by, thinking the louder he talked the more they thought of him. Reaching the changing rooms and remembering the word Hastings while keying in 1066y and he sneaked in to grab the tightest scrubs allowed before heading out onto the fluorescently lit department.

He'd slowly sneak into minors hoping the patient load was there, they were less ill and he felt more in control and more confident there. He thought back to his first day, when he'd come close to a bruised ego from his time in majors.

*

He looked over to the girl who had been staring at the floor. She was pretty with her blonde hair and greenish grey eyes. He bellowed at her.
He felt a little jump as she looked up at him. He was almost taken aback when she set her gaze on him. He wanted to make more jokes, they made him feel comfortable. Amongst his comforting noise he did find out her name

was Isabella, although she proclaimed so quietly, he almost missed it.

Later he met another lovely lady Dr. Rachel, she was different, less placid and more confident in who she was. Girls like that never fell for him, it might be his flirting style that can't handle a woman who knows what she wants. He was beginning to see a trend in this hospital when it came to new doctors. Although he was beginning to doubt his eyes or think this could all be one big prank. So far no ugly people which made him even more nervous, he needed somebody like that so he could be out of someone's league. He wondered if someone reading his thoughts would think he was horrible, but then again he was sure lots of other people had the same thoughts just fought them instead of embracing their truth.

he focussed inward and reiterated his strategy once again. Be loud and the centre of attention, eventually everyone slips when they think about you enough. He followed and bellowed that morning until they met the boss. Dr. Abdul Assem, or was it Mr.? He seemed nice, he didn't act like an old boy and suddenly he was at a loss on how to interact with the consultant. This was a whole new challenge for him.

Dr Abdul looked down at him with a piece of yellow paper, "you'll enjoy chatting to this one!"

He looked at the consultant who stood there once again with his kind smile, something he wasn't used to seeing in consultants, usually they would be cynical, and he would be able to joke about the good old days or failing that, a sport of some kind.

"Umm, looks good, did you see the cricket?" He fished.
Dr Abdul looked at him. "Why do you think I'd be watching cricket?"
"Umm, no reason, just it's on and we're doing well." He stuttered, feeling completely out of his depth.
Dr Abdul smiled. "We, haha, how do you know I support the same team... Is it the same psychic ability that told you I would like cricket?"
Suddenly sweat was pouring down his brow, this was meant to be a sure-fire way of getting in with a consultant early, to make his life easier. Just before he could think of a way out, he was spared.

"It was amazing and Stokes is brilliant, isn't he?" Dr Abdul gave his tired smile towards him and made him stand there unable to respond for once in his life.
"Now take a read of the sheet and come back when you're ready!"

He walked off and as he passed Izzy he offered her a smile, she smiled back. At least his tactics were working on someone.

*

He had just finished the clerking in what he thought was record fy1 speed and quickly went up to Dr Abdul with his "I think you're gonna like this one sir!" that he used to sweeten all authority he had ever encountered. Izzy walked past again, and he hoped she heard how great he was.

He focussed back on Dr Abdul and his smile which gave him the confirmation that it was indeed a job well done.

As he headed towards the patient and saw the very clear writing on his sheet of paper, which was his way of being cocky about his work as you could read everything he had done and thought, a slight palpitation crept from his chest to his throat. He worried, a *little* he reiterated, as this was on his head, but he didn't want to go back and double check, that would have been bad optics for his character that he wanted everybody to see. He looked at the case and realised he could always ring the specialist (the surgeon who knew the patient) and sound even more cocky to them and spread his mirth. He patted himself on the back before grabbing a phone and putting on his best Etonian waffle - a mix of nervous, coy and confident into one note which he delivered in concert to the old school consultant (*thank god* he proclaimed internally) on the other side. His smile grew to the affirming noises on the other side.

You are on fire, he smugly looked at the dusty mirror in front of him reflecting his greatness back to him. However, the mirror did make him wonder why it existed. Did making the room look bigger actually trick everyone, space, time and reality so more patients fitted into the majors. He stopped his thought to focus back on his smile and the fiery aura he imagined around him.

*

It was all of a sudden. He was being told off and really made to sweat, this time by a woman who was dressed in a disarming animal print shirt, but she currently was very armed now.

"Now look here, when the consultant says discharge, you don't go and discuss it with anyone else, you don't go shopping for advice, you listen to the boss! Get your head screwed on okay!"

She walked off and left him standing there wondering what had happened. He hadn't asked her for advice, and it was Dr. Abdul that should have been shouting at him. He kept wincing at every bleep in the department. He could hear everyone's chatter around him and with each bleep he felt his chest thud. Now he was meant to be a man, a lad, so he just looked down not wanting to overreact to what had just happened to him. He shuffled along before reaching Dr. Abdul. He waited for Izzy to finish who then seemed to quickly run off. He thought she probably just had been told off as well, or had to redo something, it would make him feel less foolish if that was the case. He was sure he could catch up with her later, she would want to catch up with him later for sure.

His running thoughts halted at the pit stop which was the tired smile and kind eyes set upon him. It made him feel more secure as he listened to what the consultant had to say.

"Everything can be managed a million ways. I'm glad the registrar agreed with me this time. It's a good learning opportunity for all. You never stop learning here."

He looked up at Dr Abdul and smiled, feeling a little more at ease. He wondered how Dr Abdul knew already, he put it down to the superpower of the consultant.

"Sorry, it was so hectic, and I panicked, I didn't want to come to you and ask again."

"It's not about me, that patient has now had two agreeing opinions which is reassurance to us and him, that is half our job after all, to reassure. You'll find that more so when you do minors."

*

Those words still rang in his head as he started his second month in the department, a whole month of 90% minors had kept him feeling good about himself, and because he was able to deal with reassuring people, he was also getting along with the staff on that side of the emergency divide. He walked up to the desk, placing himself in the middle of all the doctors and nurses writing furiously.

"Good morning gals and guys." He confidently proclaimed as people looked his way, smiling and greeting him. He did notice that today Izzy had a normal fitting scrub top for once.

"Ya Saved the hairpins for yer hair." He smiled at her, verbally grabbing her into a conversation.

He liked to think the others would stand aside as a spotlight shone on the both of them to do their mandatory routine of what he imagined was the slow dance of seduction. He could tell it was working, after all she smiled more, maintained more eye contact and laughed at what he said.
"Yeah, I guess I was lucky, or maybe you stopped taking the tight ones." Her eyes flickered as he bathed in the sass he was just given. Sass was a new dance move, and he was ready.
"So good night last night?" He asked, hoping to continue the duel.
"It was alright nothing special," She started walking away.
"No fun things? No new lovers? I mean how am I meant to know what nothing special constitutes for you?"

She laughed as she kept walking, she hadn't answered but she did look back at him.
He smiled to himself, whispering, "She looked back."
He looked at the screen before selecting "chest and shoulder pain" from the waiting room. Time to reassure him he thought, as he walked to said waiting room.

The waiting room was this weird place where the emergency department felt almost normal, a place where people can wait in a department where waiting is blasphemous. He watched as all the hopeful faces turned to him, he could feel their collective hive mind saying *"hope it's me next, I've been waiting for ages. I definitely was next in line after the guy who was called before."*
He could feel the worry going through the hive mind, the worry about waiting, their health, but also their anger, he tried to ignore it all as he called his patient,
"Jason Argonaut!"
The man looked up as he felt the room's collective disappointment. The patient walked towards him as he let his hand guide the way to the double doors of the department.

Jason was a spritely man with a slim build, he noted Jason looked light on his feet with a very nice complexion. Luckily this attractive man was a patient and not competition in the hospital.

"We're in cubicle four," he exclaimed as Mr. Argonaut entered behind the curtains, although took a slight gasp when there was a child.
He quickly noted the mistake and corrected "I meant five sorry."

He watched Jason take a seat on the plain plastic school chair. The patient then looked longingly at him, like a lost family member, or the wife of a sailor at sea.

"Hello, I'm Dr Rich, Mr. Argonaut is it, or Jason, do you mind Jez?" He slowly ramped up the volume directing all his positive energy towards the patient.
Jez looked pleased to him as he went, "Thanks doc, I like Jez."
The chuckle let him know he was on the right page.
"So, tell me what's been bothering a chap as athletic looking as you?"
"Well, I have been having these chest pains and today there was a little shoulder pain. I know I shouldn't be worried doc!"
"Tell me about these pains then Jez, it can't be your ticker since I imagine you keep it in good shape?"
Another chuckle: another point on the board, "I think I might be doing too much; you know it hurts when I move my shoulder, at the front really thudding and sharp and right at the back around the shoulder blades."
He nodded enthusiastically and made grunting noises which if you didn't know this was a hospital might indicate a totally different kind of interaction.

"Hmm yes, so movement makes the pain worse? Or brings it on?" he said professionally and expertly.

"Yeah, it's fine until a move I think, there might be a slight dullness to it when I'm not," Jez was now nodding, mirroring his behaviour, always a good sign.

"Yeah fair, I mean I think what it sounds like the muscle is acting up, there's nothing scary about what you've told me, let me *reassure* you!"

"Ahh brill doc, Thanks. Should I just use the painkillers and it'll get better?"

He felt impolite, he wondered if maybe he should do a bit more for Jason. He was confident about the case but felt like he may get another dressing down from an angry disarmingly dressed woman.

"Let me be thorough and examine though, just to prove I'm right," he quickly smiled and bellowed at the patient, saving all of his face.

Jez sat there obeying as he got to work, slowly pushing jumpers to either side trying to get a good look at the chest and shoulder. He used his stethoscope and fumbled around awkwardly with the patient's clothing like a drunk teenager on his first ever one-night stand. After a few moments he got the patient to copy his movements like the leader of a spin class before nodding and letting him leave. He could see the smile on his face which made him beam as he returned to the benches with the computer to finish the paperwork. Once again, he saw Izzy sitting down and decided to take the computer terminal next to her.

"Look at that, another happy customer, a little bit of flirting goes a long way!" he proclaimed to her as he was sure he saw her giving him a half smile.
"What'd d'ya think," he proclaimed to her, waiting for an answer.
"Looks like you did well, I guess. People smiling is a good sign," He saw it become a full smile.
"Yeah, well defo MSK[15] pain, you know people panic about chest pain, but it's so easy to tell the difference. It's like all in the history and examination." He preached.
"Yeah, I'm glad you figured it out, sounds like you did a good job." She gave a laugh and made him feel like he was the man. She started walking away.

---

[15] MSK - Musculoskeletal (muscles, joints, bones and the tissue which joins them)

"We should hang out sometime, maybe drinks or something?" He asked whilst he was on this roll.

She looked back and said, "Yeah sounds good, maybe ask the others yeah?"

She had missed the "asking out" cue in the script he had written for them in his head but impressing more than one person did sound like a good idea. She kept walking whilst he waited for her to look back. He wanted to say more but didn't get the chance. Maybe she was shy at work, after all people like privacy. He never got that, why be private when everyone can know about your life.

He looked up at the screen again, eyeing another self-esteem boost or patient. He clicked on the patient and the cycle repeated.

*

It was Friday and the department always changed before the weekend. He had avoided majors again, but minors looked like majors. A flood of patients wanting the okay for their time off had invaded his haven. For the first time in his haven, he felt invisible. He didn't like the isolation. He decided to go up to one of the nurses, angling for his usual self-esteem boost.

"Alright Meg, uniform looks nice today, might be all that running around," he smiled at her.

He had already arranged for her to come to the drinks. Why wouldn't you drink with a girl with two colours in her hair and an absolutely amazing body to add to that. She looked back at him with her blue eyes. He awaited the flirtation.

"Look, we're rammed Rich, nowhere to see anyone. I think you need to get to the corridors and get to work!"

Another knock back! His thoughts around isolation grew like a cloud in his mind. He could feel thunderstorms pounding in his head.

"On for tonight, yeah?" he asked placidly. He couldn't muster a look into her eyes.

She had walked off and she too didn't even look back.

He turned around to look behind him. The corridor littered with people in chairs and beds all looking worried and anxious. He felt their selfishness as they all wanted to be seen first, to be reassured first not taking into account the state of the department. It made him think about how stupid people were, how they couldn't possibly understand his pressure or the pressure on the NHS. Mentally grabbing a shovel, he buried his thoughts, not wanting them to seep out and contradict his demeanour and character.

He needed someone calm, reinforcements to the battle and that's when he turned to the *registrar*[16] on the floor. Dr. Tomkin Nice was a loveable smiling fellow who brought calmness to everyone around him. Although he wasn't the favourite of the scary Dr Anderson nor was he close to any of the other *registrars*, he was everything Rich idolised in a doctor. Plus he looked way better than any of his other colleagues, less bags under his eyes and less belly fat bulging in his obviously small sized scrubs. The differences could easily be elicited if this was a spot the difference poster, like the before and after on a personal trainer's page. Apart from the above, the other *registrars* spoke abruptly and talked a lot about how to do things and asked questions where the answer was always "*guess what's in my head*". They also complained a lot about the state of the NHS and how it was getting harder with no support and the budget was all taken by locums[17] who didn't have the

---

[16] Registrar - Someone who is in the final branch of the specialty training and would be officially on the specialty registrar, the rank before consultant

[17] Locum - someone outside of training who filled in the gaps. Like a supply teacher.

commitment or career progression that they had. Now to the after picture in which Dr Nice fell. He was a locum, but he smiled. He always taught and, in a pinch, he could save a life. He was *Mr Cool*, or *Mr Nice,* or someone he felt he could have a man crush on.

He also had a bright fresh face and hair that was gelled to look like bed hair but wasn't, as well as maintaining a reputation for being a charmer. One that people mentioned with glee rather than gossip.

"Heya Dr Nice, a bit crazy today right," he walked over with a smile to the only calmness in the department.

"Oh, Richy boy," He sang in key to him, "it's a bit chaotic, but does get the juices flowing doesn't it. Plus, ya can only see what you see, so in a way it makes it easier to take your time, I think."

This was followed by a big laugh which he joined in with, getting energised from the interaction.

"Plus, I heard you'd organised nice little drinks with some of the new gals. Have you invited any guys or are you scared of a little competition?"

Once again there was laughter. The more he watched Dr Nice laugh, the more he joined in and the more everything around him slowed down a little.

"With a little Dutch courage, I think I can go a long way," he smiled back, and another laugh came on. He felt it was like a school or a pride or whatever the plural phrase for laughter had surrounded them.

Having said that line it made him think about the phrase, *Dutch courage*, he'd looked at the Wikipedia article in the past, when he'd made the same joke on multiple dates back in London. "Strength or confidence gained from drinking alcohol." Dating back to The Anglo Dutch War, or The Thirty-Year War, when soldiers would drink gin to calm them before battle. He liked to think of himself as a soldier in three different scenarios.

1. In dating or flirting he was the one battling with women's inability to see how beautiful they were and how much they wanted to have sex as well, because they do deserve pleasure, because of how amazing the women around him are.
2. In the hospital he had to battle to keep the patients away and reassured or quickly admitted and thankful.
3. At the gym in an eternal battle with his body to maintain its physical appeal.

He was snapped back to reality when Dr Nice had stopped laughing and looked at him with a glint in his eyes.
"Say what, why don't we go and teach you how to shove a tampon up a nose?"
He loved these moments. It was busy and he would have to be around the beeps normally, but because it was a learning opportunity he could vanish and avoid the corridor.
"Oh yes! I do need to learn after all," he said, nodding aggressively.

He followed behind Dr Nice ducking and dodging. Like stepping stones they leaped from one bit of the department to the next, avoiding the stress and anger he could see in each person they passed. Both doctors and patients today were unsatisfied. Today, no one was looking for reassurance, they were looking for their money's worth. It was days like these that really pushed him. He could feel his anxious thoughts creep, making him revert to being placid. He shook his head and decided to just focus on the man in front of him, who skated effortlessly to a cubicle! A cubicle, he couldn't believe it. He let the words echo; - cubicle. ***Today*** they were seeing a patient in a cubicle.

He noted in contrast to the trenches they had left behind, the cubicle felt like a luxury hotel room, with a very well-dressed older lady. She had a string of pearls around her neck and wore a pinkish red cardigan with a lovely white blouse and flowery skirt. She looked prim and proper, well apart from the clamp which held her nose shut.

Next to her was a table and not only did she have a wheelchair, but a *zimmer frame* as well. On closer inspection of the table a **whole** sandwich and a **full** glass of water rested. *A feast for a king, well queen,* he proclaimed internally with a little bit of sarcasm but a very wry smile. He was patting himself on his back for his wit.

"Alright Ms Goldberry, let's take a look at that troublesome nose." Dr Nice matching his name in the way he spoke to the older lady.

"Oh, dear me, it just wouldn't stop this time. I told the doctor I don't want the blood thinners anymore, and he told me to stop eating hot food. Imagine giving up hot food, not easy there boy!"

Dr Nice laughed and once again infected the room, forcing him and the patient to continue the laughter like a Mexican wave. It was impressive.

"Look Audrey, as it's not stopping despite us trying cautery[18] and the clamp, we do need to use what we call a nasal pack[19]."

Dr Nice paused, letting her take it in. Before she spoke, he interjected, predicting her fears. "It's not comfortable, but not painful either. Although it does mean you have to come into the hospital."

He watched Dr Nice invite her to furrow her brows with his accepting and empathetic smile. The *registrar* then turned to him, although he didn't initially notice as he was too busy picking up his jaw from the floor. After hastily putting his jaw where it was meant to be he saw Dr Nice gesture to him as he spoke,
"Now I have this young good-looking man to watch and learn about how to sort out noses,"

---

[18] Cautery - using a stick with silver nitrate, a chemical which can cause small burns to stop a bleeding vessel. Primary used in noses to stop bleeding or recurrent bleeding

[19] Nasal pack - there are different types. Most famously rapid rhino. They act as a device which puts pressure on the inside of the nose to stop bleeding. Usually need to be kept in for 24 hours minimum.

Dr Nice's kind eyes allowed him to join in with the conversation. He felt like a puppet as he said his next line.

"Thank you for letting me watch." He felt very uncouth and uncool, but he imagined the plain statement is what Dr Nice wanted. This was Dr Nice's approach, different to his own. Most likely better than his own, but he would keep that in his thoughts. He wouldn't want anyone to know he thought someone was better than him.

"Alright I'll bring the stuff, why don't you climb onto the bed Audrey, sit back and have a few sips of that glass of water."

She followed all the instructions, her now being the puppet to Dr Nice's words.

He was left alone with Audrey. Her demeanour reminded him of his grandmother and instantly he felt like a young boy all over again. She was in control. He had no comments that could rope him back on a level playing field and that was with one look. Her mouth curled as she then dealt another blow to him. He noted that she was the one dictating the patient-doctor relationship.

"So dear, you're a student then."

He winced a little. It always hurt when he heard that. He responded in a very hectic, confused manner, this despite hearing this question many times before.

"Umm no no, I finished *uni* just 2 months ago. This is my first job as a foundation doctor, so I'm training."

"Yeah, that's what I meant: a trainee, training to be a doctor, yeah."

"Well, you know I've finished training to be a doctor, I'm now a doctor, training to do the job."

He felt himself fluster. His hands waved around, hoping he was doing some sort of spell which would allow him to incept her mind or better just control what she was saying.

"I see a foundation year student. Interesting the words they come up with to say you're training to be a doctor, isn't it?"

It was at the moment he wondered if:

A) He had an aneurysm, and if a) was true then

B) The question would be, "had it just burst" because this conversation just didn't feel real and more the result of hallucinations by a brain being drowned in blood.

"Well, you see the way it works is..." He began, ready to deliver his lawyer-like objection for his defendant, his pride.

Dr Nice returned before he could respond, making the metaphorical court no longer in session. The focus was now on Dr Nice and his trolley of equipment he had never seen. Seeing Dr Nice be so comfortable around these odd bits and ends did make him feel more like a student and not a doctor.

"You have a very lovely trainee here."

Dr Nice's smile destroyed his defence.

He didn't know if he imagined it but he swore she gave him an "I told you so look". Surely not. He shook his head and swallowed a little of his pride as he walked over to stare further at the metallic clunky metal tray on wheels. He stared at the few packets which were now open and dumped onto the tray. His mind focused on each individual item.

1. A small white cylindrical, well tampon shaped meshed item. It looked terrifying for something so small and unassuming.

2. Forceps which were like grabbing scissors, although they curved round, and he would not want them anywhere near his nose bleeding or not.

3. Spritzer bottle which also curved, adding to the menace of the tray.

4. The only thing that let his heart slowdown was the syringe.

The snap of gloves brought him back to reality. Dr Nice now had a visor on as well and an apron. Looking more like a butcher rather than the kind-hearted doctor he had been before. His eyes showed his glee before his victim.

There were no words as he watched the transformed man perform the procedure. It was like a silent film, like a ritual as Audrey tilted her head back and allowed; initially the spray to go up the nostrils, causing her to wince slightly. Despite this the man continued. Next, grabbing the tampon, and without much warning it slid up the nostril whilst the old lady hacked, splattered and screamed in pain, but the man in front was unchanged, now different; a beast compared to before.

"All done, as you can see. A simple but very effective procedure," Dr Nice laughed, it chilled the room and no one else joined in this time.
"Now Miss", he watched Dr Nice look down at the wristband so that the correct name could be said, although this highlighted Dr Nice transformation even more.
"Yes Ms. Goldberg, I'll call the ear, nose and throat doctors who'll need to admit you."

She muffled some sort of thanks and a moment later he found himself with Dr Nice looking at another patient's records, all his stress and anxiety about the department were back. He could hear the bleeps; the word *breach* repeated several times.

"Now's your turn, I'm outta here, shifts all done."

He looked up at Dr Nice as he was already walking out. He checked his watch, it was 2 pm. He was about to talk, but his question was anticipated.

"It's luck or maybe not, I choose my hours. Will ya make sure the ENT lot do see her though."

There was no further conversation and in a puff of smoke Dr Nice was gone and he was holding the next patient. The yellow paper read Mr J Osborne, **knee injury**. Before he could even take another step, a nurse approached him. She wore a starched blue uniform with lapels. It masked every single one of her body's features. Surprisingly to him it seemed to make her face appear more generic and blander as well. He couldn't judge her and didn't know whether he should flirt because she was attractive and like a well wrapped present, difficult to tell what was underneath. The only individuality was the yellow badge which read Tilly. Her legs stuck out of her uniform, but due to the tights they too seemed to fit in with the theme she projected; "I am the nurse here." It made him wonder if that is what she was like. He wondered about her personality, a rare occurrence for him when it came to women. He focused on her face trying to discern any of her features. She wore her reddish blonde hair in a ponytail and had brown eyes which interrupted his thoughts because of how much they told him to pay attention, like a schoolteacher.

"You're looking after Mr Osborne, yeah?"

Well, he had been for about two seconds, "I guess," he replied so placidly she looked at him and repeated her question having not heard him, "so you looking after him?"

"Yeah," he replied with a bit more volume, but no oomph or energy.

"Okay good, can you prescribe some pain killers, his knee looks awful and he's in a lot of pain."

"Yeah sure, anything he's had or any allergies," he replied again, no flavour just business. He felt his soul empty a little as he did.

"No just give us some analgesia, he is in a lot of pain and we're not exactly chilled enough for you to try and use whatever you have up there." She pointed at his head, and she did have a smile, but he completely missed it as her features didn't seem to shine too brightly as his brain focused on what pain killer he could prescribe. He capitulated and started to scroll in his shaky handwriting:

PARACETAMOL I GRAM STAT

He looked down and handed her the drug chart, which was coloured red, as if to warn you to be careful around the mystical powers this piece of paper possessed. What it said was law and the nurse looked at him. He felt she was unhappy with the supreme law which he had just passed.

"Are you sure?" She raised her eyebrow at him, "surely we should give him a bit more, maybe some stronger stuff. It looks pretty horrible."

She had the smile which he had missed again, instead what he saw was a uniform challenging him. After all his years at medical school, once again he was being challenged. He couldn't take it as his mind started to spiral inwards, telling him she wanted to knock him down a peg. He knew she was jealous; she must be. His life was perfect and once again people wanted to tell him what to do, because they didn't have control over their own life. He felt he projected onto her, but he didn't or couldn't or, he paused, he **_wouldn't_** let his ego take another hit!

"Look I am the doc; he is my patient and I've not even met him yet. It's been two seconds since I picked up this piece of paper," his anger welled as he started waving the paper patronisingly in front of her.

"How do I know what I can safely give? It's not as easy as writing it down. There can be consequences, well at least for me." He looked at her, still no features coming through to him. He didn't know if that was because of the red mist which had descended. She walked off and for the first time he could pick up one emotion, she was not happy, some might even say she probably was upset. He felt a pit in his stomach. He should probably apologise, although he didn't want to admit one thing, it felt good not to be at the bottom of the food chain for that one moment.

He looked back at his sheet, the patient was in the corridor, and he went off to see him. He could apologise later and say it was purely for the patient's greater good which had made him behave that way.

- Beep, he continued walking towards the corridor, - beep, he could hear some chatter by the desk. Breach, they'll breach, he'll breach, all his fault, all her fault. They don't know what they're doing. Phrases and whispers flew in the air like an unfinished symphony.

Another beep and he turned around the corner thinking he had escaped it but like the last movement in a symphony it all swelled as he looked ahead of him to the *corridor.*

The beeps provided the pulse of a drum, *beep beep*, a 4/4 tune, people whispering provided the backing bass line, like a musical he felt the whispers of *breach, breach, breach, breach.* The main riff was a course of complaints from the patient, *I've been here for hours, I've been waiting in this corridor, I pay taxes.* It swelled each section of this orchestra playing louder and louder, his ears pricked at the last underlying string section which he could make out. It was an ongoing chorus of *sorry* from the hospital staff.

The movement continued to swell with each step as he looked for trolley five, the numbers of each one hung up on a laminated piece of paper. He noted very art and crafts for what was meant to be a new (well new-ish around 2003) hospital.

He arrived at bed five to see an exactly 40-year-old man, with receding brown hair and blue eyes. He looked to be the opposite of the typical Darthington patient in that he was without a belly.

He looked again at the man who was jerking in the bed. He looked into his eyes which didn't show the hunt for the reassurance that the patients he was comfortable with would have. He approached. He thought inwardly about power-stancing and the confidence-breeding results philosophy of his privately funded school. He breathed in, puffed up his chest and tightened what he knew was his very well defined and strong pectorals.

"Alright Jeremy, I understand you've gone and done-in your knee!?" He noted it didn't come out the same way his stance would have implied.

There was silence, it lulled him in.

The patient looked up and he began to finally be able to read this man's eyes. They screamed that a storm was coming.

"I'm in fucking agony, you little *posh twat*. Can't you see that I'm in pain!"

He began to feel his pecs deflate. He wanted to try and re-power stance, but the patient didn't allow it.

"Paracetamol, I've waited for hours, I'm in agony and all you can do is look; HEY George Osborne!" His anger rushed at him but like an unsatisfying wave it broke too early to surf on. The man continued the weak white-water tone come out in an almost pleasant tone, "Please, I need help!"

He froze, he didn't know what to say for the first time in his life. He couldn't form a sentence with his mouth. His body froze, his heart raced, his mind raced, and he felt like he was one big juxtaposition. It was then that an unlikely hero appeared. The bland nurse from before but now all he could do was see how shining an individual she looked to him. With his frozen body and racing heart he watched her arrive looking at her well-formed thighs which then fed the uniform before leading to her face. She had beautiful mascara highlighting her blue eyes, a smile with red lipstick which he couldn't help but stare at and her hair in a bun waiting to be let free. The most attractive thing about her was her fingers and what they held, a small syringe. To him like liquid gold. To her he imagined it was another doctor giving the correct prescription, 5 mg[20] of morphine.

"Now here you go Jeremy, need to properly sort out your pain don't we." He took the syringe and suckled whilst the nurse squirted it down, giving him a weird image of a night nurse and a child, harkening back to when he was young. He was sure *Freud* would have something to say about that.

She looked back now, "Dr Anderson said she wanted to catch up with you whilst the morphine worked," she gave him a smile which screamed "I told you so". He felt every bit of his body deflated like a balloon. He whizzed out of the corridor before landing completely out of air into the office of Dr Anderson who had without even calling his name summoned him. Or maybe it was because she was always in her office no matter how busy everything was.

"Hey Dr Anderson," he squeaked looking up at her.
She looked up from her paper, he looked at her face which seemed stern despite the smile she wore before talking to him.
"So, Tilly just told me about the patient, goodness it didn't sound like you had a fair

---

[20] Mg - milligrams

shot at all." She continued smiling, although once again her tone was stern and firm. He didn't know how to respond. He was more just amazed that within 2 minutes someone already knew what happened.

"Look it sounds like you did everything right, you know."

Everything right was said sternly. He could feel the room's air tightened around his neck. He wondered how such positive, affirming words could do that.

"Look just everything was right, but you might want to improve on what you did."

He thought in his head about how one could improve on everything right.

She continued, "I just think maybe listen to the nurse or go for good painkillers. Here in the emergency department, compared to other wards, pain is common, really bad pain is common and you won't be able to examine or help anyone whilst they're in it. The nurses will always know. Like I said though, you're doing everything right."

"Sounds yeah, good, I'll take it into account," he gasped through a closed mouth, which refused to open beyond a few millimetres. Compelled by anxiety and fear, or fear which was the cause of his anxiety.

"Let's talk it through, yeah, once again everything was done right, but it's good to reflect."

He took a big breath before she continued.

*

He wondered how long he didn't breathe for once he was out of the room. He wondered if she had let him go because his face had gone blue. One thing he did learn was that he was good at holding his breath. He had been forced to hand over his patient to Dr Anderson. Also forced to watch how inferior he was to her when she had dealt with him in 12 minutes and 33 seconds. He was going home and as Mr Osborne left, a look of disappointment was shot towards him, hitting him hard, especially as this was followed by a grin towards Dr Anderson, who he had met for less than 15 minutes.

*

He was walking down the department as more and more of the symphony played around him. He looked up to see Izzy and Rachel chatting away. He envied their normal coloured, normal breathing faces.

Rachel looked his way, "drinks buddy, what time ya thinking?" She smiled, he felt a little comfort, "Izzy's well keen, she told me."

It was Izzy's turn to smile at him and he wondered if that was Rachel hinting that Izzy was keen for him, I mean why wouldn't she be. He felt his face filled with a pink flush reviving him from his earlier near-death experience.

"Yeah, I'm always keen, ladies. Thinking 8:30, at The Jarlsberg?"

It was funny that Friday night drinks and the potential for a bit of fun with some ladies made him have a 180 turn in emotion. He was certain that it was talent to be able to find happiness that quickly.

*

He was at the gym again, lifting some weights next to a man who had the best muscles he'd ever seen. He was envious of this man's biceps which looked so toned, innocent, but when flexed they ballooned. He had his shirt off and his six-pack had so much definition he wondered if this was photoshop in real life. Somehow this man had also not skipped leg day making all in the gym realise that calves could look amazing.

He had started to realise the more time he spent in the gym, the more he idolised these men, who made their bodies their temples. He had started going because his *Ex* had said he needed to start losing some weight and that he might want to look after himself. He also went even more after the breakup in hopes to have a few more sexual encounters which ended in women telling their friends how sexy he was. Now he just wanted to be impressive and lift more. He had started enjoying the gym. He felt positive about his evolution. He looked up at the mirror but couldn't focus on himself because that man behind him was now squatting double what he could. Showing how toned his thighs and arse was. With time and practice he could see his name in lights next to the words, "that boy has a cute butt, I want it," maybe even said by Izzy.

He next got on the bike. This was the *cool down* and his mind wandered about Izzy. She had been so placid around him, but he could start feeling signs of interest. However, before he could unpick every time, she had smiled at him or what he called flirted in her own shy way. He looked across at the lady on the bike next to him and couldn't help but recognise the nurse from before, his saviour. She smiled back at him and he couldn't help but somehow stumble a little with the stationary bolted down cycle. She looked good out of uniform which seemed to hide her hourglass body shape, wow now Izzy didn't have that.
They both slowed down after showing off to each other on the bikes. Well, he assumed that's what she did, because he'd never seen a

girl look so elegant with so much sweat. Before he could assume his power stance, she snuck in her first words, "much better on that bike than you are with a prescription."

She got him good, yet it just got him even more fired up.

"Anyway, I feel you owe me for saving your butt."

He looked up at her replying:

"Maybe I do, but surely saving my beautiful butt is a service you have to do for queen and country, I mean it is a pretty valuable butt." He imagined her biting her lip, although a small laugh was probably just as good, but not in as many *pornos*.

"It's not too bad, I'll give you that."

"You should join us for a drink, going to The Jarlsberg." He wanted to get it in early, after all, no one can say no after a good joke.

"Well, I've got a girls night, but give me a message if you guys head out then," she replied. He wanted to make her laugh again, so that she would leave thinking about him.

"How will I message you then, are you giving me your number?"

She laughed and smiled, boom he thought. Her hands unfurled as she took a hold of his phone and typed her number in. She handed it back before slowly grabbing her towel from the machine as she walked away, she looked back at him.

"By the way next time, instead of being rude, you should probably just admit you're scared and don't know what you're doing."

It was his turn to laugh except his came out anxiously. She had figured him out and what was worse; she had mentioned and talked about something which was awkward, how *un-BRITISH* of her.

He gulped before looking up to see she had walked away. Whilst he had liked the interaction, he felt like Captain Cook, in uncharted territories, because this woman was actually confident unlike him, he faked it, wanting to make it.

He gathered his stuff and once again the routine before "work" commenced.

*

It had all been a blur. He remembers snippets of getting ready, primarily that he chose a perfect peacocking shirt which he recalled got attention. He had noted Rachel looked very good in her crop top which showed her toned body and her funky trouser which showed her hipness. She had high end trainers as well as a couple of bangles and the perfect level of makeup.

He also remembered Izzy looking very "English rose" with her well-fitting striped top, her golden watch and her skinny, small arse hugging jeans.

He remembers a few pints, a tequila shot, reflux, rushing to toilets for a "pee" and lots of laughs, he was being funny after all.

He remembers walking Izzy home, but her being cool and standoffish, so much so she was barely able to give him a hug. He had chalked it down to her nervousness and shyness, she probably had never done a one-night stand. Next were snippets of him and Rachel talking with him mentioning the word "Sam" a lot.

The one thing he does remember is the slightly colder night and the leaves they had to walk through on the side of the street, which annoyingly were ruining his shiny new black Italian leather shoes. Autumn was coming, which means the fun summer dresses girls wore would vanish, although he was happy that clubbing clothes appealed to him no matter the season.

Next was lights, his phone buzzing, Rachel dancing very sexily and him wishing he was the guy she was dancing with and then darkness.

Then he wakes up next to a woman with a great body, mascara showing off her blue eyes and red lipstick. He was somewhere he didn't recognise; he felt a soreness around his bottom. He didn't know but he liked how he felt; and went straight back to sleep.

Chapter 3: Husband Made Salads.

She always woke up as the clock hit 6:50 am on a day in which she started at 9. Like Groundhog Day she hears the same noises on these mornings.
Her daughter shouting, "Daddy! I Want more breakfast."
Followed by another giggle and laugh as she heard her husband Dr James Anderson carry her daughter Millie into the bathroom.
"I think I'll be fine without a pee," Millie giggled.
"Not in my car you won't," he always responded with his voice emanating the smile she imagined he had. She knew the routine by heart, a well-rehearsed play.

It was then he would open the door and introduce light into her world.
"Time to wake up dear, I've made a mackerel salad and left it on the side for you."
She looked up at her husband's blue eyes, inviting yet kind, sometimes too kind. She held her tongue from mentioning that.
"Thanks, dear. Love you."

"Love you too," he replied. She always felt like he one upped her in the relationship, but daren't complain, who would complain in her scenario.

"I'll take Millie then I'm off to the practice, but tonight we said date night yeah?" He Paused "The babysitter is coming from 7 so we can head for a few drinks earlier."

"Sounds like a plan dear," she replied, sleepy but happy. She wanted to snooze a little longer but knew she then had to start her routine. Get up, brush her teeth after giving a kiss to Millie and kicking her out of the bathroom to get her clothes changed. Say goodbye and love you to both of them again before heading towards the kitchen.

The cafetière was all primed, ready for hot water, her cereal in a bowl and milk by the side in a small jug. Her husband was so good to her, but it did make her feel guilty. It made her feel like she took him for granted. She didn't and she loved him, it was always like he was playing a game of who was best in the relationship, and she hated losing.

She sat down in her night gown and pyjamas as she watched the news like she did every morning. She rolled her eyes as each story went on, she had been feeling that everyone was wrong for a while and the recent anger around the hospital shutting down had only entrenched her views around people's stupidity.

She looked at the screen, they were interviewing a white-haired old man. A man who she recognised due to his peculiar oval shaped glasses. His name Dr Ebbideh Henon flashed on the screen with the title of local GP underneath it.

"Look, it's more about what we can offer people closer to them, which is what the government had promised. Nothing else. Thing is, travel times to the city are sometimes an hour or longer for people without transport, which a lot of the community struggles with. So, it's just to say a bit of practical planning around what happens is important."

She rolled her eyes, she hated how convincing someone who was wrong sounded. It was like he had a power of communication and was using it for the forces of evil, or at least he was talking before thinking. She knew the hospital acute services were closing but it was to give better care to people in a place that was better resourced. But of course, the local news decided to interview no one else, so his words unchallenged will ring true to the locals. Views she then would have to deal with at her upcoming meeting this afternoon.

She wolfed down the rest of the cereal and the coffee before heading to her closet to wear her outfit for the day. She opened a cupboard to reveal rows of very organised coat hangers, each with a day on it. The clothing looked almost similar, but she had planned her looks from when she rose to consultant level. It was perfect, giving a bit of room to keep people's attention with a good fitting pencil skirt and then a blouse which was patterned to disarm anyone and make her look relatable, finished with a cardigan or blazer depending on if it was meeting day or clinical day.

She remembers when she first started doing this, it was after a conversation with Abdul, the old dog, who mentioned appearance can affect perception and communication. He probably doesn't remember, and she would never admit the effect over the years he's had on her. After all, she had lost the respect she once had when he was her supervisor and boss. He seemed mellowed in his older age, and it made her angry to think he'd given up. Of course, just like her husband he was kind, and it made it even more difficult for her to win the game between them without coming off badly. After all she can't be driven in this world, she can only be a bitch apparently. Well, this bitch wanted to deliver good proper organised and regulated care to the people. She laughed to herself, she was a ***proper bitch***, she proclaimed sarcastically into the patriarchal air.

Well, this ***bitch*** dressed in her perfect outfit, she then headed down out of the house and into her car. As she didn't do the school run, she was always able to drive her one true outside work passion. Her Tesla, it reflected the power she knew she had and also meant she was never late, not with the way she bombed down Darthington winding country road. Longer but more scenic routes were appreciated by her and maybe a handful of other drivers. Everyone else let themselves be congested on the main dual carriage road, however they all arrived at the same time to gates, just her being happier than the others.

The drive was splendid as the sun slowly rose up, the only benefit of daylight-saving time. She could feel the crisp breeze flow through the windows, time was slowly marching as summer did to autumn. Crumpled leaves under her wheel flew to each side as the roaring engine swept them up. She smiled at her wing mirrors to see the canvas of red and yellow, the colours of passion, that she left behind.

She arrived and looked towards her car parking space. She also enjoyed it, exactly 23 steps from the back door to the emergency offices and then another 21 steps made her get to her office. She had worked long and hard in her career and one of the best bits about being a consultant was the parking space. Before then that was straight out of your salary if you were even allowed a space, or you'd be on the waiting list for years. Even longer than some of those old boys' golf clubs.

She took her steps, her heels clattering on the floor, echoing, telling everyone she was there. As she arrived, she looked down the corridor to the other office, a cloud of dust still stinging in the air from the plaque which definitely needed a clean.

She walked over to peer and see the balding grey-haired shell of a man sat down staring at the computer with his seeing glasses on his balding head and his reading ones perched on the tip of his nose.

"Alright there, do I get to call you a six eyed dog then," she proclaimed as he was forced to look up at her.

"How do you do Beth? I tell you my eyes can't deal with all this online paperwork, especially with these new Fy1s." He smiled at her, kindly, which annoyed her, because it was too *kindly*.

"Yeah, it's been 3 months, they're almost done, aren't they?" She asked rhetorically.

"Yet I don't feel like I'm done, I've got to have these end of placement meetings and come up with stuff to say that isn't generic. I also feel the pressure of inspiring a new generation, like somehow if I don't get them to do ED it'll be my fault, I won't be able to retire," he said with a hint of his old self.

She smiled, for once a real one, "It's a tough job being you isn't it, I'm surprised they don't retire you yet."

"Yeah, I think they should get someone proper and smart like yourself, then you can have the dusty placard," They giggled together, like school children.

He looked down again at the papers, before looking up. "What do you think about these kids? I just can't find the standard to compare them to, I feel like it's different being an Fy1 compared to my day, the house officer years. I

mean you are definitely more acquainted with this worrying, self-entitled generation, right?" He raised his eyebrows, sarcasm in his last statement, which made his face wrinkle more, the look not helped by the combination of his 2 pairs of glasses. She did think he would benefit aesthetically from forehead Botox. She would save that one for a later date, don't kick a pleading dog, as she said, hopefully one day they would all say.
"Well, they say each generation is an improvement, plus back in your day bed rest was the best treatment, or maybe even a chicken broth was your best bet against meningitis."

She stared down again and for a moment saw the Dr Abdul form 15 years ago, young, only 2 wrinkles on his forehead, rosy cheek nose and clear glasses with a full set of hair, thinning slightly, curly slightly, but hair, nonetheless. She felt nostalgic, which made her feel old.

"Seriously though," he paused looking at her, both of them sharing a look they hadn't for 15 years. His dark eyes captured her brighter ones. She looked away and considered his questions. She thought for a moment, like a clip show or a fast-forwarded recap about her encounters with all three of the new doctors.

*

She had met Isabella or Izzy, easier to say and less pompous, probably summarised what her personality was like.

She was a little placid about everything, although she wondered if there was more to her inner thoughts, maybe a little sass. It was the way she wore the loose-fitting scrubs and the way she did the minimal make up with her hair tied back that screamed it to her. Assumptions had been made, but you couldn't sit down and let everyone monologue. It had been on the first day she had seen her popping in and out of the curtains again and again. She seemed almost scared of the patient every time she popped out. She had then quietly approached Abdul before coming back again in and out, in and out, ignoring the nurses, trying to sort everything herself, yet with no confidence.

She then watched her walk endlessly around the department, not doing much but her face signalling like she was overcome with work. After all that, she had managed to get the patient she was seeing home in a pretty safe manner. She had gotten the job done.

It made her think about her first days, but it was cloudy when she did. She doesn't really recall ever being uncomfortable, for some reason, she had always thrived at work, or she had blocked off times where she hadn't.

She decided to talk to her about the rules, but it is important to disarm her and not to frighten her, she got ready to use her favourite positive phrase that her seniors had used to help her get by; *you did everything right*, rang through the air.

*

She thought about Richard, she had seen him several times, to be honest, she felt like she had met him a million times before in her department. He felt like a blur of men who frequented specialties like Emergency or acute medicine. Full of themselves, no doubt or hiding doubt over a facade of flirtation and cockiness. They always ended up needing help but would never admit it, they also all hit the gym and somehow managed to have the same body types. It intrigued her, was there some kind of privately educated boot camp or did they all get genetically selected?

They were also the loudest and therefore always thought to be the smartest in medicine, the louder you are the more people perceive you know. She had discussed him with Tilly, an old friend, before he had stepped into her office. She wanted to rile him a bit, give him something to think about. She watched as his face changed colour in front of her, while she spoke about what had occurred. She found it funny the way his face had doubt, something she imagined he had never shown to anyone else. A punch he deserved for his treatment of Tilly. Although knowing her she'd just jump on him when she could. Although that made her probably the most empowered woman that she knew. She watched him walk out, he did have potential if he just showed little humility and placidity at the right times.

*

Finally, was Rachel, now what could she say about her apart from being impressed that someone so young and with little life experience could be so well measured and mature. She was almost jealous of how composed and well-adjusted she seemed, it almost felt Rachel coped better with life than herself. It was her god damn eyes which screamed contempt.

She hadn't spoken to Rachel but had heard everyone else say she was good, did the job, chatted and joked with the nurses and even had been on a few nights out with the other staff.

She had also heard she got help when she needed it, and nodded a lot, like Churchill (the dog that is, she was definitely not an impressive yet complicatedly flawed "hero") who was always happy to help. Plus, Tilly was happy with her, and if Tilly is happy you have to be good, she wondered if Tilly would jump on her too. The thought made her smile internally while she noted she should mention it next time they hung out. She didn't actually have much to say about Rachel, which may be even worse because surely everyone should have something said about them.

*

The thoughts had raced so the moments in her head were seconds to the outside world. She looked back at the man whose eyebrows and forehead had aged back to the old Dr Abdul.
"I guess I could give you a sentence summary like you used to love from me," she said in a nostalgic tone, feeling the combined age in the room like an anchor towards mortality.
"Those were the days, you could sure say a lot with so little," he smiled, their banter acting as the chain trying to keep the anchor from hitting the ground, trying to make them appear youthful. She dug her heels into the ground as she pursed her lips before unleashing her criticisms. she felt she was

allowed after all she had worked hard to get to a position where she was allowed to be judgy.

1. Izzy, placid and no confidence, she needs some.
2. Rich, too much confidence needs more placidity.
3. Rachel, keep doing what she's doing.

She paused, "Although don't tell them I said that, Rich might take it as a signal that Izzy needs to spend time with him, which would be a disaster for her!"

Once again the forehead scrunched.

"Really I thought Izzy would appreciate that she's always laughing at what he says, smiles too."

She smirked, "you men are all the same, can't you spot the please stop talking I'm trying to get away from you and I don't want to say fuck off because I'm polite laugh?"

"Didn't know that was so common it was a laugh. To be honest, he'd probably take that as she was playing hard to get."

He laughed with her; she hadn't heard him laugh like that for a while. A genuine laugh, not just because she had forced him to with her laugh.

"Thanks Beth, so you've got the big meeting this afternoon?"

"Yeah, I'm hoping it won't go too long, it's date night!" She rolled her eyes whilst at the same time, she felt Abdul's compassionate eyes fall on her.
"Well, how is James doing?"
"Yeah he's doing well, Millie and him are great, sometimes I feel I'm not great with her like he is."
"Come on now, you try your best, plus I'm glad you've brought back your date **nights**," he smiled and continued, "I'll call you out of the meeting if it's getting late! How about that?"
"I'll be fine," She felt frosty, her mind instantly made paranoid thoughts about the boy's club kicking her out, was his kindness just a part of it, she tried to compose herself.
"Thanks though, but I can handle them better than you."
She laughed and Abdul followed, unlike the last one it was back to his forced laughs.
"I'll leave you to the hard work then old dog," she smiled, the best smile she could as her mind raced with paranoid thoughts, she turned and clopped her heels back to her office before closing the door and let her bottom fall onto the cushioned chair.
She let her racing heart settle and pushed her thoughts back to the corner of her brain. She hated that side of her which was afraid any

moment she wasn't involved in the action. She'd never had a sick day and when she was young, never missed an event when possible. Burning the candle at both ends. She was afraid of letting people progress without her input, or even worse talk behind her back. She tried to remember her therapist's breathing exercises, or maybe it was counting or something about sheep in a field. Whilst she tried to focus on remembering the activity, she managed to feel her heart slow down. She counted backwards from ten and her thoughts stopped. She took a deep breath before looking at her emails. There were 20 unread already, although lots about maintenance things, hospital status changing every 20 minutes and some fun yoga classes which she imagined two people would turn up to as they were located in the hospital.

After scanning and deleting, she looked up at the clock, the meeting would be in a few hours, if this was a normal job she could prepare, but instead she looked at her pile of paperwork slowly gathering in her "in-tray". The significance of each of her signatures on the paper reports felt dwindling as her years within the department had carried on. She got out her Parker fountain pen and started working on the "In" tray pile. Each paper signed was then sorted into the "out" (known as the someone else's problem) tray pile.

*

How could a meeting last for so long and yet not get to talking about what she wanted? The clock ticked 5:45 pm. The old man in front of her who looked plucked straight out of a 1970s political broadcast droned, his monotone akin to the hum of a hard-working fridge.

"The funding stream must be appropriately adjusted and if you look at page 23 of the briefing, we can see that the deficit due to certain departmental spending has reached a critical zone, whilst royal surplus way outstrips this and may even improve if services are consolidated via the funding stream p2305 proposed."

She couldn't believe she had listened to that sentence, she hated that she barely understood it. She felt insignificant there but knew she had to hang around. The agenda would get to her, she would break this boring boy's club.

The talking continued, this time her brain decided to replace the words he was saying,

"I'm boring, I bet I give my wife terrible sex. She does a great job of laying back and thinking of England. Won't you all respect me and my tiny penis."

She smiled and held her laugh, she forgot how creative she could be. She felt like if this was a still image of the man in front, she'd be drawing a cock on his head. Maybe some balls on his already ball'd chin.
Time ticked.
She could hear the small second hand on all of their expensive watches click slightly different timings, like an unrehearsed rhythm section.

Tick,
Tick,
Tock,
Tick,
Tick,
Tock,
Tock,
Tock,
Tick,
Clunk,

The clock on the wall read 6:15. She waited but on went the monologue, like some bad student play, with a backing track of this horrible rhythm section.
Clunk,
Tock,
Tick,
6:16,

Tick,
Tick,
Clunk,
Clunk,
6:17,
Clankity,

That was a different sound, whose clock did that. She looked around to all the eyes staring at her. It appeared that she had mistaken that last sound for a clock, not the jaw snapping shut from Mr Ballchin or was it Mr Chinballs, she couldn't recall.
"May I repeat, the next agenda point is about the liaison consultant with Royal free Infirmary, the one who will run this test of change. I see we have one of the candidates here Dr Anderson. Although none of your colleagues have turned up."
She wasn't sure what emotion he was trying to show, he kept the same tone of monotony throughout. As she stood up all the white hairs on their faces and ears came to a stand.
"I just think we need to have clear clinician, and doctor leadership here, and given that I'm here shows I'm ready for that role. Plus, I worked at the Royal and know how it works and the best way forward is to integrate our systems as well as funding streams. Now this may have an initial cost." She paused allowing

them to silently raise their eyebrows, she could feel the air fill with their gossiping thoughts like ants at a picnic.

"However, the projection and cost benefit analysis our department has formed with a small two-month trial with plastic surgery has been wonderful."

She then nodded towards the only young person in the room, the one working the projector, she recognised him as a junior doctor from some other specialty, probably here for brownie points. He had after all volunteered to get a computer working and projector working and hadn't been able to leave since.

A pie chart of gold, milk and honey came on, it showed a profit, and she could feel the metaphorical lips being licked and the pupils dilated. She swore some of the managers had dollar signs in their eyes.

"Very good Dr Anderson, I'm sure in the ballot this will play on our minds. Now the next agenda point is about the allocation of the new junior doctor's wellbeing fund."

She sat down and started to slowly zone out. She would have cared about wellbeing a few years ago but had learnt to try to keep to her own. This was the second to last agenda point, she didn't mind though because she felt the win was already in the air for her. She had given what those old men wanted more than undressing her with their eyes. She had given them making money within the NHS. Now health was a commodity that was never out of fashion.

Click,
Clunk,

She was oblivious to the sounds, she glanced and saw 6:52 as the last agenda point was opened to the floor, after it was always:
"Any question or anything to add?"
There was silence, like a classroom ready to be dismissed, no one dared ask a question, not when everyone else wanted to leave. The silence deafened and crashed, and a small note of a hum could be heard in the room from the projector, this hum then began to fade perfectly into the sound of words from the monotonous leader Mr Chinballs.
"Dismissed."

Everyone stood up in a rush like Millie on pizza night or like people rushing out of a club with its lights on not wanting to see what they or anyone else looked like at that time of night. She watched them all leave before looking up at the clock
6:57.

Her Porsche was good but not that good. Damn that James, he wins another point she sighed frustrated trying to hide her guilt with anger.

*

7:09 and she almost runs a red, but she is now coming off from the dual carriageway. Down into the estate towards her lovely, detached family home. She parked up in the drive as she looked up at what she and her husband had achieved. It was so much easier to get things done in twos she thought. She was a sap after all deep down inside. It's why she couldn't help feeling bad, she was not the wife she was meant to be. If her mother could see her now, not at home cooking, the kitchen would never be able to host guests in and a dining table which most of the time was just lap trays in front of the television. Whilst feminists around the world rejoiced, she couldn't help but hear her mother smack her lips in a tutt.

The door opened to the laughter of her daughter and another young girl. They seem to be in fits as she spots her husband chatting to both of them. Her paranoid thoughts tried to slowly encapsulate her thinking, a small thought of *"I bet Millie and him would prefer that babysitter, she does after all have a tighter body and probably would give him more sex"*.

She pushed the thoughts down. She stomped into the room. Again, she enjoyed all eyes being on her.

James smiled, "Alright dear, I was just telling them about the time you had to drag me to bed after our last dinner date, too much whiskey makes daddy…".

"Piss-ey," Millie retorted quickly with a big smile. She had tried to copy her dad's Scottish accent.

She wasn't sure if she should allow her daughter to speak like that, but then she is the daughter of a Scottish man.

Her eyes then focused on the young babysitter, she looked around her early twenties, possibly late teens, she wore her two-tone coloured hair down, a little autumn with little reddish yellow at the bottom, she looked like the fall season. She wore a black top which glittered and some red coloured chinos and all-star converse to complete the look. She looked older than their normal contingent of babysitters for Millie.

She must have been staring too much because James introduced her, "This is Catherine, or Cat, she is helping out, she's a student at the practice and needs a little help with cash. Last night we were chatting about her, remember?"

"Oh yes of course," she lied. He looked at her with a knowing look, knowing she had lied but he let her wriggle free. Making her feel even more guilty about doubting him.

"Nice to meet you Dr Anderson, I've heard so much about you, your husband here won't stay quiet, I wish he'd teach me something instead of babbling on about his wife," Cat charmingly smiled.

It made her wonder if this was a ploy because her smile was familiar to her, it was the same one she had during any hospital meeting which she needed to impress.

"Well, he is an utter sap isn't he, useful for something," she smirked and caused some laughter through the room.

"Well, we don't want to miss the reservation, why don't you get ready dear." He interrupted, taking back control of the room.

"Ready," she said, lifting her eyebrows, of course he would be the man to pick up on subtle changes in her face.

He saved himself quickly, "well I mean you look wonderful, it's just surely you need to get out of uniform like we tell Millie."

He scored and it was game set and match especially when Millie piped up, "yeah mummy we all have to get out of school clothes."

Defeated but happy, she was able to go into the room and for once look at clothes which weren't labelled or planned perfectly. She was looking at her clothes that turned her into a civilian. They lay at the bottom of the cupboard on the floor, the "kids" would call this arrangement a *floordrobe*. She hardly ever wore the assortment of outfits on the floor, although had spent a bit of money on them she would no doubt hear from her mum and dad. James would never say anything though, he was too good.

A few quick uses of her make-up brush and lipsticks allowed her to top her fierce work look transforming it to her fierce yet sexy date look. She then stared at the different outfits which she had picked up from the floordrobe. A small hum filled the air as her mind took the notes and played Roy Orbison's pretty woman. She proceeded to try the outfits with shakes of her head and nods as appropriate of course. All of them a little bit un-ironed but due to her slight gain of weight over the last few years stretch ironed them right out against her body. She settled on one bought from Sainsburys nonetheless, a sparkling black dressing with golden glittery shoulders, it wrapped her figure well and made her look at least one and a half years younger. Not as young as that student. With a change of shoes to glittery platforms she stepped into the room and took it in. James had his kind eyes, but they couldn't help but look and Millie smiled and chimed, "Mummy can I have that dress. I wanna look like a princess too."

The student had nothing to say and was sheepishly looking at James before looking down once she caught her eyes.

"Shall we go? Are you designated this time then?" she smirked trying to get in early before he convinced her to drive the Tesla. Once again, he beat her to the punch and caused another feeling of guilt over how nice he was being.

"I phoned ahead for a taxi, it should be here in two, looks like I know how long it takes for you to get ready, shows my obsession. I probably wouldn't go on a date with a creep like me," he got the room laughing again. She was a little jealous that he stole her big dress reveal but also relieved that she could drink tonight. After all, tomorrow was a late shift and James' day off, they could allow their elderly bodies to recover well.

*

The cold weather seemed to pierce her in her tights and dress. She looked over and was jealous of the tweed and disarming shirt her husband wore. He had his half-moon shaped glasses hanging from the top corner pocket and his navy-blue chino ironed and crestless. He didn't look cold. It only took a moment before she noted the tweed jacket was on her. Guilt surged, He smiled. She smiled back. The taxi came and they climbed in and James struck up the conversation; a habit of his.

Normal conversation always deteriorated when the taxi driver found out he was a GP. The NHS is shit, we all need to pitch in to help out, how awfully busy doctors are, how he can't see his GP and what he should do about his mum. She frowned but always loved her husband who handled people so well. He was able to leave the taxi with the man appreciative of the talk, like a small therapy session. Jealousy and guilt mixed in with love, her mind and stomach lurched about the man in front of her, she took his hand as all the emotions intensified. Into the nice wine bar, they went.

*

They had shared a great starter platter as well as charcuterie, with a lovely Merlot straight from Argentinian Catena selection. James had bullshited about the area and also chose a mid-range priced one. It went very well with the steak and his eyes. She couldn't help but just listen to his confidence and his bullshit, she loved it about him.

"You see they said Camus was all about absurdism, but I tell you I bet he was doing it just for the chicks, you gals love an absurd hero right?"
"Yeah sure, we all love someone we don't get."
"Enough about what I spent the afternoon doing,"
She looked at him, wondering about his workday compared to hers. He managed to lift her out of seriousness with his own absurdity, "contemplating what chicks dig is within the remit of GP."
They both shared a laugh.
"How was your day? How was the meeting, are you the sexy boss now? Do I have to call your secretary to know when you're free?"
She smiled at him. "Well, they liked the pie chart a lot, as well as the money making, it did end positively. Plus, I had a nice day, I actually talked to Abdul. We hadn't properly chatted in a while."
"Well Abdul is great, although you seem to change your mind on him more than Katy Perry."

"When did you get contemporary?" She laughed, "Are you trying to impress your students?"

"I think even they know I just ain't cool, Millie on the other hand, she's young and she thinks I'm well cool."

Another pang of guilt, was he suggesting she didn't spend enough time with Millie, or that Millie didn't think mum was cool? It was weird how much of a daddy's girl her daughter was. She paused her thoughts again, taking a large sip of Merlot to hide the fact her smile was fading. Her cheeks turned bright red. Wine did that to her.

"Thing is I loved Abdul's passion, but now he's so placid, it's not like him."

"I'd say you got on better when you pretend there was a common enemy. Not everything has to be a fight Beth, sometimes we can be content, we can stop moving forward because we're happy."

"Abdul was never like that, not when I was his SHO and *registrar*, I just feel like he's hiding something or that we aren't the friends we used to be."

"Well, I don't think you can be the friends you used to be, if that's how you feel about it."

This was the first time James didn't smile with his sentence. He continued, "I do understand

why it's tough. Life doesn't make it easy as we get older to continue our friendships from our youth, we change too much."
For once it wasn't guilt that surged through her just defeat.
"Yeah, I know, but I feel everyone has lost it, the passion," She swallowed her pride, "I guess that's why I want the Job at the Royal. You and Abdul might not need it, but I need to move forward."
His smile returned and the next sentence warmed her heart, "you've always done the right thing, I always think you are doing everything right. I just want you to be happy. That's all I care for."

He finished his glass, followed by her finishing and they topped up. A few flashes later they were having whiskey at the bar. He had made her fall for whiskey or at least threatened not to be with her if she didn't. A Scottish man with a wife who doesn't drink whiskey, worse than a catholic marrying a protestant, plus she was posh and southern too, which she needed to make up for.

With him the whiskey always flowed and so does time, one moment to the next, the taxi arrives. Kissing him on his soft lips, a French one too, more tongue, hands where they shouldn't be, erections, nipples and members, arriving home, paying the babysitter and the taxi driver for the trip and to take her home to the dodgy student end of town. She swore the student checked out her husband's cock. Then tiptoeing past Millie's room which held her snoring as loud as any old man, a trait she had inherited from her father. In their room their mirror showed her and her husband ten years younger as her dress slipped off and her uncomfortable, yet beautiful laced underwear was revealed to the Scottish man. He had enough belly to love, enough to make him mature and wise. She slipped him out of his fun underwear before sliding hers to the side, releasing her breasts as they clambered into the bed together. Grunts and moans filled the place, he was her boss here, she felt pleasure and she could feel that he did as well, it all sped up, her rosy cheeks flushed further, every vessel in her body dilated and caused her heart to race and her body to contract and surge with release. Everything was in flow for 10 minutes. Afterwards they lay to each other's side. Moments passed as he hugged her bringing her close, she wondered what his mind had started thinking about. She imagined he thought about how amazing that was and how in love with her he was. However, all she could think about was the shift tomorrow and how best to manage the department, how best to teach the newbies and how horrible it would be to wake up. She felt kindness and comfort, but unsettled, she wondered if you were always meant to feel amazing and in tune as well as always think of the person who was there forever according to the marriage vows. Not that it wasn't exciting, just more that she wasn't excitable anymore when it came to day-to-day life with James. She had one purpose and she wondered if it was worth it. After all, passion for your work is admirable, it's what the people who have legacy have. Legacy was forever an orgasm for 10-150 seconds depending on how long he thrust for while she peaked.

He kissed her forehead, "hey honey, I love you." There was 10-150 seconds of silence, she was too dazed to figure out which number was true. He pulled her close.
"I love you too," she replied exhausted, whether it was from the sex or her conflicting feelings she didn't know.

Chapter 4: More Dance More Appetite

She loved a good night out, but the come down was always worse. For that she always had to have the perfect comforts. She wondered if people would frown at her for being like this, after all she was now **Dr** Amis. It sounded weird to say out loud and her mind told her it was wrong, well the comedown part of her mind. Her other half of thoughts, the positive side, was beyond pleased with her accomplishments.

She looked up at the television playing RuPaul's drag race. Smiling at the competition unfolding in front of her. She was cuddled up in her duvet, with a hot cup of hot chocolate and the pizza hut pizza box revealing cheap but filling pizza slices laid on the floor within perfect arms reach.

She had several fun nights out since arriving in Darthington, it was small but there was just enough going on that she could keep it varied. Another lovely chicken slice went into her gob, she chewed as she turned the TV up, she was after all a loud chewer, people were always too polite to tell her, well everyone apart from her come down brain.

Tomorrow were the last two days in her first job before the dreaded rotation. Although to her this meant more people to suss out, maybe more people to join on her quest for the everlasting party. Darthington could be the new Ibiza, that could be her life goal, she giggled to herself. She wasn't exactly the most suited to seriousness and doctor-ness, but she enjoyed it. She always did things she enjoyed, that was her motto, well a very clichéd motto, but life's greatest truth are probably clichés. She took another bite, she likes pizza, that was also a cliché, further proving her point to both parts of herself.

The rest of the day ends up being a blur as her dopamine and serotonin slowly fill up in her brain, able to be less critical, analytical and more emotional. She wondered what the next rotation held in store for her. She would be doing what they call a tough job, with night shifts and weekends, things that would get in the way of things she enjoyed. Although adrenaline and late-night delirium were their own high as well, some of the few legal highs along with caffeine that were left in the UK.

Not that it was inherently wrong, after all people probably couldn't be trusted with drugs, she barely managed and a few of the others last night definitely couldn't manage. She paused before she had her usual "are drugs okay" inner argument, instead she thought about the people she had met at work as well as the patients.

*

Her first day had been interesting, she had led her two new colleagues around the department, she felt excited about her new life. Plus, she always liked getting to know people, she was a bit of a gossip after all. She had met them in the corridor and tried her best not to let the covers and prologue determine her impression of them. She couldn't help her mind focus on those thoughts as they snaked down to the changing rooms.

Izzy McCullen - the no frills textbook but that would be good to read.
Richard Twain - the daily cartoon in the telegraph probably.

She watched them each go into the rooms and thought back to the mean comments her mind was making, there was probably more to them than what she had said but there can also be more to a textbook and a cartoon as well. She also thought about friendships and the reason she had come to Darthington. She wanted to get away from her bad rep, but she still wanted to party somewhat. Reinvent herself somewhat, maybe to even like medicine. She didn't really know if she wanted to be a doctor, she liked people, she liked gossip but more importantly she loved her free time.

Both of them reappeared wearing scrubs, both unfitting. She thought Rich was being brave trying to squeeze in a small as it wasn't as flattering as he probably thought. She wondered if Izzy knew that trying to pinch everything up to draw less attention to her clavicles and potential cleavage probably made people look more. She looked down at her scrubs and wondered if anyone had opinions about her, or maybe no one would have opinions on any of them because no one really cared.

The day seemed to whizz by as she got to know her two new colleagues a little more, she found it funny that Rich seemed to be hitting on Izzy who responded out of politeness but knowing men like Rich probably saw it as flirtation.

Then they split and they each saw a patient. Her one she couldn't recall fully because it had become a blur of so many patients she had seen by the end. Not that it wasn't exciting, it sure did get the adrenaline rushing but as she did more of the same management to every patient she began to work on autopilot.

Someone would come in short of breath, they'd be coughing up sputum, they'd need oxygen, she would write up antibiotics, intravenous fluids and take blood tests before letting them head for a chest X-ray. The X-ray would confirm everyone's suspicions, including the patient themselves, this was a bad chest infection. However, before she could get the gossip from the patient or know about their life to distinguish them from the others they went to the acute medical unit where something else happened to them she imagined. Some holistic all-knowing doctor did more than they did. She hoped so because she wanted a bit more of a challenge in her future. She swore she saw more and more as the colder wind meant coats and cloakrooms on Friday and Saturday nights. Everyone thought she was good, she didn't even remember half of who she saw or what she did, I guess it meant her subconscious was a better doctor than her.

*

Bringing her mind back to the room, she thought back to that one evening they had spent together, this had really revealed their personalities. They had a few drinks as a team although it did slowly whittle down to just two of them. Most likely due to the mixed signals between the two new doctors she worked with. Both Rich and Izzy hadn't dealt with the fact they were heterosexual and of the opposite gender.

*

It was a few Fridays ago now. She set the scene in her mind, they were at The Jarlsberg pub. They had been sitting in the bar for fifteen minutes before Rich had made a crude remark, or what she imagined he saw as a flirtatious remark. Izzy's face contorted into a polite smile with a giggle. It made her laugh at how unexpected the face had been. She found it all funny not clever, but we all do laugh at farts still. They grabbed some more drinks, this time she was buying. She looked at Izzy who was helping her get some drinks.
"Funny chap isn't he, predictable but still funny." She glanced to see the response of the blonde girl next to her.

"Yeah, do you not find him a bit intense; I'm always worried I spend too much time talking to him, not sure why he chooses me."

"Aww he's just one of those guys wearing his heart on his sleeve, plus he can't help if you're attractive, can he?"

She furrowed a little, she could tell Izzy didn't like the insinuation.

"Well, a hint is a hint, plus guys like him have an ego. I'm not looking for any good looks, or funny or anything, just someone nice."

"Most people are nice, underneath it all, surely," She enquired looking for any give from the girl in front, obviously she kept her thoughts hidden. She took the silence as a response and changed the conversation.

"Shall we get some bubbly then?"

"Bubbly?" Izzy's surprised reply almost acted as a no.

"Let's just do it, I love a night where bubbles go all the way to your head! The only thing that beats that is a night where something else goes for head." She felt her voice and words physically wink then nudge the girl standing in front.

"Rachel!" Izzy gasped, definitely getting that one. Smiling back at her, she wondered what her university days were like, after all medics are funny people, they can't do things by halves, even the quietest medic were all go-getters. They had to be to get into the field and survive. She thought to herself, we *all have an ego to wrestle here.*

"How about you get some bubbles and I'll get such a dry white it counts as bubbles," Izzy looked at the girl with a wry smile, she appreciated the compromise and nodded,

"But I pick your wine." She replied, they both laughed.

"So not a girl for Rich then," she enquired further trying to live vicariously through this potential will they won't they love story.

"More like he's not a boy for me," the girl replied, showing there was more underneath the surface. She liked finding out more about people, she was a right gossip girl. *xoxo.*

"Right, needs to be nice," she rolled her eyes as she watched Izzy hold both drinks with a steadiness which she couldn't manage by now. Proving that one of them was sensible.

*

They had been "walking" into town. Izzy had left after Rich's attempted seduction and goodbye hug to try a kiss. This was after all not freshers and she hadn't seen anyone successfully pull that move off in years.

Although now a more contemplative Rich "stood" next to her. She hadn't heard anything about how hot her body was for 3 minutes. He kept talking about a "Sam". Although talking needed inverted commas as well. He was barely managing all three actions of "walking, remaining upright and talking" at once.

"Y'see, Razza, a great name for you. Sam was just the one for me, she could tolerate everything, I know I won't get a good one like that again."
She nodded, and with her skills of active listening replied with a "hmm yeah, sure."
"Y'a get me Razza, plus you wanna night out, I love a night out, Darthington is so sleepy. No one else does. Sam would never come along. We became a sit and watch box set couple, I felt like I was slowly wasting away. However, I guess I got a handjob when we did."
He was almost wistful in his nostalgia in front of her.
"You say it's sleepy, but we are meeting up with people from the hospital and we have just taken some stuff for a big rave night."
"Yeah, one rave night, in London there were hundreds all at once!" He exclaimed with his hands swinging violently as he lost, regained and lost balance again before falling over with his jacket in the bushes. They both laughed.

The high started to hit her as she lifted him out of the bush feeling all of his soft coat on her skin, it made her want to caress it. She kept some of her wits before holding his hand as they walked towards town.

They both stroked each other's hand as their chat descended further into nonsense, or what is sometimes known as the truth.

"See Sam would disapprove here, this is fun, who are we joining anyway."

"Some of the ED nurses, the fun ones."

"I hope that redhead is there!"

"I hope so too," Rachel proclaimed before they both smirked at each other.

"Bets on then." They caressed each other's hand which to them was a shake on the deal before they started to sway left and right and giggle and probably gurn which made their mouths have a curious note like a dissonant, resurgent note on a reed instrument. This continued until they got to a warehouse right next to a roundabout.

"This is dingy," Richard looked up with his dilated pupils.

She laughed at him, "ooh can't handle the sleepy town."

"Fuck off," he replied with a smile before they entered the building.

She remembers meeting up with a huge group of fellow co-workers. More bubbly, well bubbles were in the Red Bull which mixed with the Jaeger. Then dancing around like idiots, with blurred movements. Another blur and then she noticed her grin turn to a gurning laugh as the words fuck off squirmed out. Primarily because she had lost two of the group and lost the bet.

*

She looked back at her clock after her shower. It was 10 pm. She neatly climbed into her bed; she didn't really miss not having company in bed, but she missed having flat mates. It did mean she was queen of her own roost.

Her age showed to her the next day as she sat in front of Dr Abdul for her end of placement meeting, she hoped he remained positive, because she had a two-day hangover for the first time in her life.

"So how has it gone for you Rachel?" His eyebrows arched towards her. She realised there was something worse than negativity, asking her to chip in. Damn this new age bullshit. She pulled herself together.

"It's been fun, yeah I think I sort of get it."

"Get what?" He probed. She felt his probe hit her mind. She didn't want it there. She didn't want him to know the inner workings.

"Yeah, like being a doctor."

She held back and didn't say innit. She wasn't that cool, and it probably wouldn't show how professional she obviously wasn't. She forced quiet the criticism building from her comedown and hungover mind.

He brushed aside her comments. She wondered if she saw a little disappointment in his face, after all she wasn't being at all articulate.

"So, you've had good feedback from the other docs, plus the nurses and to be honest they know best."

"Yeah, guess I've bribed the right people." She smiled then quickly hid it, after all she had lost a little bit of her filter in her current state, and it was a risky joke. She noted the high risk led to a high reward of a chuckle from the weathered man.

"Look I've seen you practice and you're good Rachel, you know your guidelines and you finish jobs we've all asked. All the feedback is to keep doing what you're doing, I did want to add though, start thinking about your style and maybe future career early on. Especially since you're comfortable already and I think we are all impressed."

Her own *style*, she watched him write down that goal on her portfolio page and she wondered if that was worse than not being complimented because it meant she now had expectations to find this *style* when she just wanted to come to work, get paid and enjoy her free time.

"Thanks sir", she formally replied

"Something you don't like?" He raised his eyebrows

"Not at all sir," she wondered why he questioned her, but he seemed to relent on the second answer.

"Very well I'll send this off and you can go find Izzy for me?"

She stood up, smiled and walked out before gesturing to the final colleague to go for their meeting before she realised it was now time to rotate and start the cycle again. She wondered which of the type of doctor she'd be quiet, loud, satisfactory, worrying or a distraction. She'd come out satisfactory and they wanted good, although she felt that wasn't so much a category but more so a by-product that different types ended up being dependent on the consultant's personality. She stepped out to the chorus of breach for one last time. The band played their last encore to her. She wondered if she would miss the live version of this song. She guessed she could get the band back together in the future. She smiled, ED was not for her, she wanted to have her weekends for her *extracurriculars*.

*

She sat in a stuffy room on induction. Induction had been a marathon of "this is how we do it" and "everyone else in the hospital is wrong". She wondered if she would get along with the two people sitting next to her. She was now on perioperative medicine. A weird branch of medicine to fill in the gaps of knowledge of surgeons to what induction arrogantly called "actual medicine". A role which only existed because of the complexity of everyone and super specialisation. It was also a get out of jail free card for the surgical team to feign ignorance about everything but cutting. This time this was her cynical mind speaking, without any come down, however she was craving the weekend fast. The rota given to them showed her she couldn't have all of them.

Her colleague to the right was a more senior doctor with some curly ginger hair and "hip" glasses. He smiled and laughed a lot, a people pleaser she imagined. To her left was a very well dressed Fy1. He even had a bowtie. He stunk of cologne, and he had a serious contemplative look. He wore glasses perched on his nose, although the way he looked above them to the lecturer made her think they didn't have real lenses on them.

"Always escalate to your seniors, you shouldn't be making decisions on your own and it's very important, especially as we have some medico legal issues before and the biggest thing we find is things weren't escalated."

They paused before continuing, "also this job is great for autonomy and developing your own independent thinking."

She felt a vague headache come on as they continued talking. She wondered if anyone next to her would understand her joke from 1984 around doublespeak. She whispered in the bow tie man's ear, "doublespeak."

He coughed with no response and having overheard her the curly haired man gave a small giggle in her ear. She wondered if both had got it and one liked to please and the other wanted to show his superiority. It was funny that it didn't match the seniority their badges portrayed.

The talk continued with its doublespeak. Once it finished and they were allowed to stand and mingle with everyone around, some lovely sandwiches were supplied. Although each sandwich had their own drug company leaflet attached to it about the merits of

"Benidreem" the new vegan vitamin D supplement. It promised it would change lives and make all elderly people smile and have a family according to the pictures.

She grabbed some orange juice and a ploughman's sandwich; it had a big red warning next to fat content which she chose to ignore. After all, she was looking for more junk in her trunk.

The curly haired man approached her, "Dean Perez," he almost giggled holding out his hand to her. She shook back.

"Good 1984 joke, although this job should be fun. We get to be the smart ones on the ward." He smiled before chewing his sandwich loudly, louder than her, which hypocritically was slightly off putting. Out of the corner of her eye she could see her fellow Fy1 chatting to the consultant, repositioning his glasses and miming a beard stroke on the pencil thin chin strap he had.

"So what job were you on first," Dean enquired. She knew the jig they did.

"A & E."

"Wow, you must be handy in an emergency, I'll come to you with everything then." He joked, the 5th time she'd heard that today. More introductions happened. She mentioned her life, how she lived alone. She got the usual response of it being "rough". He mentioned his fiancée and showed off, in pictures on his phone. The ring around her finger. It felt like a get out of jail free card with regards to how flirty he could be. Plus, she knew he was trying to make himself more wanted by being unattainable. They each got each other's number, under the guise of her being able to discuss with a senior. She realised he was a cliché, but to be honest she had felt a little lonely and she didn't mind the attention. Plus, he did have a certain "good looking medic" vibe about him.

They then sat down to have more induction, this time it was about leave and the rota. The bit where they praised rota coordinator for all their hard work whilst simultaneously telling them they had to sort it out amongst themselves. They were flexible, as long as we were flexible. The doublespeak continued and she giggled with Dean next to her when he referenced it back. She had to give him something for his ego.

*

Another Saturday was spent at the warehouse, although in the morning she had gone for a surfing lesson with Dr Perez. Platonically of course, especially with the help he gave her to get in and out of her wet suit. She didn't know if she felt guilty. She found herself texting him quite a few times, with each of their responses getting longer and longer. They had seen a festival for the following week which made her keen to get tickets. She made sure to ask if his fiancée would be keen as well. She wanted it to be all above board; she really liked him. She had said it to him that morning at the beach as they shared some more about each other. Both being vulnerable, staring into each other's eyes with ice cream, a slightly romantic thing he should be doing with his fiancée. She felt bad not because of guilt, but because of the lack of guilt she felt.

All this running through her head was not helping the high she was having in the club.
The others around her were on another level. Tilly especially who was dancing around with everyone. What a powerhouse.

She looked down at her phone, a new bumble match it read. She ignored it and wondered again what a good level of pullback from Dean would be. She decided to hold off replying to his last text. Maybe a little blank until work would be best. She pressed the off switch before going back to try and dance with her friends, another shot would probably help slow her mind down. She was right because after grabbing everyone for tequila, using her hard-earned money on her favourite pastime of shots the room spun once, twice, the light shone and shone and every song that played was her favourite. The hits kept coming and coming.

"This is fantastic," she shouted to no-one in particular. She imagined everyone was nodding due to her statement and not as a reflex to the music.

She saw stills of Rich approaching Tilly but getting a knock back before brushing it off and dancing with some of the other nurses, and by dance they stayed an inch away and he showed off his lack of rhythm. She enjoyed the fact he, from what she heard from Tilly, was scared of what he found sexually enjoyable.

He came up to her, "don't you miss our little trio?"

"I don't know if I'd call it that, we didn't exactly interact too much."

"Yeah, but musketeers yeah, plus me and Izzy had to go on without ya. As we are now part of the great and bonafide surgical team!"

"Well, I am the smart one you come too, a boss of sorts. You gotta listen to me."

"Hmm I don't mind it. Quite a sexy boss."

He was back to himself. It had been a record five minutes before he had implied something sexual.

"Well, I'll take it as the compliment that it's meant to be Rich."

A moment before another beat going at 110 bpm came on.
"Ohh this is my favourite song."
"Mine too," they both shouted as they danced to completely different songs in their heads. She loved her pass-time, however recently the two-day hangover was starting to make her work week seem long and tiring and she had lost little of her hyperactive edge, but it was worth it for the feeling of euphoria she was getting now, she would probably never give it up.

*

She was waiting for her annual leave, every week was harder, because the comedowns were getting a little longer. She was managing at work and they told her she was. Today they were on a consultant ward round, meaning she could get away with thinking little. She was thinking a lot but more about how awful she felt and how hard a workout it was to keep both your eyes open with an interested smile as they rounded around the ward. Stepping into cubicles of patients who stared up at the group of people hoping for some interaction, but they got minimal. They wanted to talk to the consultant, but he instantly turned his back and started talking to her and Dean who was perched behind her.

She held onto the folders trying to balance two on top of each other whilst writing in one like some acrobat, but no gold medals or tens for her as she almost toppled several times as she tried to keep up with the pace of the consultant. The notes jiggled and Jenga'd in her hands as he talked to her.

"Now we have a fractured neck of femur[21] here today. We need a bone profile[22], so get them sent off. She'll need bone protection and since she was feeling faint before falling it might be worth getting the ECG[23] and lying and standing blood pressure (BP)[24]. Make sure you fill in the proforma please."

---

[21] Fractured neck of femur - broken hip bone.
[22] Profile - blood tests including vitamin D, calcium and phosphate, the main components which affect our bones with regards to remodelling.
[23] ECG - electrocardiogram, a tracing of the electrical activity of the heart.
[24] Lying and standing blood pressure - check to see if there is any blood pressure drop when standing, as it can cause dizziness and falls.

He acknowledged her existence with a side glance, she imagined he did not want to exert too much effort by moving his neck. She used one hand to hold her pen and another to balance the folders. She managed to just about wobble and write in a barely legible scroll across the piece of paper known as the proforma in front of her. She ticked the boxes he mentioned, but there were lots left to fill on the piece of paper. none of which had really been clarified in that quick fast talking, stock exchange floor rattle the consultant had given her. She couldn't keep up and the supportive senior, Dean, was following the consultant, nodding further and agreeing. He was asking questions that were actually answers, getting a smile and nod from the consultant.

She ticked the box for meds reviewed as well as wrote patient alert, comfortable and no new concerns. She wrote the plan of ECG, lying and standing BP. She hurried off. Stopping a moment to look back and gather her list from the patient bed. The list which would be her guide for the rest of the day. The bible. The star which led her to Jesus. She made eye contact with the patient; he had a pleading look. She imagined he just wanted someone to tell him where he was, what was

going to happen and reassure him he would still live. She couldn't offer that. She offered a small joke.
"Don't wanna lose my script yeah," she… well she made a half laugh, half sigh escaping her mouth which she couldn't describe with her vocabulary.
He chuckled dismissively as they both knew no one was being comforted here today.

She raced along scribbling ECG and LS onto the list with small squares she could tick once completed to get her dopamine receptors going crazy. Her MDMA at work.

She caught up to the ward round as they started to walk into the curtain of the next patient, before she could relax, she was given the Jenga tower from Dean. He smiled at her with a quiet *sorry* which was meant to make her feel he understood her situation. She didn't think he did. Although he was only a few years her senior. She let the power dynamic go as the folder fell to the ground and everyone for one second acknowledged her humanity before the consultant turned to the patient. She wondered if this patient got told what was going on, instead she saw them talking whilst the consultant's stethoscope was in his ears. Like a librarian he raised his index finger to his lips –shh- he mouthed to the patient before he continued his examination. She quickly scribbled down the whispers Dean gave into her ear. They comforted her when they shouldn't have. She felt a little dirty before the consultant turned around with another fast-paced business-like summary. Although he didn't mention the findings on the chest. She didn't know what to do with the "lungs" she had drawn but imagined as he didn't mention them it was normal and an arrow with the words clear underneath was written.

Her mind went automatic and an hour and a half later, she stood in front of the nurse's station with a smiling team.
"Did you hear me?" A pause as eyes darted around her body finding her lanyard.
"Rachel, right?"
She looked up and the consultant seemed different, "let's get some coffee, what do you have?"
"Just black with some sugar would be brilliant."

"Excellent you and Dean get in the office, and I'll bring it through, and we can catch up."
He strolled off. A different man to the one she had just documented like a ghost-writer

for. She wondered how people manage it, to know the inner thoughts of these consultants and document them accurately or is it like a lot of biographies in which the truth is a kernel and the fluffy popcorn around less than true.

She sat down with Dean's eyes catching hers.

"You guys have it so tough, being an Fy1 is the worst."

She saw his attempt at empathy, but her brain had no fight left in it. She accepted it with a small smile, "yeah, thanks Dean."

They smiled again at each other, "guess you're glad you escaped it!"

"Well now I have the problem of too much responsibility and being an SHO. There's less support up here."

They both laughed.

"So when the consultant gets back, are we doing the whole summarise each patient and write the jobs on a separate piece of paper before doing them?"

She asked, wishing this inefficiency didn't exist.

"Yeah, sounds good, then we can split them up right," he replied eagerly. She wondered if he ever questioned the inefficiency or had he always liked it. She wondered if they all gave into the habits of their seniors eventually.

The coffee came, another half an hour was spent writing the stuff they had on the list onto another sheet of paper. Just a lot neater and clearer. It gave them their purpose for their day. Like a video game, this was their objective to finish level 15 of her perioperative job. Day and level had become one in her head.

*

Level 17 was particularly hard; she was five days away from her leave. They had a difficult perioperative patient, a heroin user who was also withdrawing. She had watched him writhing in front of her as she dropped her bag into the doctor's office before getting to the nurses' station cursing herself at arriving at 8:38 instead of 8:55. She couldn't use the "ward round is starting soon" to excuse herself from getting involved.

She went into the doctor's office to drop her bag, take out her lanyard and like a mystical girl in a Japanese anime she placed her stethoscope on. Feeling the transformative powers from civilian to doctor, because her clothes didn't differ from the people on the outside. Well, the civilians enjoyed their clothes a lot more. She felt her loose linen clothes restrict her. The rules they had around professional wear added to this. The length of her dress, the top she could wear. The fact her nails couldn't be painted. All rules aimed at women and not at any of her male colleagues, Dr Perez himself with his chest on show and his bohemian necklace was just expressionism for him, for her it would be unprofessional. Her modest top constrained her; the words unprofessional felt like the belt strangling her. She gulped her angry thoughts down her throat, almost choking before and stepping out to see the patient in her sight still writhing, but for once, no nurse came up to her to ask for something. She looked across to see Dean and the bowtie Fy1, Christian. They were chatting and laughing.

She decided to avert her gaze again and approach the two wanting to feed off their calmness.
"Hey, so the new chap in Bay 1 Bed 1. Is he alright?"
Dean looked at her, his eyes catching her off guard before she looked down at his hand then the floor then her great sexy boots. The last bastion of her outfit's freedom. She looked up at Christian, but his funky bowtie made her nauseated.
"Well look, he's got drug seeking behaviours and you know the nurses referred him to the

substance misuse liaison doctor. He can see him once discharged or his GP can sort it out. It's all we can do, we can't help them, it's not the right place."

She nodded along letting the logic hit her, it was true, it was hard in the hospital. She felt her brain collide with the phrase "we can't help". She wondered what this substance misuse doctor had that allowed him to help.

"Okay, that's cool, I saw him down in ED a bit, I guess I never dealt with it much. Probably lucky, I guess."

"Or cherry picking," Dean joked, his voice calming, but she knew if she relied too much on it there could be trouble.

The screams were a little louder, interrupting the other patient in the bay. They looked anxious, although no one moved, not even the ever so confident Dean. Eventually the nurses started approaching him with what some called hard love. She wondered if they were the only ones who did any helping in the hospital. Maybe them and this substance misuse doctor.

She thought back to her initial meeting with him.

*

It was a particularly busy day in the emergency department, and she had seen Rich dance around the department trying to stay in minors or avoid the corridors. She also saw Izzy circling another lap, probably waiting for results.

She had a man with a swollen ankle she was going to strap. The conversation explaining his X-ray hadn't shown a break, had been quite circular and even a little terrifying. It echoed in her mind as she had gotten the material for strapping the ankle.

"Oi, what do you mean it's not broken, it hurts like it is!"

"The X-ray is normal, but sprains can hurt as bad as a break."

"Yeah, sure and I bet the next doctor that sees it will tell me it is broken, it fucking hurts. You just don't get it!"

She looked at him wearily.

"I think, given the examination and X-ray it is unlikely. Why don't we strap it and get some exercise?"

"You just think I'm making it up- don't ya? Just like everyone else here. Look, I'm on methadone. I'm not a user anymore. Everyone else has had painkillers and I've been ignored."

She tried to back off a little feeling she had no answer. Feeling like she was out of her depth. Acutely, unwell, dying of pneumonia that was fine, but a well-ish man shouting, not so easy to handle.

"Let me get the stuff, chat with the boss to make sure and then I'll come and strap it up."
"Fine whatever, fucking hell."
She watched him put his head in his hands. A sign of frustration and giving up. There was no further anger as she slipped out of the curtains.

She had made a judgement based on what Tilly had told her. Probably because Tilly had met him and knew what he was like. Due to his use of methadone you had to be careful, you can harm them with a strong painkiller prescription. She did want to help, but she found it hard when she was feeling anger and frustration as well.

Before she knew it, she was back in front of the curtains, but two pairs of shoes were peeking through. She wondered if it was a friend of the patients and felt her heart race. Which it hadn't done at work before. She liked adrenaline, but not this kind. She preferred adrenaline from surfing than running from Mike Myers. She'd definitely hide if the latter was the case. She peeked through and the relief came in a whole-body relaxation. Another doctor was sitting with the patient. This doctor wore his own clothes in the ED department, to her he felt like he lived in a different world. He had come in wearing a woolly cardigan, with some nice chinos and leather boots. He wielded his doctor's bag in one hand and a stethoscope in the other. The patient had been unpleasant to her. However, he was smiling, understanding and nodding along to this doctor. She wondered what magic power his cardigan held. She stood with her head peeked through, they hadn't noticed her. Whilst they remained in their own world, she was able to watch the scene like a west end audience.

As she imagined herself as a theatre goer, the lights seemed to focus on the two as if they were the only two people on this particular stage. The scene started.

Noon int. Emergency Department
Darthington Hospital.

Dr Ebbideh
Hey there Ed, we've met before, haven't we?
Ed

Yeah, Dr Ebb was it?
Dr Ebbideh
You do remember, thanks I feel important enough now. How are you doing? It's been a while since you came to see me.
Ed
Ya see doc it's working with Chloe and the pharmacy down at Winchester Road.
Dr Ebbideh
It's quite good, plus it's near the small cafe isn't it.
Ed
Yeah, hillside cafe. Do a proper greaser there, it's quite nice, a few of us meet up.
Dr Ebbideh
Yeah, it's really good, the food fantastic and dead cheap.

Ed
Yeah, given how expensive it is in Darthington nowadays, it's like it's bloody London.

They both laughed and there was calmness on stage. This definitely wasn't a conflict scene.

Dr Ebbideh
Now look, I know they looked at your X-ray, no break, but I know it hurts, which is difficult for you because you walk everywhere don't you?
Ed
Yeah doc.
Dr Ebbideh
Well look, the X-ray says it's not broken and from what I've examined I'm not worried about it being broken.
[pause]
Ed [nodding]
Yes doc, I get ya.
Dr Ebbideh
Which means tape to support it and using it will probably be the best management at the moment.
Ed
Yeah, I get it for sure, that sounds like a good idea.

This time Ed was enthusiastically agreeing with the management. The lights faded.
The scene returned to normal as the curtains behind her felt like they were redrawn.

Dr Ebbideh continued, "and surely, it's great in two days' time, if I'm wrong, which I have been, then they'd phone you back. For once the risk is so small in this situation it makes me feel good, but I don't know if that helps you."
There was silence. A good silence whilst she watched him use it to let the explanation sink in and to let the patient dictate what they wanted. Ed smiled, "Sounds good dock."

She couldn't help but be miffed that there wasn't anything different said between her and him, maybe she wasn't good enough, maybe she didn't know how to communicate. Dr Ebbideh stood in front of her smiling. She had missed him introducing himself. She quickly darted to his lanyard which had RCGP showing his allegiance and pledge tied around his neck. She wondered if he saw it as the anchor. She usually saw them as that. His badge read Dr Ebb Honan.
"Hey there, I'm Rachel, one of the Fy1's."

"Excellent, wonderful," she was filled with positivity in that instance. He smiled back at her.
"Well enjoy, this is a lovely chap you just have to let him feel a little in control sometimes or know about the good local greasy spoons. I'd probably suggest that as your learning point here. Go for some food there, especially after a hangover."

She looked at him and laughed. Although her eyes must have revealed how annoyed she had been. The next words proved that to her. Dr Ebb's spoke as he walked away with his hand in the air ruffling his grey fluffy hair.
"Plus, the woolly cardigan means your words are just that more powerful."

*

She stood in silence holding the tape for the ankle strap, but just like the play she felt the light shining on her as she snapped back to reality, like Eminem and noted it was her holding her stethoscope zoned out in front of her two colleagues on the ward. The silence broken by the swearing of the man in Bay 1.
The nurses were now approaching this man as she looked at her side to see Dean and Christian laughing.
"No way, I can't believe you managed to get that height!"

She looked over and rolled her eyes. It was Dean showing off again. He'd been pretty cool on the water and hadn't stopped showing videos, although whether that was genuine excitement from Christian or just his nose being so far up anyone seniors' arse, she wouldn't be able to tell. She wondered what kind of video Dean could show that wouldn't get a positive response from Christian, probably show him wanking and he'd have something positive to say about it.
Despite her negativity in her head she couldn't help but look at the video when Dean showed it to her. She had seen it live, actually. She didn't want to be the same, but she had been impressed so despite her best attempt at a scowl she could only manage a smile. No laugh mind you or over excited phrases, a small victory for her, nonetheless.
"I mean you saw it, tell Christian how cool it was. Like the weather was fantastic, just unbelievable, never been like that before!"
Christian awaited her. She gave a nod and the uh-ha that followed was definitely too enthusiastic for someone who didn't know much about surfing. Christian interjected, interrupting her lyric-less song.

"Well yeah, it looks amazing, it's brilliant what mother nature can do. I feel now that I'm here I need to get into surfing."

She wondered if he meant that, after all there were a million things, she had heard him want to get into now that he was here. She remembered the list of them and who he had been talking to at the time.
1. There was a time where the consultant Dr Robinson had said he enjoyed climbing.
2. With Dr. Mothinder, the surgery *reg*, he had revealed his love of spicy food.
3. With the patient Angela, who was young and a little flirty, he had said he enjoyed going to the pub.
4. With her he had said he loved proper clubbing.
5. With the matron, he had talked about his love of baking after she had brought in cookies for the ward.
6. Finally, Dean and his long-standing wishes to do surfing.
It was intriguing that one man now had all these new hobbies. He surely had a busy year ahead of him.

The consultant had then arrived in front of the laughing trainees. The steps of his shoes seemed to bring the boys to attention, like a military general. He looked around at the three of them and she wondered if he could see in his peripherals what was going on with the shouting patient which the nurses were now confronting and "de-escalating". She would have to keep on wondering because whatever his thoughts there was no vocalisation of them.

"Shall we start then."

The routine began once again. She could feel her mind slowly tiring from it, away the boys went. One to get the nurse. The other to bring the trolley and I guess she was the one to pick up the first set of notes from said trolley and play her game of Jenga with the two folders in one hand and with her weapon of choice; the pen in the other. She wondered if that was a weapon of a junior doctor, because she didn't use the fabled stethoscope much.

They strode forward whilst she did a jig to keep up and keep balance. As they were the perioperative team, they walked past the first bed with the screaming man. She showed the file to the consultant. She was awaiting what his response would be to the current situation.

"Ah 26, can't see anything here that isn't optimised, shall we leave him to the surgical team, don't think we'd offer much help here anyway."

There it was again. She wanted to speak up, say I know who can offer help, but instead she watched them all walk away. Annoyed at herself for not speaking up but also for appreciating Dean's derriere too much. She decided to perch the folders on the end of the patient bed. One sway to her right and then her over correcting to the left means they landed on the patients' feet. She watched him shoot up as she tried to gather her things, but it was too late to pretend nothing had happened.

"Oi what's going on, just when I was actually feeling okay, now the pain is coming back!"

She paused, she tried to remember the way Dr Ebb had handled his patient, "umm sorry, just had to write down a few things, clumsy of me. Probably good I'm not your surgeon hey."

He smiled at that, "you're not too bad though, you cleared up quick innit."

She wondered why he had changed his interactions at that moment, but she decided to let the ward round go on, she wanted to do something different. She felt her heart pound and race, anxiety flooding her veins, she wondered if she was doing the right thing.

"Yeah, I'm pretty talented right, I'm well wicked at it."

She hoped she came off sincere and not condescending. She watched him accept her. He smiled at her giving her the best response, "wicked doesn't suit ya doc. You can help though, can't you."

She felt the shroud which had covered and dehumanised the man in front of her lift in front, like Moses and the burning bush she could help him. Everyone said they couldn't, but here he was asking for help.

"I'm ready; tell me how I can help?"

She felt like this was a secret, she needed a private consulting room, so she drew the curtain around the bed. It took three steps to successfully close the curtains:

1. The first was to try and hold onto the polyester materials. Every time she tried to grab a fistful it escaped her hand.
2. She finally moved to the source and tried to pull at it from the bottom, only to end up nearly falling over because the side she had done only does a straight line and won't cover her and the patient to make the "consulting room".
3. Finally grabbing the other side with a fist full of frustration and a little polyester burn their privacy was created.

Surely no one could hear the intimate secrets they would share, she heard her sarcastic brain proclaim. Lucky for him, he wasn't deaf and therefore they could talk at a volume where anyone who did want to listen had to have a bat-like hearing. Luckily from her experience of the patients in the neighbouring bays this would not be an issue.

"So, the thing is this stomach pain keeps coming in waves. No one seems to get on top of it, they keep giving me pain killers, but I just want to know what's causing it. If having no painkillers means I find out the cause, then I'll do it for you."

She stared into his eyes. She saw her eyes reflecting in his. She was sure he had the eyes of someone wanting change, the same as her eyes. She hoped she wasn't misreading them as it could easily be the eyes of someone who had stayed up all night doing all sorts.

"So, tell me more about the pain then," she probed, using the connection as a lasso to pull out the issues, concerns and expectation of what she had imagined is this forgotten misunderstood man.

"Well, it's been going on for months. In the morning it's worse. Like a stabbing or a spasm that just stops me doing anything at all. I can't work and I just have to lay there waiting for it to pass."

She nodded, with the right amounts of hmms she had been taught to show she was actively listening. Not that she wasn't, but she wanted to get this right and really show she was the help he needed.

"So, it really has affected your life hasn't it. Any trigger factors?"

"Yeah, that's what I just said, but yeah I can't think of any. It's not related to food. It's not related to anything else."

She did her nodding, he seemed engaged. She continued to ask. She felt she was getting closer to some sort of answer.

"Where is the pain and where does it go?"

"You see, I just don't know when it'll come, and it just means I can't do anything."

She felt a little jumbled with her questions because the answers still hadn't cleared the air. She thought back to her teaching around pain. If someone mentioned any pain apparently the best way to figure it out was to ask them questions within the anagram SOCRATES. This was meant to tell you the kind of pain. However, usually for her it was about getting the marks in her medical school exams.

- **S**ite – Where is the pain?
- **O**nset – When did the pain start and was it sudden or gradual? Include also whether it is better or worse.

- **C**haracter – What is the pain like? An ache? Stabbing?
- **R**adiation – Does the pain go anywhere else?
- **A**ssociations – Any other symptoms associated with the pain?
- **T**ime course – Does the pain follow any pattern?
- **E**xacerbating/relieving factors – Does anything change the pain?
- **S**everity – How bad is the pain?

Surely if she asked all of them, she would pass with the patient. She imagined what it would be like if they too held a marking scheme for every encounter they had with the hospital. She smiled that she would definitely get a few extra points.

She managed to go through it and note down on the balanced stack of plastic paper and metal binder in front of her.

- **S**ite – in the whole abdomen.
- **O**nset – starts gradual and builds up then waxes and wanes.
- **C**haracter – an ache with stabbing on top of it.
- **R**adiation – not in particular but sometimes it went to other parts of the body.
- **A**ssociations – nauseous with it.
- **T**ime course – nothing noticed.

- **E**xacerbating/relieving factors – certain movements helped or made it worse, "using" was the biggest relief.
- **S**everity – pretty bad, can't live with it. Scale varies from 6-9/10.

She looked down at her notes; her picture of him before looking at him. This was the time to examine the patient. To make contact with them, to touch the patient, pretending that that was going to reveal some big answer, although she knew that at least for her limited experience the examination was used just to confirm what she knew. Unfortunately, this time she knew nothing.

"I guess I should have a feel of the stomach and then we can talk about what might be going on."

He nodded and allowed the patient-doctor ritual to continue. She felt like she might as well have placed a feather hat on top, drawn symbols on her face with her red lipstick and gathered a stick with a diamond or ruby on it to start performing this ritual as she lay him flat in the bed using the remote control. She heard the machinery whirring as it slowly lowered the patient down. As she imagined inside the bed were old school chains which creaked as she whizzed them into action. The bed finally lowered, and she was able to see the man, not as some angry user, or a patient with complaints, or an examiner keeping the answer from her. She saw a vulnerable human being. Someone who was trusting someone else to the extent of lying flat, still and letting them do an examination. One she hadn't fully explained, but he was ready for.

She placed her cold hands. She saw him wince. She apologised, "sorry, did that hurt?"

"No, you just have the coldest hands I've ever felt," he smirked. She appreciated some kind of deflecting humour in this scenario. She rubbed her hands together to warm them up before attempting again. She pressed down on each part of his abdomen. The quadrants she had been taught would show her what was wrong, but they were all soft, painful, soft, no masses, nothing there. There was no answer hiding behind the exam.

She allowed machinery to bring him up to her level, trying to get rid of the hierarchy and vulnerability created a few moments ago.

"So it seems nothing really strikes out so it's probably worth investigating more. Trying to find the answer, it's obviously what you want."

"Exactly, an answer, so more blood tests or what, like what you gonna do?"

"I'll chat to the team, and we can make a decision okay!"

"More talking won't get me my answer," he was starting to get angry again, she felt his voice change. She thought she had a good rapport, but now she was disappointed that things had so quickly reverted.

"I've been here for twelve hours, and no one has done anything for me. I'm still in pain and there's still no answer. Like bloody hell how much more can talking get done."

"Look, I'm doing my best," she admitted "we just need to do the right thing for you and do this the right way."

"Well, your best isn't getting me anywhere, I just want a way, something to stop it. Ahhh!!!!!"

He started shouting and writhing again. She couldn't move, but the curtains had been drawn back, the nurses walked in and soon the same scene as at the start of the day was going on, given no one paid attention to her she was able to slowly step back. Initially she didn't remove her eyes from the scene. She saw the nurse try to talk him down before the threats of the security team. With that, things quietened down. She had taken enough steps back that she hit her shoulders abruptly on the nurses' station desk, where her team seemed to be hanging. The consultant broke her stream of thoughts.

"Same coffee order?" There was no real pause before, "good ward round team!"

She looked up and nodded, had he noticed she wasn't there, or was she that dispensable. She looked up at Dean and Christian who looked back. She could tell they only now just realised she hadn't followed them.
"So where did you disappear to?" Dean asked, looking at her with a raised eyebrow and a fake "I appreciate you and I am aware of you" look. Christian seemed to nod in agreement, but without the latter look. Probably because he didn't care enough to even try to pretend he cared.
"Yeah sorry, I was dealing with the first chap, just wanted to help since he asked me a question."
Christian sighed and Dean replied softly, "so, did you manage anything?"
"No not really, I felt he liked me for a bit, but his pain and examination didn't fit with anything." Dean spoke again softer, he was being sympathetic or maybe patronising, it was getting hard to tell sometimes.
"Yeah, which means most likely, he's not being honest with us. Especially with abdo pain. Our job is to rule out something nasty."
"I thought it was to try and help."

"Look, hospital is hard, but we just got to get people safe in their best interest."

His soft tone did reassure her, she didn't like the way his eyes moved up and down her body, she felt a little undressed and vulnerable, but at the same time if she was undressed and only Dean was there, she knew from experience she wouldn't mind.

"Yeah, I guess. You're right. I'll just tell the chaps looking after him, luckily it's Rich and Izzy anyway."

Dean laughed and smiled, "any excuse to get the old team back together yeah?"

She nodded as they both smiled together whilst Christian had stopped caring and was probably looking at his phone for the latest hobby he wanted to pick up.

"Anyways if I wasn't there, did we document the ward round," she joked, trying to sound indispensable.

Both Dean and Christian eyes jerked wider than she had ever seen them.

"Shit, yeah maybe you could, like we didn't change anything, it's going to be a nice day. Maybe say optimised and to continue as before."

She wondered how a human could be optimal and also what was before and how they would continue it.

Before she got those answers, the coffee had arrived and the ritual of quickly going through everyone again and rewriting everything onto another list began. She called it the duplication ritual by now, but she was good at faking enthusiasm for it. So much so the consultant made no mention of her not being on the ward round, if anything he made jokes and references to the ward round to her as if she was there. She didn't break his belief and laughed along, cementing the new fake timeline that she was there. After all, some may argue reality was what the collective believed happened.

She selfishly or selflessly opted to do the jobs on the bay that housed her patient she wanted to help. Also, it meant she would catch Rich or Izzy when they came to see him. She sipped more from her coffee, the buzz of a businessman's second best high overcoming her. Unfortunately, no rounds of coke from the consultant was allowed, *anymore* she imagined.
Energy, heart palpitations and highs. Her eat, pray, love, her mantra.
She scribbled away and put her signature next to things nurses and the Multidisciplinary staff who actually helped told her to put her signature next to. She would only quickly

check it was appropriate but she trusted and knew the people asking knew more than her and in a way it was her following senior advice and no one would say you were wrong for doing that.

*

She could feel her stomach rumble with generalised pain across her abdomen. She had finished coffee and nibbling on the different small chocolates from the nurses' desk didn't seem to help with her symptoms.

It was now 13:30 and she hadn't had lunch. There were plenty of discharge summaries[25] to write, as well as other places that needed her to place her signature next too. Also, Rich or Izzy hadn't appeared. Before her carbohydrate deplete mind could rant about her friends, like a perfectly timed script they arrived. Izzy smiling and giggling as Rich made another joke within his grand story. She could tell it was "grand" from the way his hands hung in the air claiming all of the air around Izzy.

---

[25] Discharge Summaries - formally a TTO (to take out) a document which summarises the patient journey in hospital as well as acts like a script for the medications issued. Usually sent to the GP and usually a copy is given to said patient.

"Hey Rach," she watched Izzy give her a beaming smile as she used her to step out of the air bubble with Rich. He took no notice and slowly brought his bubble to both of them.

"Heya guys, how's general surgery treating ya? Miss our time together yet?"

She wondered if they ever got bored of her same spiel she gave them every time they walked past each other. Since the split of the group they had been friendlier with their current team. It was now like passing a school friend in the street, you pretend you should see more of each other, but you never really make those plans and probably never intend to. She thought this was sometimes out of politeness and sometimes because the bonds between people appeared quite fragile in this high-strung shift work world. However, she mentally stepped down from her soap box to hear the replies from the two who sat in front of her with grins.

"We miss you Rach, not a bad thing to look at in the morning, although, guess Izzy will do," Rich looked at her with a wink, he probably gave himself more credit for that than anyone else would. "However, this surgery thing is very good, it's such a good team, so much banter and theatre is like super fun. Plus, you only have a few patients, and they all have problems which me and Izzy help fix. After all, nothing better than a power couple who fixes people."

Izzy laughed and her rosy cheeks showed off more colour, a blush some might call it. She wondered if that meant Izzy had moved on from polite smiling and giggling to hearty laughs in their closeness together. She could still tell that she wasn't sold to the idea of the man next to her who she knew wholeheartedly believed that Izzy had bought his product.

"I wouldn't go and say a couple, that's weird to say but it is fun, and the teams are really good. It feels like a team because everyone gets split up less often. Less left to your own devices, people teach you how to do things, plus a few nice meals and coffee after ward rounds are nice."

"Yeah coffee dates are brilliant, really help us get into each other's pants," Rich jumped in.

Izzy rolled her eyes, "it's not really a date if there's more than two of us."

"Well, we just need to get that date done then."

She felt she was watching a sitcom, oh how fast the in-jokes come when you work so intensely together. She was jealous that they had been able to do so. She knew that her friendship with Tilly sustained and now she was hanging out with Dean, a friendship she was worried could cross lines. It'd be easier with Rich and Izzy, both who do know how she feels given their similar experience, but as their paths diverged, she imagined all three would stop being as relatable to each other. Shaking her head at Rich's last statement she interjected, "that would be if you were good enough for Izzy."

She saw the blush again and Rich smiled, "well everyone needs a bad boy right."

"A boy is the word I'd focus on there," she quickly retorted, and Rich bowed in front of her whilst whispering about admitting defeat.

"So, shall we hang out at some point this week? Or maybe a coffee?" She questioned.

"Yeah, we definitely need to hang out," they both replied in unison. She watched as both of them reacted to that fact in different ways. She wondered what was in their heads at that moment.

"Need another good drink don't we," Rich smiled whilst Izzy nodded.

"Maybe a quiet one or game night, you guys must get tired of big nights," Izzy interjected, showing her point of view. Trying to lure them to her house, she wondered if it was because she preferred it to the pub or maybe she thought Rich wouldn't stay as long, a big gamble.

"Yeah, game night, then we can play drinking games," Rich jumped up and down in excitement, completely oblivious that the suggestion made Izzy nervous, something she could see on the other girl's face.

"Yeah, that'd be great, but let's message and figure it out. You can stop treating me like someone you did a class with at *uni* that you placate when you pass them by" She decided to go in with a double-sided joke, see if she got anyone biting back.

"Well, someone misses me," Rich laughed and made it about himself.

"No, it's not like that" Izzy looked apologetically with no signs of her getting the joke.

The pause between them all gave her the opportunity to ask a follow up question, "I did also have a boring work question."

Her words jerked the scene in front of her away from laughter and fun and friends to one to help her move forward in the day like some bad writer who couldn't find an appropriate Segway.

"Yeah, go on, let the power couple help," Rich smiled, Izzy winced, and she just laughed.

"Well, that chap in the first bay, What's the plan for the investigation because I had a big, long chat about his pain. Was just wondering if I can help at all?"

"Oh well", Izzy replied, not making eye contact with her, "I think that's why we're here, doing the discharge summary."

"Discharge!" She replied, never so surprised in her life.

"Yeah, I don't think we can help him, the consultant saw him this morning. Didn't you see the note from him?" Rich proclaimed.

She wondered why she had missed that in the notes. She quickly went off and grabbed them. Looking at them with Rich, hoping to prove him wrong because she wanted her outcome for the patient, she wanted to be able to help.

"There!"

Rich's big finger pointed at what looked like five squiggles. She squinted her eyes whilst Rich tried to read it out to her. She watched him elongate each word and struggle to tell her what had actually happened.

"S-oont, sorry soft na, no non ten something must be soft non tender. No pert and a squiggle,"

"Peritonitis," Izzy chimed in, finally looking into her eyes. She wondered if Izzy was on her side at all, maybe she hated conflict. If that was the case it would mean she'd never have a story as they don't exist without conflict.

"Exactly so discharge home with GP FUP. That means follow up y'know."

"I do", she replied. No anger, no resentment, just deflation in her voice.

"See we'll do that and sort him out, you don't need to worry, easy from your guy's end, can't perioperative him if he doesn't need an operation." Rich smiled, she wondered if he could read her face, was this to make her feel better or a joke to reiterate her job here.

"Yeah, plus that way you can plan our night whilst we do that," he continued.

"True, I guess," she gave them a faded smile before nodding, "I'll text ya guys, let's make this Saturday yeah?"

"Sounds good," Rich nodded.

Izzy gave her a smile, "see we are not going to be passing ships, but less of the drinking games. I don't know if I can handle a drunk Rich visiting, it's probably against the tenant agreement."

A fierce reply from Izzy and before she could watch the tennis match between the two, Dean had placed a hand on her shoulder, "everything alright there Rach?"

He looked kindly at her, his hands hard on her shoulder yet soft in her mind.

She looked into his eyes, "yeah I just wanted to help, I just feel like that chap needs help."

Dean looked, "sometimes we aren't able to help, that's the system's fault and not ours here. At least we can tell him it's nothing nasty, something he needs to work on which is tough, but nothing nasty."

The tone of his voice pitched perfectly to relax her; they both stared in silence,

"Let's get some coffee, I'll help with your jobs and stop Christian complaining about doing everything today. Maybe a drink when we're done."

"That'd be nice," she replied, "will Becca be there?"

"Nah she's on some course, so it's free for all at my house tonight."

She decided to worry about the consequences or potential trouble of a late night, she wanted the attention, "yeah sounds good we can go straight there."

"Perfect! The earlier we finish the more time I'll have. We can order food as well. After all, Becca loves a dad bod."

They laughed as his hand gripped her shoulder. Smooth, apart from the cold band, so called "promise", on his modern non-gendered ring finger.

Her tummy rumbled, she decided she would suppress it and just go overboard on the takeaway order.

*

It was whilst she was texting the final plans for Saturday that the next burst of noise started beyond the bleeps and sighs of nursing staff. It was the shouting of a man who had been given a letter and some medication and was being asked to leave the Bay.
"Look I don't know what's wrong with me," the man from before shouted. The man who Rachel couldn't even remember the name of. He had become Bay 1, Bed 1, to her.
"Out you go sir, go to your GP."
"Why can't you guys help, they'd said they'd help."
"Count your lucky stars you're not ill, now these beds are for really ill people."
She watched the matron give a stern face before he walked off. Maybe he knew the drill, maybe he knew security would walk him out or maybe the motherly matron had done exactly what she was good at; telling off, but showing she was kind and understood the situation, something she had never seen a consultant be able to do. A skill she was lacking in as well, showing too much kindness and not enough sternness when it was needed.

He walked away, no security, no big fight, like she had seen in the ED, just walked away with no help, just a common truth amongst all people that had minor illness, "It's not a serious illness, you just had to live with it."

She wondered if it was all a sickness of a soul, something you needed to work on, like some pilgrimage, or was it no illness at all but as the Buddha put it, the suffering of life. She knew this was her comedown brain talking although this time she hadn't used MDMA, she was just feeling shit.

Dean looked up from his computer and up at the time 5:30, they were running late, but not much longer until dinner, drink and comfort. She yearned further for that comfort when he smiled at her before returning to his typing.

She felt guilty. Her typing steadied, going through all the justifications in her head. Unfortunately, her head continued producing the guilt chemical refusing to listen to her rational reasoning. She wasn't the rational being she told everyone she was.

*

She remembered the food being yummy and sharing a lot, including the bottle of wine they had. She remembered the small amount of MDMA she had done to calm her racing heart after the day. She remembers the kiss and his hard and soft hands over her, she remembers the guilt as she left the house before anything else happened.

However, she also remembers how good it felt to be held by him like she was the sexiest thing alive, because a part of her saw him choosing her over his other half. It made her feel good, it made her feel helpful.

She had gotten home and the euphoria seemed to be mixed in with the guilt, her mind telling her off, but her body telling her not to worry about it. She could feel herself coming down too early, or maybe it was her conscious. However, she decided to bury that and call it coming down. She felt comforted, important and good, really good. She finished her "euphoric dance" before bed and was soon adrift in her sleep.

She willed her mind into silence, after all she could have arguments with it tomorrow.

Chapter 5: Eat Balti. Heartburn

Another bite into the dinner his wife had prepared him. It was nice, but he always felt chest discomfort and his stomach burning during every meal. He liked the food just not the consequence of the food.

They always had traditional food and she always prepared it for him all day whilst at home. He wondered if she ever felt oppressed by him or did she in fact see this as her life choice, they certainly didn't have any kids to stop her having a career. She never expressed it to him. So, the only person to blame would be himself. It put a lot of pressure on their marriage, he thought, or at least selfishly, on himself, because he always felt he never gave enough time for the supposed women of his dreams. The more his symptoms flared, the more he thought about what he had to show for the stress on his body. As a young doctor he'd bought into his own hero complex. He thought he was destined to save lives, the main character of his own story. Although he couldn't say his achievements weren't plenty. He always felt he couldn't fill that hole inside him, that pit, no matter what he did and ticked off in his climb up the greasy pole. The more he climbed the more he realised he wasn't in control, he wasn't the main character or the hero, he was just another person, an extra in someone else's film.

Now most of his colleagues would disagree with that realisation or view it as disturbing or upsetting. However, when he realised it, he was almost set free. There were no standards he needed to meet, no chapter end, no finale, he just needed to do the best he could and that varied day to day and that changed patient to patient, but as long as he did his best, he could do nothing more. The pressure had lifted from him. He worried about Beth sometimes, he wondered if she was where he was fifteen years ago. At that time, looking back, he was paranoid, miserable. Now, despite a little British pessimism, he was content. More so his spikes of happiness could keep him going because after all there was never happiness forever. He believed it was about living your life and accepting it. He laughed to himself, it was very thin evidence to base your life belief on; a case study of one.

His wife continued to talk about their plans to escape for the winter, "look when are we going on holiday, this weather is unbearable!"

He smiled back at her, "Yeah, plus I do need my yearly dose of hearing your sisters complain about how I don't look after myself anymore."

She gave him a playful punch to his arm, looked at him and told him with her eyes that she did think he didn't look after himself anymore. He stared as she walked away and knew the warmth he felt meant he still loved her. They were distant but still produced a warmth, or at least he assumed that was what her smiles meant to him. He looked down at his plate, only half gone yet his appetite had gone again, he felt bloated and decided to stand up with his plate heading back towards the kitchen area of the open plan house they had created together.

He approaches the "kitchen"; he could already tell what his other half would say.

"Again? Either admit you now dislike my cooking or go see a doctor about your symptoms. Because I know you, you always finish what we put in front of you."

He often wondered if he'd make a good patient, he'd sit quietly but he'd probably judge and not even listen to the advice. If he complained about patient compliance he only did so because he knew that it was hard to have anyone tell you what to do. Then again maybe it was the way you came to that decision. Like an old cartoon or sitcom trope he felt his wife would know how to make him comply. Probably by making him think he'd come to that decision.

"Don't worry, it means I can enjoy it tomorrow for lunch, two for the price of one. That's how much I love your cooking. You know none of the other consultants get this level of care."

"None of them get to have me as their wife."

"That's why all of them still have their hair."

He gave her his wry smile, the one he was sure she liked because he could always see her at ease when he did it. She had never admitted it to him, so it was an assumption. One he'd based his actions on, but she had stuck around, that had to count for something.

He tunnelled the food into another Tupperware box, that would take forever to clean and still be left with a slight red tinge from the sauce, he thought to his upcoming week. Lots of hours in the department, but worse, lots of hours in meetings. He found it frustrating that services were being taken away from his hospital, as a cost saving measure within the NHS. It just didn't sit right with him. He had discussed this several times with Beth, but rightly so she showed him the evidence for a tertiary centre and the better outcomes having good experience in focussed areas allowed.

Burn, sharp and stabbing in his head as well as his throat and stomach. The stress would probably kill him. If he just let go, let it happen, maybe he wouldn't feel that burn. He took a big breath in and held it, hoping to ease his stomach. He felt his head become light before the pain passed. He finished shovelling his lunch for tomorrow in the box and into the fridge.

He walked out and closed the light in the kitchen before arriving at the one of three bedrooms in their empty, but what people would call, magnificent house. That was the official reviews at the Christmas party after party. He smiled again to himself as he walked past the bathroom watching his wife brush her teeth. In this stage of her life she looked more beautiful than she had done to him as a young man. They had their troubles in the past but ageing gracefully for her had made him realise that he had it good.

"Alright, I'm heading off to bed", he paused, letting his heartburn settle.

"Brush your teeth you idiot," she reminded him.

He smiled, "of course," rolling his eyes.

"They're not gonna get any better, the coffee and tea have made them irreparable."

"Good thing I'm not shallow," she gurgled back at him.

By the time they were both in bed, they cuddled for a moment, before both admitted it was too uncomfortable and warm and turned to the side. She was quick to drift off. He let his mind slow down until the only thing he could feel was the gurgling and burning in his belly. Once settled, so was he.

*

He was sitting in his office looking through the feedback forms he had collected about the now old new doctors. He had all their meetings and now he was staring at the computer with his reading glasses tilted down, wishing he hadn't bought them from the pound store because the glare of the screen was killing him. He slowly looked down at his keyboard using one finger on each hand he started to type into the box.

He recalled the meeting with Rich.

"Yeah, I loved it here, I just love talking to patients, I think that's definitely my strength."

He nodded as he listened to the boy continue talking about his time here and how great it was. He felt like the talking was trying to hide how Rich truly felt. He felt like he was being played up to. However, he knew he couldn't just refuse what was being said to him.

"Anything you found difficult or think we should improve?"

He opened the floor up, hoping that would probe, hoping he could hear something original or how this man actually felt.

"No, it's brilliant, you're all brilliant, I actually bought you a box of chocolates. Also, if you see Dr Anderson, I got her one too. Just because of how great you all were." He watched the boy smile, there were moments where *it* almost gave way, **almost**.

"Brilliant," he replied in turn to the trainee as he saw him whoosh out the door, for someone who loved it here. He was eager to get out.

He looked at the feedback below.

"Positive, confident, really good manner with patients."

"Really confident, nice to patients."

"Confident, confident-er and even confident-erist."

Well that last one was made up, but he knew how they would all go. He knew plenty of confident people, especially of Richard's ilk. It wasn't Richard's fault; it was just the system that would mean he would thrive. Confidence doesn't always ring of competence. However, he knew that it makes everyone think you're competent, and that is better than being so, especially with regards to career progression. He let the glare and heartburn settle and then typed, probably too slowly, the word confidence in strengths.

Once saved, he then had Izzy's form open now in front of him. He looked forward to the empty seat in his office, he saw the silhouette of the girl bumbling her words, a hallucination. He stared at what was the silhouette of her sat in front of him.
"Yeah, it's nice, I think I'm getting the hang of it. I feel a little more confident, yeah, I think I just need to ask more but everyone is so supportive."
"Looks like people said you were nice, they said you were quiet. How do you feel about that?" He questioned with a raised eyebrow, trying to see if she had the fight in her. He had seen them on and off, however he knew everyone had more than one layer, and as a doctor everyone has a character they played, he wanted depth. However, she didn't take the bait.
"I probably should be more confident."

He let the silence hang for a small while.

"I just know I'm doing the work." He watched as she let the air come out of her, he swore he saw her deflate in front of him.

"I think you are too. I think it's less about confidence but more being honest about how you feel or what you've done."

She stared into his eyes and their gaze was caught for a little while longer than it should have been, he disrupted it before his thoughts ran away after all as he knew he was a terrible man.

"Look, just be honest to everyone, because I think you're doing well and you know your stuff, you don't have to be Rich, just tell them what you've done and what you believe in. You'll find that will be enough."

"Yeah, thanks Dr Abdul." He saw her smile, a real one. It was a nice smile. One he only saw as she walked out of work, it saddened to think her smile was fake in his department.

His heartburn drove him to lose the hallucination as he looked at his computer again writing slowly with his now stiff finger.

"Very good clinically but needs to show her work off. To be honest in her interaction with staff, within reason."

He wondered if he was being vague, however it was his belief that doctors became better as they became better people, rather than through only reading all the guidelines and worse following them verbatim. He was probably being airy-fairy. His younger version would definitely hate him. That thought alone made him smile. He was sure that young doctors would read the feedback and just complain in the mess, or maybe in the pub, about him. However, that thought alone made him smile, after all it is the job of the young to ruffle the feathers of the old.

Rachel was an easy meeting; he didn't have much to add. She did look a little tired, he imagined her as a candle which was burning from both ends. Her image melting in front of him he wrote down the feedback that everyone had written, a simple, "keep doing what you're doing." He wondered if it was wrong to do so, after all he didn't want her to keep burning the candle at both ends, more so just keep doing what she's doing as a doctor. Although to separate that from the person you are outside is hard and takes years of training. Usually further strained when you get to consultant level. He held off adding more to the form in front of him. Least not the stern professors' old boys club came and locked him up for crimes of being too thoughtful.

*

He was back on the floor of the emergency department. He had inducted the newer doctors who were now all running around wincing at the cacophony of voices, bleeps and boops. All meaning different things and needing different actions, but all mixed into one big hum meaning you could never decipher exactly who, what and where needs what who and where.

However, that machine hum was better than the drone of the managers at the meeting that day. His heartburn swelled as he thought of it. Looking down at the sheet in front of him he read the patient details which he was asked to review by one of the new doctors who had looked frightened to ask to leave for lunch. He had given him permission and also made the new chap think he was savant, when all it was the experience of reading people's faces. "I'm hungry" was an easy one because he'd seen it so many times among colleagues and himself. He looked down at the case notes and it said, "shoulder and chest pain".

He had been seen by Richard a couple of months ago. Richard had sent the patient home with a diagnosis of muscle pain. This time the patient had come back with the pain still ongoing, well *non-resolving* according to the triage notes.

He looked up at the department watching everyone run around and try to find space to see their patients. He noted how hungry and ravenous they all looked to get their patient in. He could compete or just use his office like he had done in the past. He could also pull the hierarchy card, but that would mean people were aware of him and he'd definitely get side-tracked into answering another question or management would descend as he had been told someone was looking for him to discuss the flow. As if he had an answer for the flow when all these supposed managers didn't. They probably think he had some kind of magic wand that he isn't waving to spite them but in reality he didn't, he had no answers, apart from to just keep on keeping on. Like a Gallagher brother he had nothing to offer apart from inane lyrics. He walked around one last lap before popping out to the waiting room. Calling the name on the sheet in front of him.

"Jason Argonaut"

A very unassuming youngish man came towards him. He had a normal stride and on instant examination of the walking man like a person ready to judge a book by its cover he felt there was nothing to add. They sidled down the narrow corridor. He noted the corridors were only narrow due to the piling of trolleys and chairs in them, well that and the patients. This was after all in the middle of winter and just like a children's monster that always appeared in the cold, wet and dark nights, illness had done so as well. Him and Jason arrived at his carpeted office. Jason complied fully as he pointed to the chair. He could tell the patient felt a little unease from the way he sat down in the chair.

"Don't worry, it's my office, I gotta find a place to see ya and as a consultant there have to be some perks."

He joked as he saw the posture of the man in front ease into the uncomfortable chair. After all there was a quota on how many comfortable chairs one could keep in the room in an NHS hospital.

"So, you're back?" He smiled at the man, who seemed to now find his trust and began handing it over.

"Yeah, I came in a few months ago with my shoulder, it's just not gotten better like the doctor who saw me said it would!"

"Take me back to the beginning."

He always wondered how people felt to start again when seeing someone new, almost cancelling everything they shared with the previous doctor. He remembered the frustration as a junior when a patient would change a story or answer yes to a question they had said no to moments ago, giving the consultant more to go on, as if it was one big prank they were all in on.

His thoughts wandered as he went into autopilot, after many many years things had become automated.

"So, you see doc, despite what the other guy told me, the pains are still there and I'm not entirely sure it's related to me being at the gym because it doesn't seem to affect it. Nothing seems to affect it."

He looked at the man in front tentatively who seemed to be seeking further reassurance. He could tell that this man didn't want anything to be wrong with him.

"So has anything changed? What brought you in today?"

"I guess I just felt like it wasn't going, it's probably silly right doc?"

There it was again the pleading for everything to be okay. The need to dispel the uncertainty around the pain, which had only been fostered and grown in the interim. He winced allowing his raging stomach fire to settle before looking back at the man in front of him. A man of reasonable physique, much more capable than himself, but yet still so vulnerable.

His stomach flared again.

"Hmm, maybe we should make sure nothing nasty is going on in the chest. Now tell me, has anyone in your family ever had any heart troubles at all?"

"No, not that I know of."

"Nothing at all?"

"Well do you mean heart attacks doc?"

"Yeah, plus anything else around the heart."

"Well, my grandad had a small aneurysm, but that was fine, never caused him any trouble, I don't think."

He felt his glasses slide by themselves to the bridge of his nose. His eyes focused, imaging the word *aneurysm* in his head. He wrote it down in the notes before pulling two pieces of paper from his drawers, filling them in quickly too.

"Go back to the main reception and show them these two requests for an X-ray and some blood tests. We can then ask our colleagues from the surgical team to see you to make sure there's no other things we've missed with regards to your shoulder and chest pain."

He watched the man follow the instruction and knew Jason looked a little dismayed, the reassurance he sought he couldn't give to him, not yet.

"Yeah, cheers for that, do I have to wait long?"

"That I can't answer, you've come to ED, waiting long is what we do here, hopefully it's not too bad."

The man nodded and walked outside before he could take a seat which helped his aching legs, another spasm in his stomach before he settled down to the notes in front of him. He wrote down in his most legible scroll, which still turned out to be illegible. In court he would blame his fancy birthday gift fountain pen.

CP & SP
?casse (which spelt cause)
R/O Answer (which meant to be the word aneurysm)
Plan
CSR (which should be read as CXR) + bloods (written legibly)
Surg RV if bloods and CSR neg

*

He sat as the noises grew louder and louder, as people were shouting left, right and centre trying to create some kind of flow in the hospital. He looked up to the approaching squadron meant to deal with this. They each had their personalised clipboard, all worse suits of course with their NHS lapel pin badges, showing their support. Lanyards with the next fad they were supporting, which was currently the mind charity lanyard. He wondered how much was handed up from above and how much they believed in the causes which appeared around the neck like some accessory to complement their pristine outfit, as if having some sort of bling made them more human.

He was after all being mean about fellow human beings doing a job, but he wanted to take the easy cliched way out by being angry at them. Divide and conquer was truly working Mr Health Secretary. Despite all that, the un-PC truth was **Managers** just **fucking** pissed him **off**.

"Alright Dr Abdul," one of them smiled. It was always difficult to differentiate their faces. They all had very undiscerning facial features, as if there was a vat from which their ilk was born. He also felt they took turns to talk in the same tone, they had been trained to do so, to try and communicate with the beasts known as consultants. However, it came off like a hive mind, where four spoke as one.

"Remember, we're heading towards black[26]."

He nodded in response to the echoing voices. They echoed in his ear drum as if the lines being delivered were from a prophecy.

"So, discharge as many people as possible."

---

[26] Black – the highest escalation status in the hospital when there are no beds for patients to come in to.

"That's good ya told me, I was planning to keep some in for fun." He quipped back. However, the union gave him a quick vague nod as they moved forward delivering their command to more and more people. He watched as the troops nodded to the hive mind, imagining everyone now has the ability to discharge more and help the flow of the hospital, his sarcastically quipped in his head loudly and guiltily. At least he found himself funny, which is all you can ask for at his age. As he walked down the corridors, watching this new version of ED, coined corridor medicine, take place he wondered if there was now an extra instrument or notes being played in the normal cacophony of what he was used to. He could hear the words discharge and black status being whispered again and again. Like a slow note of dread held onto too long by the band, one that seemed to last longer and longer in the air with each passing year.

Like a conveyor belt he dealt more and more people a diagnosis, feeling that each one drained him of his soul. He wanted to tell them all that nothing is set in stone, and it was all based on probability, but when you were busy, unless absolutely necessary, the response was go home, it's okay and see your GP. Hopefully not too soon so that they end up

just being sent straight back like some kind of hot potato. One without a good cheese or beans filling, just something awful like salad and butter or worse tuna mayo. Why add cold into a warm meal? He laughed at the mental digression.
After his boot had kicked out those who had complained about waiting for what he considered a minor ailment and what people watching casualty would also consider a minor ailment. It gave him time to chase up the swamp of results that awaited his signature.

He checked for that man with the shoulder tip pain, Mr Jason Argonaut. The blood tests showed an excellent picture of health, with the results in red if abnormal there was only a slight pink tinge in the Arabian black sea. Like a random red snapper which had found its way into the bay and floated due to the salt content. It was his blood count which was 128. Down from 150 when he had last checked with the GP a few years ago, when he had some sort of minor ailment which had resolved just like the shoulder tip pain would, hopefully. His chest x-ray showed nothing obvious although the blurriness of Dr Abduls vision didn't help give him an expert's eye. He looked down at his plan and sighed a little. He would need to explain the longer wait to the patient so he could get hold of a surgical review.

Although the luck of the ever so fallible corridor medicine meant you'd bump into other staff easily. This allowed him to quickly clock Izzy, who was walking in front of a flirting Rich who was trying his best impersonation of a narcissistic personality disorder, hoping the ED staff would reply positively allowing Rich to feel valued. He hoped so too, God they were really short of trainees.

"Hello Dr and Dr, or should I say Mister and Ms!"

He could see them both give him a good stare. Rich with a smile and confidence expecting some kind of reward from the rest of the department for knowing the consultant and Izzy out of obligation to the senior.

"Hey Dr Abdul," they replied in unison.

Weirdly with completely different tones but harmonious, nonetheless. It allowed him to raise an eyebrow to the two juniors, who he could spot relax their neck muscles in response.

"So, I'm being mean and want a little business from those noggins of yours."

They listened intently, he thanked their medical school lectures and consultants for this generation having given them fear of authority and made the consultant feel above human. A trait that only furthered egos, comparable to the past of giving you free haircuts, food and golf rounds.

"There's a chap in the waiting room, Mr Jason Argonaut. I can't find anything for his shoulder tip pain, and I want to make sure it's nothing. Could your r*eg* have a look?"

He was crass with the last line, but he felt it eased them. However, before he could claim a victory for junior doctor wellbeing, the hive mind of managers descended and interrupted the conversation.

"We hope we have no admission. We have no beds."

He watched both Rich and Izzy neck muscles tense up all over again.

"Only as appropriate," he whispered to the two juniors, hopefully in a frequency the hive mind didn't tune into.

*

He had finished another day; he was now following up on the "interesting" cases. He noticed his man had been discharged by the two young ones. He looked at the files. It had a vague scribble saying:

"Disch, home as per discussion."

Not stating with who, not good documentation at all.

"GP to review."

An easy one to understand, which meant GP to refer, he felt somewhat at an unease. He learned not to ignore the gut feeling.

Without thinking he found his phone in his hand, the man answered back.

"Hello?"

"Hi this is Dr Abdul from the emergency department."

"Hello doc, thanks for the help I saw the surgeons, although I think I've met one of them before."

"Mhmm," he said in the least sexy way as these calls were all recorded for training purposes.

"Well, they said I'm fine and if it's not gone in a week go to the GP who can chat to their bosses, which I think is great, less waiting in hospital."

There was a tick in the patient's voice, he probed deeper.

"What is it you wanted us to do, what were you worried about?"

"Well, you see doc, as we talked about and you reminded me dad had an aneurysm as well I think, never knew much about he's not around anymore, but I guess you can't help but wonder, not that it would cause the pain. I'm being silly. I can talk with the GP. He knew my dad, he'll know."

He paused and let his gut settle down, heartburn or diagnostic acumen mixed in his stomach juices. Raising his eyebrows but there was no response, of course body language didn't translate well over the phone. His breathing pattern probably didn't say "I am raising my eyebrows tell me more."

"Tell me more?" He said frankly feeling sad he lost his ability to subtly communicate.

"Well Mum said Dad had pain in his chest and stuff for ages before they found it."

"Okay fair, let's do our job of reassuring you that I'll book you an ultrasound, you'll get an appointment by phone or post okay?"

"Cheers doc."

The line went dead. His stomach burned further, he felt a surge and into his bin he vomited, it was dark in colour and almost coffee like. He waited and paused; he felt a second of dread followed by a moment of doom before finally returning to normal. He decided to clear the bin out before heading home. He reassured himself that he had eaten a brown curry.

That night he and his wife slept in separate rooms after a fight involving him blaming her cooking and her shouting at him to go see somebody. His thoughts flew around his head. He felt well and sleep did not come easily despite his tired mind. What was a relationship to do when the stomach was no longer the portal to his heart because the stomach just didn't want to work!

Chapter 6: I eat what you feed, order 23. The orange duck.

She had noted the bread she bought from the corner shop seemed to get staler week by week no matter the date or how supposed "FRESH" she bought it. Mixed in with her opting for jam and not marmite as she had begun to realise the shopkeeper was in the other 50% of people who didn't like marmite as stocking it wasn't a high priority for him. With her sandwiches changing her moral core changed too, a fact she was surprised people didn't share more commonly. She was having increasingly stale jam sandwiches, she wondered if this added years to her face, she didn't want to blame the surgical rota. The shifts were unkind, the variety of staff confusing acting from "nice" to horrible to just not understanding, "un-understanding" or another word that held the same meaning. She promised never to be like them in the future. She wondered how one became one of those "un-understanding" people. Her morning routine had only changed slightly in that she appeared thinner due to her lack of time to eat, but extra time to drink coffee which helped on those dating apps she had joined to try and find an outside life to escape from the hospital. However, nothing had got her going. She was living a life, which seemed to lack drive or passion or whatever Hollywood movies like Hitch implied life was about. For now, her life was about making it through. Her head sounded different, a reader of her thoughts might mistake it for character development or a complete inconsistent change in character, she put it down to lack of sleep.

She opened her phone again, a few annoying messages from Rich which continued with an annoyingly flirty vibe, a few slightly funny one-liners and a whole lot of unwanted repressed lust which she tried her best to manoeuvre around. She continued the chat after all, he was one of few people she hung around with and when his attention wasn't completely on her he could be, maybe, bearable. She quickly swiped the notification across, having got the gist of what he was saying not wanting the revealing read receipt to appear informing him of her acknowledgement. The other annoying addition to all his messages was adding question marks to each little speech bubble that appeared on her screen that meant she had to have an answer of some sort. Answers always lead to more questions and further conversation, which could always be misinterpreted as interest in what he had to say. Not like she said much back and therefore he too must have been feigning interest or his lust must really be that strong. She looked at the other side of this and noted she worked with him and as always, she had enough people she already didn't like. It was nice to have someone who was helpful even if his true motives were "un-understanding". What she did look forward to was the end of this rotation. Primarily because an 8 am start had really started to push her limits of tiredness. She looked forward to medical days starting at 9am, then she could be a little like Dolly Parton. Dr Dolly Parton MRCP[27].

Today the start was different; it was an 8:30 pm start. It was her night shift. A delirious inducing four nights in a row. Much better when compared to the seven in a row of days of old, or the straight into next day of older as

---

[27] MRCP - member of Royal college of physicians, given after passing medical specialty membership exam.

she was constantly reminded by a snarky set of seniors who thought their survival gifted them better medical acumen. She would never disagree to their faces, an unnecessary battle, one she could just complain to her colleagues over beer with, which allowed for some good socialising, but left her so used to this type of conversation that with those outside the medical world she couldn't hold a conversation. However, there was never enough recovery time before she would be straight back onto the 8 am starts. She wondered how much more her risk of heart attack she raised from doing these nights. She also wondered how much more relevant she found the saying "tiredness can kill". She didn't change much in her routine, well, apart from that she would definitely allow herself a whole extra biscuit or two in the mess. If her stomach gave her the indication, although 3 am in the night seemed to suppress her appetite. She would start her "day" with something warm like soup or a jacket potato. Never with a cold filling, although the potato burned the top of her mouth as she always tried to wolf it down, this was invariably due to her being perpetually late to handover due to the inability not to snooze her alarm 3-4 times. The one positive of nights was getting some winter sunlight compared to her always dark day shifts. Where you are home in the dark and you go to work in the dark. This winter conundrum ironically provided sunlight when not required and whilst when she first started, she had used bin bags on Rich's suggestions, the "crack den look" had annoyed her mother when she had visited. She had received some black out curtains as a November birthday present.

Her potato today had a homely collection of baked beans and cheese. She wondered if it would affect her figure, something which dwindled of its own accord and luckily never grew. Good for her cardiac risk factors. She believed at least in Darthington, it garnered enough positive attention. She looked as she chowed down on her potato slowly cutting and shovelling the pieces in her mouth, like minor surgery, the potato had to be excised in the correct way and the layers gathered perfectly on her fork so that she could get the best taste in her mouth. She held her mouth open, too hot again. She made a sort of blowing cyclical motion with her mouth. Trying to get any of the air to cool down her mouth, when this did, leaving only half her taste buds intact she felt the rest of the warmth go down into her stomach as she swallowed, slight reflux settled in a moment before she grabbed the next bite, slightly cooler this time and with a few pumps of air and her salvia it was a little easier and less refluxy to gather the next piece down. As she sat down, she thought of the progress she had made and what she could aim for in her nights. Her eating became a little more automatic as the dish became an actual edible temperature. Her end of placement meeting from the emergency department still played on her head.

*

She had wandered into Dr Abdul's room unprepared for a meeting. No quips coming to mind and not really sure what the first four months had shown her beyond the fact that medicine, despite what people said, did play a huge role in your life and also a more well-known fact; colleagues were pretty horny. Life and death can do that to a male's member. Her female member equivalent (was she even allowed to think the word clit, heaven forbid) still not gaining excitement from these situations. She brought herself back to the meeting, thinking it was best to avoid that as her PDP or goal for her next four months. He began his line of questioning, relaying what she saw was the hymn sheet in front of him, her colleagues' opinions. He had worked with her a few times but not enough she imagined to really capture the depth of her, she was after all, or so she hoped, a three not two-dimensional character.

He questioned her confidence; she felt a little aggravated at this. After all, people were only seeing what they wanted to see given the way she looked. They would all say the same, she was a nervous medic who needed to be more proactive and louder. However, she was fine with the patients and asked for help when needed. She just didn't shout about how much work she had done or how busy she was. She felt it was fraudulent. However, her individualism was hard to see in the sea of "individuals" in the hospital. On some level she understood that sometimes you have to pin yourself to a flag or type of doctor to be seen at all at this stage.
"Yeah, I guess I could do with being more confident."
She watched Dr Abdul wince. He seemed to be recoiling a little, had she upset him with her words. She felt her whole weight become minuscule and her ego deflated, becoming like a rubber two-dimensional shell of herself. She felt the prying eyes of the once wincing man, who just like a flare up of unwanted symptoms seemed to have settled down. She

felt his eyes searching, but what could he want to find, what was there really to find.

His eyes rested on her; he began a lecture, one she wasn't expecting, talking of what she believed was her three-dimensional character. They stared, maybe too long. She wondered in his eyes and his facial features that as a young *registrar* he must have been very attractive, wise yet fiery, yet beautiful in an exotic way. He broke the stare and she looked down. Now she hadn't felt that before in the department. She was glad someone could see who she really was rather than who everyone thought she was. She had left the room feeling a little victorious.

*

You had to hold onto small victories as you never knew when they came about in medicine, she was racing up the hill to the hospital on her feet with her toms which she still considered the height of fashion. She was now allowed to wear the signature blue pyjamas of the people who fixed things, letting her into their gang plus on night shifts the right size tops did exist and were plentiful. Also, at night no one cared what you looked like they were unlikely to send someone home for looking bad. They needed you on the night, it was nice to be needed by the hospital.

She realised that if the hospital was a person then the relationship she had with this great big unforgiving place would be one that would fall under one of the categories of abuse she had been so "well" online-trained in.

A slow small tip toe into the room as the list projected onto the screen with everyone staring allowed her not to be noticed but she got there just in time for the roll call.
"Night Fy1."
"Hi, here," slightly panting, trying to hide her recent arrival, "I'll change into scrubs in a bit."
"Brilliant, I'll be glad to work with you Dr Mothinder Fernandez Reg." A very handsome, very angular modern looking south Asian man sat next to her and shook her hand. She looked down, publicly feeling the pressure of all the eyes judging her shake of this man's hand. For someone at night he smelled nice and looked dressed beyond the call of duty.
"Await your turn please Moh."
"Of course, Candice," the angular man smiled, basking in the attention the whole room gave him. Candice stern yet forgiving had been the day reg. Obviously still looking fresh as the woman always did. She always

wondered how Candice managed to keep her heels clopping down with authority down the halls for thirteen hours straight. How the *registrar* managed to command all including those who gave untoward looks. It helped that she imagined Candice's very well-endowed husband had given her the biggest rock possible, so that even those who were legally blind would not miss what lay on her ring finger.

The night shift officially began after reading through the list of patients still waiting to be seen. Her stomach churned as it washed the potato cheese and beans mixed in with the anxiety and rush, she always got when starting the night. She looked to her SHO, a chubby unassuming man with no prominent features, in ways he was the portal to advice this evening. He looked opposite to the angular man who sat grinning at her with an uncomfortable intensity. She tried to look away, flustering at where to focus, finally choosing the SHOs slightly creeping Tattoo from behind his scrub sleeve, a weird Arabic lettering of sorts. She then looked down, remembering her jeans were still on. The medical equivalent of forgetting your trousers. "I better change!" She proclaimed, instantly regretting not saying that more quietly and to herself. Everyone looked like they had had their bantering post work conversation interrupted with banality. The Angular Reg stood up. He looked at her again intensely.

"Let's head to the changing room, we can get fitted for our evening outfits, as tailored as they can be." A few giggles in the room and she threw one his way as well. She stepped in front taking his offer of leading the stroll down the corridor.

She was on the blue team, as it was the blue line which led to the theatre and their grand changing rooms. She tried to think of a chant that would support them, something like we are the cutters, sang to we are the mods from Quadrophenia a reference she barely got but one that hung over her from her ex-boyfriend's insistence about the film.

She had let her internal monologue drown out the man next to her external one or his soliloquy which seemed as it continued to almost shine a spotlight on him, and he looked as if to perform it to some unknown crowd from a stage where they all watched their dull (no matter how many exclamations he talked with) lives.

"You see the brilliant, most wonderful thing about being a surgeon is you get shit done. Ya get me Izzster."

A horrible nickname Rich had latched onto and convinced the rest of the surgical lads to use. She wondered if they thought it would make her loins moist with gratitude to be indoctrinated into the lads' club. Another grin was shot her way. She laughed along, easier to do that she compromised again. The soliloquy continued, the virtues of surgery expelled once more, it was described as a panacea. The land of milk and honey or hunnies, something like that. Gosh she really was in the lad's club.

Her very hip tom laden strides allowed the theatre double doors to give way. The changing rooms approached. As she headed toward the door a large angular palm laid on her shoulder, "now don't be too long, you saw we had a few to clerk, plus you don't need to do much to look any better, lucky for some of us on nights." He laughed and chuckled, there was no wink to complete how angular and unrounded that statement was, matching this man's physique. She skittled away the code memorised in her fingers, but not her mind. Into the dark changing room as the garb of the surgeon was placed onto her body. Right sizes aloud some flattery to her figure. She could feel the responsibility sag. Her shoulder must be getting reasonably toned with how much she had on them. The primary heavy lifting was carrying her Fy1 bleep, the first port of call for all surgical questions and she knew the least likely to have the answer in the hospital at night.

Outside once more to the angular man as they headed back to the assessment unit, not without a fun jibe at her shoes, she hid her dislike of his statement. She focused on what she imagined would be the onslaught of those who needed a night surgical opinion. Those who couldn't sleep through their ailment or those who wished to sleep through their ailment in the comforts and reassurances of the hospital or even worse, those who were unwell that she couldn't help.

*

"Yeah so, I've had the pain for months, right on the tip and going to the baws. No matter what happens it just keeps getting worse and worse. I feel embarrassed talking to a lovely attractive young doc like yourself, are you fully qualified then?"

"Yes, I am Mr Morrow," she answered the question for the third time this evening and that was after 5 patients. 1 am was not kind to her wits, however she did wonder if she would be glad of her youthful looks once she was what the public deemed old enough to be a doctor.

"So, tell me what brought you in today?" A phrase that had been added to her script from her time in the emergency department.

"Well, it's just that, tomorrow, I have a date, you know a really hot one, someone definitely out of my league and I kind of want to make sure I'm in tip top shape."

"Of course, and I'm glad you're here at 1am for that." Her sarcasm dripped, but her southern English accent came off as authentic. She was what they would call an innocent Bonnie Lass up north. He stared, unable to read the sarcasm in her statement, she continued.

"So, any lesions or strange change or colour to the tip?"

"Nothing really!"

"Have you seen anyone else about it?"

"Just a GP who gave me a cream, but to be honest doc, it's not done anything."

"Okay, hmm, well, are there any other symptoms apart from pain there? Is the pain always there, does it go anywhere else, fevers?"

Her jumbled thoughts coming out into the open, barraged the patient, in a cartoonish fashion. He almost fell off his examination bench.

"What one should I answer then?"

218

"All of them," she tapped the edge of her pen onto his thin file of paper notes. She imagined she sounded like an annoyed teacher; her tone of proper southern English pushed the stereotype further into a Victorian archetype.

"Well pain is only when I touch it to you know.... and sometimes it's in the testicles. Ummm..."

He paused trying to remember the words flung at him that felt metaphorically stuck in a pile next to his feet. She watched him stare at the ground further as if trying to unpick the words that had formed her prison guard-like questions.

"No temperatures, no funny things. That's it really."

"So how many times do you, as you describe it... y'know," her words were mincing in her mouth, a subject she didn't ask often about, let alone at 1 am in the morning, to a man she didn't even remember the name of.

"Not many like 3-4 times."

"Okay, so not every day."

"I meant every day."

Her face began to go red; her calm exterior began to melt. 3-4 times, he must be made of some durable stuff, wasn't the satisfaction once enough she barely needed once in a while, in fact it had been seven months since any sort of release. This made this conversation even more frightful, and the next step was examination something that would make her even redder at the prospect. She needed a chaperone.

"So next the examination, if you'd like I can get a chaperone."

"I'll be honest dear, the less people the better."

"Let's say it's normal hospital policy to have one, especially if it's general men or women squi... I mean sensitive arenas."

Her voice squealed in the high pitch of a soprano. This was not the conversation she needed now, this wasn't even a Friday night, it was a Monday night! No excuse!

"A chaperone will be coming through."

She stepped out of the curtain avoiding looking at the ridiculous man who she wondered why had made it to the surgical admission unit for a night review. She flicked through the four or so loose papers which had become his visiting file. At the back a small scrap of lined paper with his details printed on it, the name of his GP surgery and a scrawl from the GP. *Ahh his golden ticket,* she internally proclaimed.

Telephone consult:
Pain +++ tip, test tender. Surg RV r/o torsion.
Many thanks,

Dr

The rest is illegible.

The one scrawled abbreviated mildly legible line revealing the reason for the appearance of this man challenging her comfort with sexual talk at work. The one line which did not reveal much of what had gone in the closed doors and recorded phones of the GP room. For her review, which concluded it was definitely not a testicular torsion, which would be a urological emergency needing acting on or infertility and necrosis and even death could occur. Her diagnosis and management were that this man just needed to enjoy his member less.

She looked over to the nursing desk. A few nurses sat in chairs staring at some monitors and looking at the bay every so often. This is probably what hospital tranquillity amounted to. She smiled at the nursing assistant next to the sister in the dark blue garb which screamed; I am the authority, do not disturb my staring.

"Could I get a chaperone please?" Maintaining her stare at the assistant as to not disrupt the head nurse, the head nurse looked over to the assistant,

"Fine, go for it Sarah, just hurry, I need you over here."
She wondered what it was she was needed for, before her mind began the conspiracy theories Sarah the nursing assistant stood by her side with a big smile.
"For Mr Morrow yeah?"
She nodded.
"He's a funny chap, I quite like him." Sarah smiled back at her, she decided to hold off on her rant about the man. At least he had one fan.
"Well, we just have to examine his testicle."
"Fun right?" Sarah giggled, God she hated the piercing noise that guttered through the tiny frame of the very slender athletic nurse. She looked like a giggler, someone who got a lot done because of that giggle. She always wondered if she was a male doctor whether she would get a lot more giggling from the ancillary staff. She mustered a smile as they both stepped behind the curtain.

"Ohh, your hands are so cold, did you know that, I'd get those sorted, most men don't like it cold like that."
The giggling happened from over her shoulder, she wondered if he thought he was a funny guy because he often got giggles, she offered him a small laugh, not wanting to

break any dream like reality this man had created for himself.

"So, we're just having a feel of both testicles. Any pain?"

"No, just a little discomfort on the left." He threw a smile at the HCA.

"Good, no swelling all feels fine sir," she added as she finished up the exam. Although the man was nowhere near being a knight or deserving of the accolade of the title the sir. It unfortunately was just a turn of phrase she had picked up from her time within the medical world, repeated a lot as a sort of formality to try to make sure there was a barrier between patient and doctor.

"Thanks dear, guess I'm all good to go then? Had the MOT and engine ready to be on the road,"

More giggling, she saw him standing up, remembering that she needed a *reg* opinion before discharge.

"Umm, well sir, maybe sir, you should sit down... I just need to run it all by the other doctor, just to make sure, umm."

"Make sure what? Surely you're a doctor and you're happy right?"

There weren't any more dick jokes, he looked a little pale, she tried her best to sound confident but always found the manoeuvring

and explaining policy and the intricate balance of confidence in her and the system hard.
"Yeah well, we just wanna be sure, it's how it works it's a good thing yeah, a good thing let me just go out and I'll be right back okay!"
She scuttered away as she escaped from the curtain. Leaving behind her nervous energy, the giggling and the man's average testicles.

Once discussed with Mothinder, or Mr Fernandez as he had introduced himself to Mr Morrow. The Misters sat and had what she thought was quite a gentlemanly conversation, she wondered if men always had such civilised discussion around matters of the workings of their most precious organ. He seemed happier with another opinion of reassurance; he threw his thank you but kept looking at Mr Fernandez. She watched him turn to her with a nod and say, "good job". She couldn't maintain her stare and again at her fashionable toms she looked.

The rest of the night had less dick and balls and more blood and guts. Carefully chosen terms to shock and cause a little dark humour that she watched Mothinder say to her as they sat in the doctor's mess for a break. She gave him a smile; it was a little funny. She would use it she was sure, hopefully to make her junior laugh next year.

"So, Izzy, you see that's the fun of the night don't-cha think, a little bit of decision making."

She nodded as she bit down on her sandwich, stale with little jam, it was the end of the jar that had just slightly coated the crumbly bread. She wondered what percentage of the sandwich was in her mouth and what was in the Tupperware box carefully placed on her lap to preserve her scrubs dignity.

"So, what is it you want to do when you grow up?"

He asked with his smile protruding out of his face. She took note that even his smile came off as extremely angular. She appreciated the generic joke and question asked to all Fy1's. After all, in the eyes of the hospital they were the algae or the bacterium, they still had to become more than single celled organisms. A more appropriate term would be when you evolve or escape your cocoon or something else that preserved the imagery beyond implying she was a child. She was a post graduate medic, nearing her thirties so she was a grown up. She wondered if the stale bread had given her such a chip on her shoulder. She relaxed her body into the couch in the mess.

"Well, I've not decided, nothing jumps out at me."
"Well, I'll have to convince you to stick around with me, I can show you the ropes and make you love surgery."
His angular hands landed on her shoulder, rough and coarse, weirdly they retained a slight comfort to them.

The end of the shift was always the toughest. The adrenaline slowly coursing but weaning as the consultant who no matter how enthusiastic pulsated in her ears with monotony. Sometimes she didn't even recognise or remember who the boss was, they were a blank face, like in Charlie Brown with a trumpet noise as their voice.
They rounded the patient left on the unit. Making plans and listening to her and her SHO and reg justification for everything like the Spanish inquisition by daylight. The time to finish was 8:30 but invariably it was 9:30 when she, the SHO and r*egistrar*, stood in the canteen. No more adrenaline left in her system as she chowed on the hash brown roll she had been offered by the angular man. He was in good shape, which surprised her when he piled the five items into his breakfast roll whilst the SHO in contrast had a small egg

roll, the ironic contrast between body shape and plate hadn't eluded her.

"So, tomorrow guys, we need to try and have a break together, or maybe it'll be Izzister's turn for theatre."

He winked at her, and she was too tired and weak to do anything but appreciate the attention.

The food chowed down, and caffeine avoided. She closed her eyes before opening again to see the familiar surroundings of her bedroom. She was out of clothes and in her airy pyjamas. Her black out curtains were drawn. No more crack den, now she slept like a regal princess. No peas in her bed, she had checked, she giggled to herself for that joke. She knew she was funny, just no one ever gave her a chance. Looking at her phone before bed she looked at the three messages on her screen.

Her sister, "Hope the night shift went well, give me the deets later okay!"

Her mother "how was your day?"

Finally, the bumble message "How was your day?"

She rolled her eyes, weirdly men who she matched with seemed to ask the same question as her mum or sister, sometimes in the same words, would she have to write out the same three messages to each with some variation, why did it matter what her day was like to a complete stranger. Then again what else could be said to someone you didn't know and based your interest on a touched-up picture of themselves. She wasn't exactly original, but she liked to think she raised salient points. She decided they could all wait. Her head hit the pillow.

*

After another snooze it was 7:45 pm.

The dark curtains had tricked her and tricked time. She wasn't a morning person, or an evening waking person, which probably just made her a person. She looked at her bedside table, her phone lighting up. One message extra. Rich of course with another question mark and long winding message with euphemisms. She counted three question marks; he was hunting for three responses. She would give him two. First, she needed to have her potato and due to time limitation it would be a microwave then oven job, oh the tricks she had learned for efficiency.
Night after night, she had gotten involved in lots of different scenarios. For once in her life she hadn't thought so much about every small detail, she had let the days or nights flow, including her time in theatre with Mr Angular man. His body was the opposite to his

surgical skills, whilst rough and ready and very jagged, he operated like an artist with intricacy. The painting produced was an appendix removed, in a small jar whilst the rest of the bowel rested like a page from grey's anatomy as she held a retractor looking in. Everything moved, like an animation. She had seen this as a student but only from a far now she was in there looking in. Part of the crew, she saw the confidence it must give you to touch the organs of someone, although she couldn't remember much about this beyond his appendix being the problem.

"Got the appendix, I'll sew it up and help Izzy close," he smiled at her. The gasmen popped in and out, solving one puzzle after another in their newspaper. She wondered if that was part of their interview. She imagined a gruff bearded man looking at a young well shaven man in a suit asking him to do a sudoku followed by the crossword and for extra honour points finish the cryptic crossword. Despite her sarcasm she did envy their job and almost viewed it with excitement.

She watched as everything was meticulously placed back into the abdomen, the person had become an abdomen to her. An abdomen she saw being sutured up, first with the return of the inner layers, then muscles, and finally the fatty tissue. She was given the stitch and she felt the coarse hands guide her and watched the wound slowly closing, like a piece of her own art. They cleaned everything up as she watched the theatre team finish up. Like a well-rehearsed play, she stood awkwardly as the scene unfolded in front of her.

"Alright Mr appendix here, or Mr no appendix can go back to the ward."

The equipment counted. The swabs marked off. The box was taken away by one of the staff in blue, whilst the scrubbed-up people around her expertly in one motion managed to take their gowns, gloves and mask off and into the bin. She struggled as her gloves stuck to her hand due to perspiration, blood and other unidentified bodily fluids. By the time she had them off and into one of the many sacs of contaminated delicately handled rubbish the no appendix had already been unwrapped, moved onto a trolley after a big one, two, three *slide*. The machinery was ticking along, and her surgeon was sitting at the computer filling in the note. She scampered out of her gown and let her mask drape around her neck.

She approached her boss. He smiled back at her. His hand grabbed her shoulder again, she felt a little jitter around it. Like a jolt of energy. God it was hard to be comfortable when men and women are involved.

"So, I feel like I need you as official assistant on the document, you put in like three stitches,"
she actually giggled, not a compromise. God had she become a giggly girl.
"Time for the mess don't ya think?"
"Yeah," she giggled again. Why was she giggling?
*

She was paying a lot of attention to the interior design of the doctor's mess, a couple of tired leather brown sofas, just about big enough for shorter people to have a nap. The wallpaper slowly peeling off, small amounts of what is probably just about safe enough dampness was evident, no black mould yet. The fridge was laid bare apart from a milk cartoon, the biscuits half eaten and crumbling with a small sink which had vanishingly small amounts of soap. The computer in the corner was prone to overheating and the fan jittered in it continuously like a ventilator trying its best for what is obviously a dying patient. She was sitting next to Mothinder as he bit into his bagel he had prepared, like a carnivore he continued biting into it, showing no mercy.
It was the last night of four and her delirium was beginning to set in, gigglier and less aware of her actions. The room's dark pastels blended into a *Lowry* style gothic picture in

front of her eyes creating a new reality for her. The only bit of colour was the ridiculous gold chain Mothinder wore that she had not noticed before. She kept smiling and staring at his chest. He gave a wry smile and wink, and said something about his eyes being up there, something very Rich-like or was it something arrogant people did, it was the way in which things were said. She couldn't even remember what he had said, flicking her eyes down to her lap and reaching in her pocket to get away. Her phone provided distraction as she kept smiling at the man next to her, for no particular reason just more out of not knowing what resting face she should have as well as trying to avoid any comments about her usual resting bitch face, horrendous comments like you should smile more often. Comments completely unrequired.

"So, are you seeing anyone then Izzy?" He enquired.

A reasonable line of questioning that in her delirious state seemed barbed, she shook her head as if trying to clear the merged pastels to look more clearly at the conversation in front of her.

"No, I'm single right now, heh" She giggled.

"Ooh, remind me, you're a postgraduate, aren't you?"

His inquiry probed, she felt pastels colours surround her vision, another shake and another giggle.

"Yeah, I'm closer to my thirties, I guess. Feel like an oldie now."

"Hmm let me guess, 28?"

"Yeah" She didn't know the combined feeling she had just felt flow through her, a mix between impressed and offended, "impfended" if that was allowed to be a word.

"Yeah, I did think you weren't far from me. Well 31 and 28 are pretty similar, not achieved as much, have you?" He laughed but it felt a little jagged as it hit her face and left an invisible bruise on her cheek, or more aptly her ego.

"I'm joking of course."

She had to pretend that the words didn't hurt, after all a joke couldn't possibly be hurtful, it wasn't a very funny joke she had thought before another wild hook came out of his mouth.

"But you know, that's why you really need to think about the future, don't ya think, like we all tip toe, but we need honesty too ya get me, need to say things and get things done. Ya get me?"

She wanted to say no, instead she nervously giggled and nodded. His statement was redundant and full of no meaning.

"Because I can already feel the nights drag on me and like you'll be even older at my level."

This was horrible and uncomfortable. What had brought truth, he probably thought he was being nice, but this was intrusive and none of his business.

She chose to ignore him, not offering a laugh, her facing scrunching, him not oblivious to the change in atmosphere tried to save the room with his brand of "honesty".

"Look." His hand coarse and rougher than had been in surgery laid on her shoulder, she felt the vice tighten, she felt it in her head due to the squeeze on her right shoulder, her face looking into his eyes, they too were dark, the *Lowry* pastels she imagined in them had begun to blur around her.

"I'm an honest guy, I just really worry about juniors, and I want you guys not to waste time ya get me?"

She felt like every time he said you got me it was preceded by some inane statement which actually had nothing to get.

"Like if you want kids or a family, you know you have to meet someone for at least like a year before moving in like 2-3 before proposal marriage and then maybe kids but that puts you at like 32. That's a tough age to be a mum you know. Plus, then career wise you'll end up being just a GP. Just really think about it.

Although I guess you might not want a kid which is fair but I imagine you do want a guy. I'd just say sometimes you girls can be picky."

Now that did have meaning, horrible meaning to her and not what she wanted to hear at 4 am in the morning, she prayed for her bleep to interrupt, but like a cosmic joke it seemed silent, it wouldn't have been if this was a nice fun conversation. She wondered if there was, like on her old phone, a self-call option, a sort of get out option. No sound from the damned machine as the pastels began to blend like a washing machine screen.

The washing machine of pastels began the end cycle, she swore she could hear the loud noises of it, like a plane taking off. Despite her apparent discomfort the pastels kept talking.

"You see, time exists and at our age we gotta be smart. Ya get me!"

He patted her shoulder; she felt his edges pierce her skin.

"Right?"

Now the cycle has finished. She looked up, a little panting a little raw and red, she felt her skin come up like a sunburn. No tanning. She watched his eyes checking her all over, feeling as if she were naked in front of the man, as if he was judging every aspect of her.

She pulled away.

"I don't think I want to talk about that, I think that maybe, umm, the ward needed something or let me check yeah check."
She finished and got up seeing the angular man's eyes fixate further on her.
"Come on look, you can't all be giggly and only listen when you like the advice."
She was becoming a lobster.
"Umm, no of course, I get it I guess, I'm just nervous about the ward and it's the last night, we've done loads yeah, it's just always busy, so much work." She could feel that her words didn't mean anything, she wondered if she should add a ya get me onto the statement.
Mothinder stood staring. A confused look, at least he wasn't angry.
"Anyway, why don't you check on that ward," he replied. His eyes finally averted as he took another almost cannibalistic bite out of the food in front of him, she had never noticed how sharp his canines were.

She had managed to make it to the second corridor with the blue line leading her closer to the ward, usually she would stay away as showing your face always created work on a night shift. However, she required a cooler place to allow her skin to recover, using the time alone as an Aloe Vera. She felt herself becoming a little tearful; but to react would be to lose.

She let her eyes become a little puffy holding in any form of cooling liquid as she decided to slow her pace following the blue line, the ward would arrive soon and distraction ahead she knew would come. She needed distraction, she finally got to the front door as she felt her ears go from red to pink.

*

Sat in hand over next to Rich as a buffer between her and the angular man, not that anything else had been said and he had approached her this morning with a quiet reserve and was even complimenting her suturing skills. She zoned in and out of the conversation as each patient was mentioned and someone from the team piped up defended the night team decisions, sometimes to grumbles, sometimes to a curt well done from the smartly, anti-infection control, dressed consultant. His sleeves down and gold watch glistening, his tie hanging down with its sensible yet colourful patterns, showing more character than he ever did to the junior team.

Rich looked over at her, she saw his hand miming a drink, she understood the universal signal and the likely plan that would follow, habits she had been told, keep you going in times of chaos.

She had already imagined and correctly predicted the conversation that occurred between her and Rich in quiet whispers making them look like students who were rebellious in the back row gossiping away. Their words formed a smoker's cloud.
"Jarlsberg 7:30-8:00".
She nodded back with a smile.
"It's a date," she mimicked in her head as he spoke the words in slightly louder volume, a stage whisper rather than normal whisper. The words landed in her face like the puff from the shared cigarette. She coughed a little, making the simile or metaphor real for one second.
She felt the eyes of the room, but no one took any notice, after all they had learned to ignore most of what Rich says. Although no doubt he would interpret the situation differently, it was easy for her to be cynical about him, although she did envy his easy-going self-confidence and his ability to continue in his beliefs to the point of almost deluding himself. She was being unfair. She watched him looking at her and what must be her exhausted exterior, there seemed to be some kind of caring about more than himself in his eyes. He turned to her this time no smoke,
"Plus, it sounds like things have been hectic, you deserve a break, you smashed the nights,

especially nothing to hand over, you're brilliant you know that don't you."

He smiled with such confidence she chose to believe his complete unevidenced statement about her. After all, he hadn't seen her practice.

"Thanks Rich, I appreciate that, you're brilliant too, I guess." She gave a small giggle. She watched the angular man give a silencing look to her and Rich, causing both to react in the same way, the look stiffened and forced all of their muscles to contract. Her belly ached as she awaited the end of handover.

The end came after a long delegation and quick teaching case from Candice. She sat in silence whilst listening to Candice talk about an interesting case and teach a lesson which whilst useful could have been delivered in one minute and most likely had been delivered to the many people in the room many times before. This would constitute their mandatory teaching time; it would be the department claiming it was an hour of teaching a week to all the staff and thus they were definitely a training post. The lesson was, "always do a rectal exam in cases where you have any suspicion of rectal disease." Surprisingly not a silly idea but not ground-breaking either. In the case had the person not mentioned done so an embarrassing admission of piles may have been avoided. Examine what you think might be wrong, she wondered if she could just deliver that lesson when it was her turn to do the Friday morning presentation.

The room dispersed, people hummed and chatted, she felt a jagged hand hit her shoulder,

"Good working with ya sport, not too bad at all, just keep that chin up and maybe smile a little more, it'd do you wonders."

She felt the tension rise before letting it dispel with a small smile and an escaped nervous giggle. He smiled back and rushed off. Noticing him pull a small gold band from his pocket and reach it towards one of very well-defined fingers.

The walk down the hill to home was in a pleasant breeze but one in which bright pastels merged into one, she almost crossed the road into a car. Luckily the person driving had their wits about them and had not just finished four-night shifts. It stopped, beeping, she felt embarrassed and apologised like a dishonoured Japanese lady with bows of her head and her hands in a prayer sign. The driver honked again before pulling round and driving past. She walked back onto the pavement before her house. At least there was no shouting from a pulled down window, she probably just made the driver think she was mentally unwell.

She felt everything slow down as she entered her room, slowly the stench of her old clothes and lack of cleaning due to night shifts permeated through the air. Their dishes undone and the house slowly dusting up, she found it funny that her body reaction to almost dying was to want to sleep, night shifts really did remove any innate drive out of you. She closed her eyes, once, twice, noting she should get out of her jeans and trendy toms.

She closed again and then opened them, she went to stand up, confirming to herself she needed to change. The clock read 19:15, she had slept. She looked at her phone and there was a small text from Rich.

"I'll come to pick you up at 19:30, better get dapper."

For once no question mark, but a definitive statement, one that she should probably reply with a delayed time to. She realised she liked the question marks he sent if it meant she avoided definitive statements and trips to her home.

19:45 and she managed a quick shower and make up, applying a darker shade to her lips, she looked at the mirror as she wore her underwear. For some reason having not done washing she had left an interesting pair of underwear she hadn't worn whilst being single. The dark pants with small lace and flowers across, the top bra matching with more lace, a slight push up element, to try and show what she had accepted God hadn't given her in exchange for a waistline that stayed small no matter how many jacket potatoes she ate.

She managed to get some jeans on which hugged her figure and went to find a top that hung over her shoulder just enough to show a little of what she got but still leave some mystery. She always went for the English rose look; simple and elegant her mother would tell her. She smiled as she started to hear the engine of a car outside her home. Taking a deep breath and having one more moment of silence she then headed to her door to greet the man who appeared in front. Wearing an ironic baggy shirt with a tweed jacket on and she swore the same figure-hugging jean she had on Rich stood in all his assumptive glory.

"So, are you ready darling for a pleasant drink?"

Another question mark. She smiled back at him.

"Yeah, it'll be nice to unwind a little. My mind has been far too focused on work."

"Tell me about it, plus you've finished nights, you must be in a party mood then yeah?"

She kept quiet this time.

"Or do you want a little intimate date with someone as amazing as me, yeah? I know women like an obnoxious or what I call confident man!"

This confirmed that his statements were definitely worse than his questions. Although harmless and fun most of the time.

"Shall we?" He ushered her to his car. A nice Volkswagen Golf, one of the newer models and when she stepped into the car, she could see it had all the latest features, this was a high-end model.

"Nice car," she proclaimed without much thought.

"Yeah, top model, I got it once I finished med school, such a nice graduation present, plus gets me around everywhere, which you need in a small place like this to escape."

She had let him talk whilst her eyes glossed over what the top model really did feature. She could see the sound system was top range, there was a sat nav inbuilt into the car with a screen available to the back seats. The seats had lovely leather and as she placed her bottom on it, she felt like a member of the royal family.

"Watch this" a crooked smile took over the man next to her face. A button next to the control panel lit up as she suddenly felt a small heat across her bottom. Warming, it was comfortable, she knew Rich was enjoying getting her lower half warmed up and knew the next line.

"You didn't think you'd be feeling all cooked up so early on a Friday evening did ya?"

A roll of her eyes before Rich smiled back at her.

"I did not plan for it, no" she gave him sass back and it seemed to only encourage Rich.

"Well, it definitely means it's only gonna get better from here, how will you manage to keep your hands off me?"

"Well, it seems that you'll only manage to keep me going with equipment, and I think maybe your car is a little bit better than you."

She smirked at him and this time it was his turn to laugh at her. His laugh was then drowned by the revving, his dials almost flying off the metre before the car jolted up the hill towards the hospital and beyond that the Jarlsberg. The clock read 20:00.

*

At the pub she looked at her glass of wine. She normally held off too many drinks, but after nights she needed her heart to relax. She needed the wine to protect her from a stress induced heart attack. Her coolness only extended to a medium glass despite Rich insistence she needed large. He did however convince her to share a bottle. Claiming she would get the next, she felt she had lost to his tactics, like a manager whose team had been undone despite it being better on paper.

"So how were the nights then? You looked pretty done this morning, I think you may have napped during the teaching session."

"Well, it was just really busy, and I just had a rough last one."

"Ohh how come?" Rich eyes meeting hers, she could tell he was hunting for gossip.

"Well first night we had a man who basically wanked too much!"

"What's too much? Because I feel you're the kind of person who may not really know how much wanking is enough!"

"What's that meant to mean? Kind of person." She sniped at him, she saw him smile at her annoyance, it didn't surprise her that he must like this kind of exchange. He was a confident charming man but not a nice man.

"Well, you know I feel you may not be the biggest fan of it."

"Look people can do what they want, I don't mind that, it's just not my style."

"Well then how much is too much for you, young lady" his hands waving round, causing a slight scene as his wine glasses wobbled and was saved by him, yet he seemed to be happy with his save rather than acknowledge his initial mistake

"Well, he said 3-4 times, I thought he meant week, which is still, like you know, surely there are better things to do with your time. I was then corrected, and he said 3-4 times a day. Which was funny." She giggled at the last sentence and for once appreciated Rich's hearty laugh which followed.

"Yeah, but see, you can't be doing it right! There's nothing better than an orgasm. I imagine even better for you girls, less mess and longer lasting."

She wondered why she had gotten herself into this conversation. She against her better judgement with a little night brain drunkenness downed her glass of wine to add in some regular drunkenness to her state as well. Her glass filled up again before she had even set it down onto the wooden table.

"Although my shitty humour aside, you said a rough last one?"

She saw some self-awareness and caring from him, not novel but she wished more of it was on the surface.

"Well, it's just with that r*eg*"

"Mo? Yeah I really like him."

"Yeah well, he's nice sometimes, but we just had the most horrible, weird conversation."
Rich eyes intensified, there was no silly sex jokes, his hands now resting on the table, no flailing whilst he responded.
"What happened?"
She had never heard that tone from him.
"Well, he basically just said I was too old to be single and if I didn't do something about it I'll end up either alone or not having a choice in my career, and he kept saying he was being nice and doing me a favour by telling me this at 4 am in the morning, someone he had known for like four days. I just hated it, it made me feel horrible, I couldn't talk, and I could barely look at him without feeling awful."
Rich had no flails, his eyes serious, no bellowed tone, just a slow voice.
"That's ridiculous, you're brilliant and you don't need to worry about hurrying, someone will be lucky to have you because you're amazing, just because he's jealous about rushing things doesn't mean he has to take it out on you!"
She smiled and felt a small warmth overcome her from his statements, she could also take them seriously, there was no laughter no sexual joke. The warmth was much more comfortable than the car seat earlier.

"Look you need to just enjoy yourself, never ever bother with him again anyway, he's not that good. Plus, any more trouble I'll stop him, yeah?"

She nodded as she followed his enjoy yourself advice. Gobbling another glass before it was full. Pastel colours appeared now again around the whole pub, and she was acutely aware of all the noises around her. They soothed her, the small bleeping of the fruit machine, the music blaring making her move her shoulders a bit at a time. She looked over as the hand flailed again.

"So, are we hitting the town? I think others should be coming!"

She did wonder when they would, after all Rich had invited her but her assumption was, he'd invited the usual crew. That his proclamation of a date meant it was definitely not a date.

"Yeah, Rachel is well up for it plus she's bringing the SHO from her ward and a few of physios and Occupational therapist (OT)'s, might be fun, I bet they know how to party much better than us, after all we're all stick in the muds as medics, just chat about work and pretend it's funny! No outside life."

"It's hard when you're doing so many shifts." She replied, she definitely noticed the slurring of her words this time it was Rich's turn to giggle at her. The noise soothed instead of jarred like it had done at work.

*

She stood with Rachel, a Physio by the name of Beth and another OT by the name of Sandra. Sandra was the youngest with clear blue eyes, her body shapely in all the right areas and toned in the others, despite her name being old fashioned she was not.
Beth stood next to her, similar in physique, nice in all the ways you would want just a little older. Rachel smiled at all of them.
"Let's go guys, salt, drink, lime."
Why had she done this? She felt it burn through her inside, suddenly more noise and pastels. Before her throat could rest another shot was in her hand. They repeated it again.

*

The world was spinning around her as she said goodbye to someone who sounded a lot like Rich at the door. He had hugged her and asked for his gentlemanly kiss, she had delivered it on his cheek or was it a polite quick one on the lips, there definitely was no tongue. She looked at her clock; 01:33. She closed her eyes in a spinning bedroom, she needed to get off her toms and slide into her pyjamas, she also needed to have her uncomfortable yet complimentary underwear off. They were definitely not for sleeping in.

She closed and opened her eyes again, determined to get up and change. Standing up she looked again as light peered into her eyes. Her clock read 08:31. She felt everything spin, her head more acutely aware of all sounds and smells around her. They grated unlike the night before where they had enhanced. She felt her stomach churn at the idea of stale bread and jam. Urging her towards her toilet to add yet another smell to her home which needed a post night shift clean.

She did not want stale bread and jam ever again.

Chapter 7: Cheese and Ham, Toasted!

He had been looking at her the whole car journey, he couldn't help but look at Izzy who sat in the warmed seat next to him, he wondered if it made her feel any different towards him, he hadn't read that in any dating advice book.

He could see the jeans she wore hugged her figure, a good move on anybody with her body type. He saw black lace emerging from the top. Was she dressed nice for him he wondered, snapping himself back he failed to change his inner monologue subject. He continued as he examined the rest of what was in front of him. With the precision of someone who was trying to get as much as possible from what she was dressed in. Her top hung perfectly loose trying to make him imagine more, or want more, another two lacey straps lay across her shoulders. He had never quite noticed before how exquisite her collar bones were. Now he wondered what the word for a fetish of that was.

*

They had been in the pub for a while now and after sharing a bottle of wine his lovely time had been interrupted with the arrival of the party. He couldn't believe how the *reg* had spoken to someone as nice as Izzy, really he couldn't think of a bad word for her, he let that thought sink and it made him wonder if it meant he had something stronger for the girl sitting opposite him, who was now greeting the rest of the group with her amazing smile. With words like glad to see you and it's been so long. She was, after all, so nice.

He had joined in with one shot before rushing to the toilet, his reflux going crazy with tequila as always, chewing a small antacid he took a moment over the toilet determined not to be the first person to vomit. He was after all the man and society would, no matter how much it said it wouldn't, judge him on higher "holding your drink" ground.

He had returned to the giggling girls as he took his seat next to Izzy who was now more slurry than he had ever seen her.

"So, it looks like you enjoyed those shots." He began to dig.

"As if anyone can enjoy tequila, it's just usually the quickest way to enjoy other things." She giggled. This was a different side to Izzy he was seeing. Jumping on the opportunity he got his metaphorical drill, getting ready to dig deeper.

"Oh really. I mean I don't think I've ever seen you flirt."

"Oh shut up Rich, look let's just say some of the men in Darthington are nice, but like in a little brother way."

"Oh I see, maybe you're looking for a big brother?"

He joked, he thought it was good and nonetheless the response of his laugh followed by her giggling confirmed this to him.

"Well, you get what I mean, everyone is nice here, but sometimes you need a little fire, plus I kind of don't want to waste my time on people who aren't right." Her slurring is more evident to him.

"I guess so, I get ya." He moved in a little closer as did she as the conversation became a little more intimate. He stopped for a second the tequila settling from his stomach to his blood stream, the truth serum that it must contain or be extracted from moving his lips to ruin the moment.

"Surely though that puts a lot of pressure on you and them, I mean if you're meeting using apps then maybe sparks don't just happen. I mean you base attraction on a blurb and a photo, and I'm good at making my photos look a lot better than me! I imagine you're the same." He smirked with a little rebalancing of his whole body. She gave him a big smack on the shoulder, it was more painful than playful, he wondered if that was her intention.

"Well, I've not seen you on the app yet, so I wouldn't know that would I." She gave a few sneezes mixed in with the sentences.

"Plus, I like the freedom of being single."

"Amen to that for sure."

They clinked their two glasses of wine together, he wondered how much she would remember of buying the second bottle for them to share. Hearing her gulp still didn't put Rich off, the drunker he got the more he noticed all her previous features but more. He really couldn't help but look at her that way. He had decided he worked too closely with her, and they were friends but the way she acted around him made him fall and he hated it when he couldn't control who he fell for.

"I feel we should definitely do more hanging out, like enough of just work, like I said before a game night maybe like we had before." She looked at him, giving him a weird hope in his body.

"The one with Rach, I mean she just won everything." He recalled.

"I'm pretty sure I won settlers." A confidence in her obvious lie.

"You didn't!" He quickly refuted the truth she was trying to create.
"I'm pretty sure I did!"
He frowned at her as she scrunched her face up trying to remember. He was sure she was wrong but maybe she needed a few wins. Her scrunched face was cute.
"Or maybe we should go to a live gig, like we did a few weeks back."
"I don't think we have." This time he was unsure what her last glass of wine had contained, it was the opposite to his truth serum.
"Oh maybe that was a date or another time."
"Well then you're the one who should be inviting me."
"I can't invite you to my dates, that would be weird."
"Probably I could sit and give you advice, I could be your hitch, you know the movie Hitch."
"Yeah, I know Hitch."
He heard her having another gulp and he could see the bottle nearing empty, their conversation flowed. It was nice and easy, and she kept smiling. There was even a bit where they danced together on the dance floor. Until Izzy fell over and proclaimed it was her home time. It was then more of Rachel's friends including her SHO Dean arrived. Izzy was

already slowly meandering outside. He knew it was his duty to escort the lady home and sometimes knights got rewards for their quests. He thought it was bad to expect *it* after such a fun night, or did it just show he was more than the little brother type.

*

The air was cold outside her house, he had been holding her hand all the way home as she rested her head against his shoulder, steading herself on him. She was definitely an assistance of 1, a light assistance of 1, he imagined that was one of the greatest compliments someone could say about your weight. So much so he had thought about it several times before saying it to her, to get her giggling, he internally patted himself on the back. He was funny. He just needed the reassurance to make sure. Hiding away his anxiety at the door, she struggled for her keys. "Thanks for that, it was a really fun night Rich." She smiled at him, staring at him or maybe beyond him, she was definitely swaying. He wondered at that moment what it would be like if she always stared at him or maybe always let him inside her house, showing her inner life to him. His stomach lurched a small pit growing larger, heart rate rising, he tried to find words, he had none, but he always had some. There were meant to always be words in his head, but she had vanished them. He shook his head thinking of the latest dating video he had watched, something about assertiveness.

He looked back at her, she was definitely looking at him or past him, one of them was definite or maybe, definitely maybe at least. He took a big breath, he managed to say assertive words but in the most anxious way possible.

"Where's my goodnight kiss?"

She smiled, with a glazed look in her eyes, he wondered if her brain had interpreted anything in her current state. She placed her lips on his lips and let them softly interact with hers, sending his previous heart rate into a dangerous arrhythmia. He didn't know if he passed out or remained still but with one blink she had already turned around and closed her door.

"See ya soon, we'll get something organised."

He heard her voice echo.

The door shut in his face as his heart jumped and galloped, he considered a visit to the emergency department but decided against seeing what the tracing of his heart would be like due to a kiss. It was that moment he realised he wasn't as much of a lad as he thought he was. It made him almost scared to think what she thought of all this, or worse the possibility that she probably didn't think much of all this.

*

He had been enjoying the change to being the surgical man, there was suddenly less pressure and more getting by on his own confidence and a little brown nosing. It always helped that brown nosing is what public school had taught him, anyone in authority seems to always like the traditional techniques, especially when they were old school consultants. It felt like he was part of the club and nowhere was that club more key to survival than with the department of surgery at Darthington hospital.

Although this particular Monday he was suffering from his first ever three-day hangover after the Friday night, he had continued to drink right until 4 am Saturday morning, trying to keep up with Rachel and all her friends and it didn't help how "sick" he felt around the whole Izzy situation as he had unimaginatively called it. Not that he had much imagination with regards to this.

He looked around the ward he was based on for the day, it was him and Izzy covering their favourite ward, the general surgery ward which contained one vascular patient who had to wait to transfer over to the "proper" hospital. It also meant they held the so-called

Darthington vascular surgery bleep. Which in itself posed its very own challenges. Vascular surgery entailed the whole body and when the piping that carried blood failed or blocked or burst there were disastrous situation that one couldn't just fix with a few cannulas and assessments, it would need a surgeon, luckily the patients never stayed long and very few people ever rang their bleep for advice, knowing that those who manned it could not provide what they were looking for.

He was in the most dreadful part of his hangover when Izzy and her scrubs arrived. His heart continued skipping beats and his stomach churned. She had the right size with no pin ups and her collar bones again showing to him, what a weird thing for him to fixate on, he wondered if she would ever find it cute, him saying her collar bones were the most attractive bit of her, probably not, he saved the mental note to avoid saying that.

He looked beyond her around the ward, the tinsel was finally gathering around the hospital. The Christmas cheer was fully coming, they were on the week of Christmas, and something had transformed in the hospital, the pressure seemed to simmer down despite there being more and more patients to see. There was almost an acceptance that less was going to get done, secretaries off, consultants with no real routine lists, clinics running bare boned. The District General Hospital was reflecting the sleepiness of the town it provided for. The rota coordinators had emailed Christmas rota plans, lucky for him he wasn't working, he wondered though after reading the email prefaced with I am away for 2 weeks what would happen if the plan failed, there definitely wasn't a plan B, he imagined that is why the consultant on call got paid lots as they would have to assume the responsibility. All he knew was he was going to have a proper Christmas lunch and enjoy his luck for his first year of medicine.

The cheer and colourfulness of the ward was brought to life with a Christmas tree, hanging tinsels as well as some mistletoe around, allowing all staff to get away with being flirtatious or at least make one comment each, all this really did change the atmosphere of the hospital. Although he always wondered how the patients felt now that their bed sides and windows and what was already little personal space was invaded further by glitter which now was everywhere. Worse than bacteria in a hospital it had spread now covering every inch of the hospital. He wondered if the pandemic had started across the country. He chuckled to himself, winning the attention of Izzy momentarily. He would save that one for later. It would do very well in the boy's club.

The ward round was uneventful as more "continue as before" were written in the notes as patients lay either recovering or worsening post-surgery. Nothing much ever changed in surgery, the simplicity allowed him to know how to act in the limited number of situations that did arise, it was black and white here and he liked that. In summary they would either get rung about them to do the discharge summary to get them home once enough time had passed, the physio was happy and the drain stopped draining, or they would ring the medical *registrar* and have a plan for their complication post-surgery. Very rarely were people opened up again these days. When they did that was the only time they weren't rung. Usually they would arrive to a registrar and nurse who would look at them disapprovingly for even leaving the ward with a reminder of their bad behaviour issued to them in the phrase, "I had to call the r*eg* the patient needed sorting out and you guys weren't around."

*

The day had not disappointed him, he had managed to prove again why he was good at this medicine malarkey. There had been a faint on the ward in which he responded to in a, in his own words, textbook manner. What he also enjoyed was the fact everyone was impressed. He could see it on their faces including Izzy who hadn't responded like him. The patient had been mobilised from a chair, then went limp and had to be lowered to the floor. The red bell had gone, initially causing everyone to look around and have the hope that it was a mistake. Before muffled helps were called from the curtains in bay 2. This allowed everyone to walk hurriedly to the situation. He walked in first and saw the man almost on the floor. Limp. He felt his brain rush, everyone remained silent whilst the alarm blared. It took him one moment to balance himself and then he started speaking with authority.

"Let's get the crash trolley," he bellowed as everyone leaped into action.

He went down next to the physio, the one from the other night Beth, noting how attractive she looked with her worried face and dirty blonde hair in a ponytail with strands across her clear eyes. He whipped his thoughts around to the patient, his grey skin becoming slightly mottled. He knew that they needed to get him on the floor, flat.

He shouted instructions and spoke directly to the physio, they all complied, as a team they got the patient flat on the floor. He then went to feel for the carotid pulse in his neck and felt for air.

Bingo!

He confidently bellowed again.

"Get his folder Izzy. He's got a pulse and quiet breath sounds. We need to know what we can do for him."

She hurried off with a nervous smile that he saw and couldn't help but internally comment on. It was nice on her face. He wished she would offer it more to him. The physio had placed a hand on his shoulder.

"Shall we see what he's like."

"Of course, Mr… uh…"

"Cartwright". The physio filled him in.

"Mr Cartwright!" He shouted in both ears.

The body stirred and grunted.

"Good, good, Mr Cartwright," his bellowing voice now showing its true strength as the man stirred further the louder he was.

Like a phoenix rising he watched the man be lifted by all the staff., with his eyes open he seemed a little groggy.

"Wha… hape…" he attempted to speak. He tried again and reassured everyone when he was able to finish his sentence, "what happened?"

"Looks like you had a funny turn with the physio Mr Cartwright."

"Did I," he replied.

"They worked ya too hard didn't they." A stock joke and a few laughs from his audience, he resisted the urge to bow and over egg the situation.

"Yeah, do you know where ya are?"

"At the hospital, after surgery."

"Yes, and your date of birth?"

"3rd of November 1943"

"Brilliant and what time is it?"

He then heard his stomach rumble as the patient stared at him and his offending abdomen.

"I'm starving and so are you doc. It must be near lunchtime."

It was the patient's turn to get the audience to laugh. He wondered what would happen if he could take Mr Cartwright on the comedy circuit. He finished up his examination and once back to bed reassured everyone including himself at that time the crash trolley and Izzy arrived.

"No worries guys, it's all sorted," he said with an air of greatness.

He deserved to feel good and both the nurse with the crash trolley and Izzy gave him a face which he interpreted as a well done. His stomach rumbled and he knew Mr Cartwright was right, it must be lunchtime.

*

He always wondered why he felt so sad looking at Izzy lunches, he had watched her defend them before with multitude of reasons including that it made her feel comfortable, an argument that couldn't be beat, but the bread she had seemed to be crumbling in her hand and there definitely wasn't enough spread in between the two pieces of drying white bread. His lunch was no longer the gruel or protein-based foods, with the shift pattern and with his growing tiredness that he was trying to hide his food habits had slipped. He had to get something from the canteen as he had not been prepared. A nice warm cheese and ham toastie rested in his lap dripping with grease onto his plate. Despite his diet he definitely looked buff or bulked up and hoped that the horrible weather and loud jumpers which may be hiding the slight fat his midline had started to gather on his new diet. It was after all the winter bulk. The most prominent change in his wardrobe apart from jumpers was going for slightly bigger sized scrubs from his ED days.

He took a bite as some grease dropped further on the plate and slightly at the bottom of his top, a stain which he would ignore and if anyone noticed then at least he knew they were looking at his crotch, small victories are seldom found in the hospital, and he would hold onto them. He bit again as Izzy looked at him. She smiled, finishing her mouth full before speaking.

"Well done today, I thought that was very good."

He had never noticed her to start a conversation with him sober, usually he had to try, he wondered if she was impressed or starting to feel the way he did about her, or if she was being polite. It was hard for his brain to decide; his mantra of small victories chose the former.

"Yeah, well when it clicks it clicks, plus I mean how sexy did I look to you guys and the physio, gotta say you were all impressed."

He smirked and she gave him a giggle and a small smirk as well.

"I wish I hadn't said anything. Your head is already too big, so much so you can't co-ordinate your eating."

He laughed along with her; he did enjoy a little roasting.

"Anyway, who's our r*eg* today?" He asked as he knew they would have to catch up eventually with this mysterious man.

She looked down and instantly her face changed, it hurt him to see her look so concerned. He felt his urge to protect her, albeit a probably sexist urge he was sure to be told.

"It's Mothinder this week, but I don't know where he is. I'm not really in the mood for catching up and there's nothing really to catch up about. I'm quite lucky I have only today before I get the whole Christmas week off."

"Aww, but I never got your present ready for you," he smiled at her, she seemed a little taken aback.

"Umm, a present, I mean that's so nice of you, why would you do that." The most nervous thanks he had ever seen seemed to float from her mouth into his hands, fragile and breaking.

"Well, if you don't want it then you don't have to."

"No, no it's fine, that's good thanks."

It was another fragile smile; he didn't know if this was a good sign or not.

Just like God had spoken to stop his wandering, their bleep went off. The noise pierced the room as people around them all looked down to their pockets hoping it wasn't them, like Russian roulette they looked around to see who it was that would have the bullet come from their chamber to their head. It was him and Izzy whose little gun had rang.

He could feel the sad eyes as he walked to answer the phone, like walking to one's own execution.

"Hello, Richard Twain, what can I sort out for you?"

"Yeah yeah very good this is the vascular bleep ya? Dr Nice here we got a chap with a rubbish toe that you guys need to look at."

"Hey, Dr Nice, remember me it's Rich from ED.

There was silence with no response, he must just be thinking and remembering the good times they had.

"Yeah cool, look, can you just see this toe."

Weirdly no familiarity in Dr Nice's voice, he put it down to a rough day or something, after all they had some good memories he was sure of.

He decided to reply with even more confidence to put the next point across well, "I think most of the time you phone the guys at the royal, then they get us to admit with their plan."

There was a pause, he awaited the good news of a job well dodged. Especially as he was talking to a friend.

"Look, that's your job, that's your team, yeah come down and see them and sort them. I've referred them to you."

The phone hung as he felt like he had just been a young schoolkid told off, a small surge of anxiety welled up, his smile for once faded slightly, he gulped once or twice then headed into the room again and looked at Izzy.

"What's up?" She asked her soft eyes, almost soothing him. However, his embarrassment was beginning to redden his ears.

"Look, we have someone to see in ED."

"But I thought,"

"It doesn't matter, we need to go."

He saw that she was surprised at his sternness, his lack of joke or sexual innuendo but his heart was racing again because when he was looking at her hurt face, he was thinking about the phone conversation. He gulped a third time before guiding and walking behind Izzy towards the emergency department, this time for once his head was unable to compliment the body walking in front of him due to its distraction. It had been a while since either of them had followed the red line.

*

The Christmas in ED was decorated quite differently to the wards, whilst the wards had gone impressionist, old-school renaissance, ED was minimalist modern, angular one that took a while to see but appreciation came from those who looked.

There was a little mistletoe hidden in each corner, as if to say have your affairs with each other in the corner please compared to the wards asking for kissing on display. Some tinsel here and there in the corridors and in minors, within majors as they walked through the department it was even more subtle, mostly on the notes trolleys or around the computer desks, away from patient areas. The glitter minimal, like a ward protecting itself from the pandemic it felt like everyone here protected themselves from interacting too much with Christmas and if they did, he imagined they would hang up the decoration with glitter in hazmat suits with rigorous decontamination afterwards.

They found their way to the minors cubicle where their man lay, he wanted to complain about the hunt they had but once in the full department the smell of a dead toe was too hard to miss and their noses guided him and Izzy towards the curtain which hid their supposed review. Whilst this wasn't protocol, he wandered what lay ahead for them and how well they would manage.

The smell was hard to keep a smile through but the man to which his toe was producing this was even more difficult to keep a smile to. The man and his toe had an air of anger and his response to the two of them stepping in wasn't ideal.

"More students, bloody hell it's a dead toe, can't I just see the guys who're gonna deal with it please. These hospitals are getting worse, I swear."

"Hello there Tom."

"Mr Bridges," the man had snubbed at him, his words smelling a little more awful than his toe. A great feat he noted and internalised. He tried his best to keep a smile on, to appear more comforting, maybe a joke will break the air. He threw it out there.

"Sorry, we young forget to respect the elders, sometimes,"

He withdrew from his tool belt his best patient pleasing smile. These were the privately educated big guns, the Boris Johnson smile.

"Elders, goodness son, you gotta a lot to learn, what's that nurse next to you doing, wagging her tail at your whim, just get me sorted out."

"Look Mr Bridges my name is Dr Rich and this is Dr Izzy," he decided to emphasise the lovely smart lady next to him, he buried his train of thoughts about Izzy before continuing talking to the man.

"We are part of the surgical team, so we are the ones that will be getting you sorted, okay?"

Grumpy but accepting, the best one could hope for in the scenario. For a second his train came back, he wondered if Izzy was feeling something for him after what he assumed was quite a brave display of protection. Maybe they should find a mistletoe, his thoughts almost running away about the feeling of having her body close to his, sin on sin, holding her waist and her quite nice bottom. He pulled himself back before anyone could tell he had vanished into a misogynist steam train fog. Jumping off the train before the doors locked and pulled away from the station.

He unboxed the toe from the sock, removing it delicately like he was about to look at an expensive engagement ring. He and Izzy stared at the toe, he wondered if she could also see it staring back, the eye on it being a wet looking ulcer with an emerald tinged pus expressing. As his hand approached it he noticed, no gloves. Wincing back, he tried to put on his best smile.

"Probably should get gloves on," he added, this time he could feel his nervousness well up, almost breaking through the wall of calculated bravado. He shook it off, he was

Richard Twain after all, which meant 90% bravado at least.

The next challenge was placing the gloves, the 10% of him having caused his hands to be far too moist and sweaty, much more than his forehead or shirt would have shown. The gloves knew about his hands and his deception, revealing his crimes to all those around him in the department, showing them all a glimpse beyond Rich, the sexy confident doctor to Rich, the probably nervous feeling a little out of depth, Fy1. They stuck to his skin as he pulled down on them, the thin cheap plastic stretching and thinning over his palms, sticking to all the droplets of moisture created by his fight or flight centre. The first pair invariably broke and the second much larger pair stuck around his hands leaving gaps where fingers should be, alas it was as good as it was going to get for him as he placed his hands over the dead toe and the oozing ulcer. He expected a wince, but the man now distracted by Izzy and whispering away to her let him get on with probing and pushing around the site. He did wonder what he was meant to assess, he wondered what more information his index finger could gleam. However, given his teaching of examining the complaining body part/organ that he had learned from teaching the other day he felt obliged to poke around and to eventually in the notes write ***toe examined***. However, all it yielded was yes there was a dead toe and an ulcer with pus. Maybe that it was cold to touch, but it was dead after all and that it didn't hurt or have sensation but then again it was dead after all.

What snapped him back was the laugh of Izzy, he wished it was only for him. He wondered why that man didn't make her nervous because she laughed the same way she did around him.

"Alright sir," he decided to interrupt before unwanted feelings of jealousy took over. Minor jealousy only, nothing serious he internalised.

"So, looks like it is definitely necrotic, I think the pus and ulcer are probably what we need to do something about. So, we'll have a chat with the bosses and make a plan."

"I thought you guys were the surgeons, surely you're the bosses."

Thus, he let the dance begin again between the patient and junior doctor. Luckily due to the way the emergency department was run his sparing skills about convincing someone his review was important and that a registrar or consultant needed to make a final decision had gotten really good, Olympic good, if he wasn't to flatter himself too much.

"Fair enough," the patient said in a pleading tone to get him to be quiet. Once again they dispersed from the room, he and Izzy stood by the minors desk both their eyes scanning each other, he could tell both of them were trying to summarise what had just happened. For once she broke the silence, he couldn't help but smile at that concept.

"What an annoying man, we were just trying to help him," her frustrated face was sexy to him, he liked it, probably not conducive to like the frustrated face of someone you want to be your lover. She went on and the way her southern accent tinged in frustration stirred him a little.

"Just some people when we're trying to help them, I just can't stand it you know."

"Probably should have told him, he'd have been nicer if he saw that side of you Izzy," Rich raised his eyebrow and let his smile settle.

"Plus, I've never seen this side of you" He added, getting her to smile back at him with a soothing laugh.

"Well, what should we do? It didn't look nice, but I don't really know much about what we do with "not nice to look at", I guess, I mean I just, what should we?" Her nervousness was a little contagious, he wasn't sure if that was good or bad.

"I guess we chat to the vascular team at the royal. Just say what we see."
He awaited her approval, a small open mouth and nod led him to believe she was on board.
"I guess I can chat to them, probably should tell our reg or just mention it." He delivered again to the slightly vacant girl who had changed at the mention of word reg.
"Izzy…".
"Yeah sure, yeah I'll get that sorry, I will okay"
"Yeah, all we need to tell him is we've done everything,"
"I guess so ha, dead toe going off,"
"Yup, I'll do the grafting and the selling over here," his boisterous tone coming back to him ever stronger. His smile reached new levels in his cheek bones. Etching dimples in his eyes, damn he knew he looked good when he was confident. He wondered if Izzy thought that about him, hence the silence, maybe she was impressed, flustered, hopefully a little turned on. Unspoken of course, it's coyer and more attractive if a lady is couth. At least Shakespearean romantics would say so. He watched her walk away. He wondered if he should say what he was thinking. He decided to do it, surging with confident energy.
"I like watching you walk away," said with enough bravado and a pinch of sarcasm.

She looked back, again she looked back with a giggle and a smile.
"Thanks Rich, I guess."
"Just take the compliment!"
The giggle came again and washed his ears, his inner ear follicles standing to attention.

She was out of sight, not out of mind, he looked around noticing there were so many beautiful women in the department, the people down here really did look after themselves. He noticed his favourite red-haired nurse in the background, if he wasn't so infatuated he would have moved towards her, or was the reason for his lack of movement was the fact he was standing next to a phone and an actual computer, god forbid hr actually had a chance to have both a conversation and the information to hand. He put it to his loyalty rather than convenience however made the mental note of promising to flirt with the red-haired colleague.

He picked up the phone. The automated message played as always - a little buzz, the hissing of a low-quality recording followed up by what sounded like a robot woman's voice, he wondered if sex dolls would sound like this in the future, surprisingly for once it was doing nothing for him, it may be the subject and the words used.

"Bzz, hmmm, please say the department or ward you require."
"Vascular on call."
"Did you say Variety Onsten, calling Variety Onsten unless you say cancel."
"No no,"
The phone was already ringing. Slamming it down he attempted again to make the call.
"Did you say Vance Orrington, calling Vance Orrington unless you say cancel."
"No, no,"
Ring ring,
"Sorry, hello, It's Vance Orington."
"Cancel!"
"Sorry, who is this?"
The redness in his ears returned as he slammed the phone this time on a human voice. He picked it up one last time. Pressing 0.
"Operator" he shouted for the whole department to see his anger fly out of his mouth in a cloud into the phone speaker and visibly travel down the line. The curls of the line bulged straightening before a voice escaped from what he imagined was the robot on the other side of the phone.
"Hello switchboard, how can I help?"
He breathed, his face going from red to purple to blue back to white.

"Can I please be put through to the vascular on call service covering us and the royal infirmary please."

He managed his nicest poshest voice to charm. He made a mental note to pat himself on the back as it was impressive that he did that through gritted teeth. He heard the hiss and crackle of a phone trying its best to reach out, beyond the concrete walls of the hospital and out into the ether before landing and going through the glass and drywall of the fancy modern royal infirmary hospital.

"Hello, Mr Vaskineous, vascular reg on-call speaking."

He wondered if his name had been changed to sound like vascular, maybe that's how he got selected to be a specialist, so dedicated his name and person became the specialty.

"Hello, Its Richard Twain from surgery at Darthington,"

"Oh yes, good old Darthington, they still running that place, I'm surprised,"

"I guess we're just about managing but we have a chap here probably needs an upgrade,"

"That's the nicest way to put it."

"Well, we have an old boy, with a nasty looking toe,"

"Plenty of those around Darthington, I heard webbed as well."

There was a large bellowing laughter that he decided to copy on his end, it built rapport plus it's a classic joke about Darthington. In a way genetically it was funny because it was true.

"Well, this chap has a background of peripheral vascular disease, and his toe is black with an ulcer, it's probably wet gangrene."

"Ahh if it's dry let it die, if it's wet, we need bex."

"Bex?"

"Biotics, sorry it's my slang, plus rhymes better."

"Of course, I'll get them started."

"Perfect get him on the ward and ready for transfer later today or tomorrow unless things get worse. I imagine you wouldn't be so calm if things were already worse."

"Yeah, probably."

He wondered if his voice did reveal so much, he wondered if for once he sounded normal confident and not fake confident, he also wondered if he would panic in an emergency, he always thought he was better at being calm even though his inner monologue might disagree with him, for anyone peering into his mind they may notice his neurosis more so than his confidence. Even though his confidence is what always seemed to blast out of his mouth. He was well versed in the art of saying what people wanted to hear. Including knowing what to tell himself, another pat on the back for his abilities.

He had realised the phone remained glued to his ear despite the silence, he wondered why the man hadn't asked for the details. He probably should have told him the details. He put it down slowly and looked over at the screen searching for the man's name so that he could add him onto the ward screen. *The flow was most important*; he remembered the managers smiling at him when he was down in the emergency department.

He walked onwards as he saw Izzy in a trance walking towards him. Her mascara looked slightly different, and she seemed to be focused only on him, it warmed him slightly to think she would devote this much eye contact to him, it had to be a sign, he was starting to really lose his mind around this girl. It was the way she interacted with him, it made him feel close. Like he meant something, or at least someone else would think about him. Of course, who wouldn't wanna think about someone like him, he hid his neurosis deeper.

"You manage it?"

She didn't respond momentarily, he saw her eyes were wetter, he wondered if she had been outside in the wind.

"Ground control to major…"

"Oh," she quietly replied, softly, maybe even fragile.

"You alright?"

"I'm... I... I"

He realised that she hadn't been outside, she was upset.

"Hey Izzy, why don't we head off for a small break?"

"That would be great Rich."

She smiled at him, so vulnerable and welcoming, he grabbed her arm, he felt her give in to his hand, her soft arm resting in it as she let him guide her.

As they walked down the corridors dodging and him smiling with a Disney prince smile or at least that's how he would describe it they noted their old consultant Dr Abdul.

He caught their attention.

"Rich and Izzy, can you help me out please."

It was at this moment Izzy pushed herself from him, as if to say it was embarrassing Dr Abdul would see the display. For once he was a little hurt, he usually liked sexy secrecy but why would she be embarrassed, he was great after all.

"Yeah sure, what can we do?" Izzy responded immediately to the man, with a smile, he tried to get an angle from where he was standing to see the type of smile but he hadn't managed before Dr Abdul replied and distributed what the books would call textbook communication eye contact to the two juniors.

"There's this chap who has come in with shoulder tip pain, can you guys get your reg to pop a look. Cheers."

He watched as the eminent figure of Dr Abdul held onto Izzy's shoulders, he saw her quiver before Dr Abdul brushed past and the figure disappeared into the shadows of the ED department.

He wondered if it was a good quiver or bad quiver, she never quivered when he had touched her, although there hadn't really been any physical contact since that night.

He watched her face, she looked a little woozy, he knew pale was her sexy look but she looked a little paler than her normal sexy.

"You alright, we can still do that break?"

"Y..y.. eah, I mean can you maybe, it'd be nice if you talked to Mr Fernandez."

"Mr Fernandez, how formal, of course I can, you know my one skill is talking."

She laughed, like she did that night.

"So why don't you go up to the canteen, grab me a coffee, I'll scout this man and we can have a chat in twenty minutes."

She smiled, it was comforting, he wondered if this was what it was like to care for someone, he knew he was falling. Hopefully into something marshmallow, well not her bosoms; those were probably small and soft rather than large, like jelly babies, he probably would never tell her that. The problem with falling was it wasn't bungee jumping or skydiving there wasn't a safety mechanism built in. He smiled as she walked away, at least there was adrenaline before the splat.

*

A familiar face welcomed him in the cubicle.

"Ahh, Jezza."

"Heya Dr Rich."

The young man replied back.

"That shoulder is still bugging you then."

"Yah but all the tests were fine."

"I don't think we needed a test last time did we, now did you follow my advice? It doesn't look like you quit the gym."

They both chuckled. He enjoyed the patient chuckle, the reassurance given in a laugh.

"So, I'm just waiting for the surgical team. They said they'd get a specialist to make sure."

"Well, I am the surgical team."

"No way you're quite quick up the ladder to specialist."
"Haha, well you know what I'm like."
Another laugh.
"Anyway, if it's all negative, I'll chat to my boss but I'd get ready to go home. Okay. Just pack up and I'll catch you if anything needs to change."
"Ahh, you're great Dr Rich."
He didn't verbalise his victory, no one likes a sore winner.

*

This time he had his own phone when it rang through to his reg. No robot voice to thwart him. His ears now a lovely shade of pink after the day's activities washing over him.
"Hey Mo."
"Sup Rich."
A more tired than usual Mo was chatting on the phone, he could hear the eye bags from his voice.
"I got this guy downstairs with shoulder pain."
"Shoulder pain doesn't sound like us."
"Yeah, the ED consultant wanted our opinion, tests were all normal."
"Fair, what do you think?"
"Looking at him he seems fine, could always bring him back if we want proper scans and stuff."

"Nah his GP can deal with it, tell him as it's chronic to go to the GP they follow up and stuff, get a surf and turf. Ya get me?"

Rich laughed, he didn't get him, but he felt that was a moment to laugh as if he was a studio audience member and the sign for laugh had come on, he wondered when applause would be appropriate.

"I sort of get you, although not really a surfer dude as you can imagine!"

This time he got to hold up his own audience sign.

"You now serve the ones needed up to the ward teams and turf the others to the GP. It's the rule of all acute on-call teams in the hospital. Nothing can go wrong with no responsibility."

"That is true."

They both chuckled, although with the nature of the conversation he wondered if it sounded like evil laughter. He stopped himself.

"Anyway, I'll sort it out."

"Cheers, Rich, it's good, I heard about the vascular patient as well, he's coming up before transfer yeah?"

"Yeah, he's being serf and turfed to vascular service."

"Good yeah, I'll pop by and see him."

"So, Izzy told ya about it."

"Yeah, Izzy, did something like that."

"Cool, we'll catch up later."

The line went dead as Rich watched the man with his shoulder walk out of the emergency department, keeping a small eye he watched as he left through the double doors, officially no longer within the department, he liked the idea that he could not be burdened by that responsibility. He went to write in the notes and update the discharge letter to the GP.

He avoided writing "the patient has been turfed" although the subtext was there.

Despite the relief of lack of responsibility, he felt a wave come over him, he reassured himself, he was merely being like his registrar who would in turn be like his consultant and that lineage had provided good care to people for years. Surely nothing could go wrong with an approach that has worked for years.

Don't   fix   what   ain't   broke!

Chapter 8: Interlude

Christmas eve 17:32

She had arrived home on Christmas eve. There was no snow in the countryside. She looked in the mirror at the bathroom, her tired eyes hidden with just enough makeup so her mother would think she was looking after herself. She didn't want to cause unnecessary worry. She looked down at her badge.

Dr Isabella McCullen, Foundation doctor, Emergency services.

The Badge sounded more impressive than she had been, she liked the way it made her mother look at her. She was part of three sisters and a brother, it was hard to compete. She always got on with her father but that was before the divorce which had changed him. She had tried to meet up on several occasions with him, but he was struggling. He hadn't seen the badge, but she hoped he would look at her like the day she got into medical school. She missed his cooking sometimes, especially his marmite bread sauce. They always had marmite bread sauce every Christmas. Except for the last few, there was no more marmite sauce, she wondered if her mother had hated it all along. She missed her father or maybe she missed the marmite.

She looked away from the mirror, guessing she had been in the toilet long enough that an excuse was needed, she pulled the flusher, quietly apologising to the planet under her breath.

She stepped outside into the main corridor. Looking down to the light flashing from the living room, one of her sisters stepped out looking up to her on the landing.

"Sheesh Iz, I feel like you need something to perk ya up!"

She always wondered why her sister had such a broad accent, nothing like her own queen's English.

"Yeah probably, you know the drill D!"

"Yup, a small rum and coke, really small rum with a little Christmas spice."

She smiled, she didn't drink rum often but this was Christmas tradition with her, Danielle, Paulina and Benjamin. Their parents had chosen long names with fun nicknames. She imagined her mum and dad having fun doing that. She hoped they at least used to.

She arrived down in the lounge and was welcomed by everyone. A few jokes about being the smarty pants followed by Paulina saying she was technically her senior in the medical world and everyone else pointing out that there were no kids here and therefore in the room Izzy was more useful. They all laughed.

She always liked laughing compared to giggling and her family never giggled.

Her mother looked up at her with a smile. As she sipped away at her rum.

"Take a seat next to me, Izzy. You look far too tired, I'll need to teach you how to do your make up to hide it, especially with all that work they must make you do at the hospital."

"I will do Mum, I'm glad not to think about it."

She sat down next to the warmth of her mother, it was comforting after all the shifts and after living alone to be next to the comfort of someone, on a couch. Especially someone without an ulterior motive or someone a spark didn't need to be forced upon. Someone who just loved.

Another sip and her drink was done. She felt a little woozy and lightheaded and swore she could taste marmite in her drink. She wondered how much Dani thought a small amount of rum was, given she was a university student now small was a different thing to the younger sister. Afterall, she remembers the measures not being of licensing law standards when poured for her by her *uni* friends.

The conversation flowed, there were jokes, no forced ones that were followed by bellowing laughter, no talking about body parts, complaining about seniors or the way they annoyed them and no fear when she finished her drink people would offer and push to get her another. Not that she needed another, she closed her eyes for a second before awakening in her bed. A small letter posted on her forehead.

"Sorry you're so tired Iz, Benji carried ya up. See ya tomorrow early start for the family for Christmas. Love the fam."

She smiled at the word love, she felt loved here. She knew she had to come back. Darthington didn't feel right, it had at the start but not any longer. She would come back when she could. Her family were the ones that made her feel safe and comfortable.

Christmas day would come and remind her it wasn't perfect, they'd be no marmite and with the extended family visiting she would be put to work and her mother's neurosis transferred onto her. Her confident mum who in front of others would become quiet and giggle. She wondered if that's how her colleagues saw her on the wards. She closed her eyes with the clichéd thought that *we are doomed to be our mothers or fathers*. She justified the cliché to herself; the world's greatest truths are clichés.

Christmas Day 04:00

The rear-view mirror angled to reveal her id badge hanging precariously from her hip.

Ms. Bethany Anderson. Lead Consultant in Emergency services.

She had to sneak out to climb into the Tesla in the winter darkness. Her phone had alerted her to a trauma call at the hospital. Not that her hospitals did official traumas, but it did occur once in a while. She was on the on-call rota and given the way the department was staffed she found she was always on the on-call rota.

The car zoomed down the main road to the hospital, the scenic route not an option for her. She always had to have clothes ready for the call, you had to emit you were ready, especially when leading.

She hoped the noise could be explained to her daughter as Santa Claus, although against her husband's wishes she had refused to wear the Santa hat to work. He called her a spoil sport, she called him unprofessional, it was the first fight of Christmas day.

She hopped out of the car and with a slight jog ended up in the emergency department, the lights dim, the tinsel barely reflecting and mistletoe spars. She made it to where all the noise was.

The bodies were all around the trolley, everyone shouting, everyone speaking, noise and more noise but no symphony. She had to conduct this noisy band.

"Alright everyone!"

They all looked back and within moments she was wearing a vest which spelt out what they already knew.

TEAM LEADER

"So, update me now."

One of the many bodies around the trolley walked over to start talking to her, in a weird sense all of them in their scrubs melded into one person, the adrenaline in her making her eyes acutely focus on the information being delivered like a narration.

"This lovely and pretty unlucky 87-year-old gentleman was at the pub for Christmas eve with the old boys club, he is after all an old boy. Yeah, driving back he swerved and hit a poor tree. However, he was poorer than the tree. Yeah, so he went into the steering wheel, crushed probably a chest injury and oh yeah, his leg was trapped and had to have firemen out as well."

"Okay," she paused for a second to read the badge of the doctor talking to her. He was pretty junior.

"Let's get a bit more of a concise summary please." She recognized the registrar.

"Tim give us an update."

As more adrenaline coursed through her veins, she wondered why they had gotten that young man to explain, probably because they were busy. She wondered if Tim wanted to prove a point and continue leading, she saw his face, sweaty and filled with anxiety. Whilst the adrenaline drove others crazy for her it was like an orgasm, better even and did the opposite it slowed time down.

The man, Tim, from which she imagined a raincloud of his own sweat hung above him responded back to her, finally in one dance of his lips handed over the reins.

"87-year-old man, crash at 40 mph an hour into a tree. No visible head injury GCS 8/15 on admission rising to 13/15. Chest wall injury right sided pneumothorax with thoracentesis clinically fractured left neck of femur fracture and ankle fracture too. Right side lower limb fine, fast scan abdomen, no free fluid."

"Thanks okay everyone, let's recap on all of the other trauma areas."

She began the trauma dance, one foot in front of the other, watching each step, like a ballroom routine gliding across the clinical information and converting it to actions. The ask and respond nature is probably more like salsa. This was even better and more thrilling than any form of dance she had been part of. It felt good to be good at it. Like a performer with the crowd being the men and some women in front of her and maybe even god watched her. Or was God the critic of the show?

Time would tell.

"Airway?"

"We have him tubed, getting sats[28] around 88-90% difficult with that right chest but not rubbish. Pco2 stable"

"Breathing"

"Well, we have the pneumo-thorax[29], but nothing on the left, his respiration is maintained at 25 breaths per minute. "

"Circulation!"

"We got a HR of 85, regular, normal Heart sounds, no indication of pericardial effusion[30] from the crush injury. Blood pressure (BP) is not great at 100/45."

"Not the worst," she smiled.

"Let's check those pupils." She wanted to be clear, disabilities weren't too clear of a phrase, but it helped them remember.

---

[28] Sats - saturation, the percentage of oxygen in the blood stream usually should be above 94%.

[29] Pneumothorax - a collapsed lung.

[30] Pericardial effusion - fluid around the heart.

"Blood sugar 5 after some glucose in his veins. Pupils blown on the right but not left!"
She took a breath and felt time slow down a little more. It didn't look good.
"Basically, we need code red[31] going through him, we need blood plasma, we need family to chat because this doesn't look good, and we need a scanner. Before we even think about the Royal."
There was a moment of silence, she wondered if it was seconds or minutes, she wondered why people were waiting as if trying to avoid the instruction of their boss or wanting her to fail. She pushed aside the paranoia.
"I said the plan, let's get it going, you!"
She pointed to the junior member who had provided the colour child book narration.
"Get the code red going for this trauma!"
She watched as they hurried, imagining that if they did have a tail, it would be between their legs. She felt the world run at her pace, she felt her heart thudding and pumping, it was black and white there was the right way to do things, which she knew, she always enjoyed a trauma call, which was an interesting concept

---

[31] Code red - comes by different names but in many hospitals activates pathways to get blood transfusions and alerts specialties who need to be involved in trauma.

because the patients were very ill at the other end, yet she found a perverse joy from this.

"We need to get that chest drain, we need more fluids and some blood for him. He needs a full CT, the donut as we call it and all those standing behind me from other specialties need to stick around, the donut will decide who is needed and who is useless!"

She heard a few chuckles, nervous of course. The nervousness reminded her who she had, her resources and the fact she knew everyone around her wasn't good enough. She took a breath before being frank,

"I think this will need to be done at the Royal, we don't have enough resources here!"

The blood arrived with the porters and the young doctor came back, like a dog returning a stick.

"So can we get the ambulance service ready for transfer, if you could phone the royal ED department to get them ready."

"Yes of course!"

He ran off chasing another thrown stick in the distance.

The lines went in. She followed the anaesthetist to the CT scanner[32], formally

---

[32] CT scan - computerised tomography, takes a series of X-ray using a circular donut like shape to create a 3rd image of the body.

known as a donut, for no other reason that it looked like a donut, the health service was never particularly creative.

It scanned the man, who looked more machine than man at the time. It all felt more like a textbook or even a flow diagram, it's how she kept her cool, it wasn't particularly cruel, it was what was needed in these situations because by following the plan in a machine-like way you get results and get over the panic.

The scan finished and everyone looked at the screen. She looked at the radiologist and radiographer who understood with one look to send the images to the royal, she looked through the scan.

"Subdural, spleen gone, large bowel perf, fractured neck of femur, and pneumothorax with rib fracture and lung contusion. He needs theatre soon."

She didn't let the radiologist add anything, he merely nodded along.

They ran back to the department with the trolley following them. The squeaking of everyone's rubber shoes and crocs as they struck and marked the floor.

Back at resus an ambulance was ready and the young doctor sat next to her with wide eyes, she saw that the adrenaline was finally running through his veins and the fear and flight was replaced with fight.

"Okay someone needs to go across and you need to phone to tell them about the fact they need theatre."

"I'll head over, umm, I know The Royal well just finished there." Tim finally spoke through his sweat laden lips and facial hair.

She felt her brain tell her it was a power move by her junior; the royal was her dream to be able to do what she just did again and again and again. She felt her junior self-tell her to go, to be the best, this was her chance.

"No!"

There was suddenly a big silence, not the commanding one but the one where everyone would judge her. She needed it back, she hated being weak. She was the boss, her head wondering what they would say about her, probably already complaining about her attitude. It was always harder for her compared to Abdul who remained calm and commanding. She wanted to be better. She knew she had to ride with them. Her brain clicked and saved her from them really digging the knife into her back.

"You need experience running the department, it'll be good for you I can head there and then back home! Now let's make sure we don't end up with people in danger from waiting too long!"

She heard the collective yes of soldiers to their sergeant as she climbed into the ambulance.

The clock read 06:59.

She felt like there was something she was missing but as she hopped in with her hand over the airbag supplying air into the tube into the man's lung she was engrossed in the flashes and beeps. Completely engrossed in her plan and hoping they would see her leadership here and at the Royal.

Her mind tried to remind her about the time which now read 07:01, she ignored it as another beep meant she had to move around and push another drug through the drip.

Beep.

Beep Beep Beep.

Ho Ho

Beep

Ho

Beep

Christmas Day 09:30

The handover always took longer on medicine. She envied the surgeons who rushed out after a night shift while she waited with her hands tumbling with folder after folder. She looked at her writing which got messier and her signature with her name barely legible beneath it. Rachel Amis Fy1 GMC 7290207.

Her eyes were comparable to Theresa May at the end of her tenancy like a racoon she was trying the Brexit look. The ward had multiplied its Christmas cheer, with every day of Christmas crescendo-ing in decorations, trees and gifts. Everyone was jolly and happy to be at work. She wondered how many partridges were strewn around; she couldn't spot any pear trees though. Looking around the nursing staff's finger she could see the gold rings of taken mothers of Darthington. There were at least five today. She looked into the bays with their decorations, wondering if the elderly wished for doves to find their peace.

The tinsel had fallen all over the handover room and the takeaway curry in there started to fill the room with a weird aroma when combined with the mince pie smell. Of course, the only takeaway open for food last night was the mango leaf. It was a godsend, and they made their revenue every Christmas at the hospital she imagined.

She watched People walking in and out of the handover room with a few mumbles of "merry Christmas" followed by "can you look at this" or "what do you think" or if she was lucky a few words of niceness. She wondered what people thought of her sleepily telling them she'd finished her shift, a zombie in front of them. She was wearing a stethoscope; it meant she had all the answers regardless of day or night. The resentment built throughout the hospital corridors as people asked about her Christmas plans, her family and how she would enjoy the day, resentment soon became jealousy. She decided to nod along and look down at her screen, the glow keeping her artificially awake.

The walk home became a wander as she started down at her phone screen slowly counting the time with a giggle every so often, she received a message from Dean. To the outside reader they read like generic texts but to her they were now established inside jokes -well they were generic inside jokes. Like American comedy they were uninventive but put a smile on each of their faces and better yet passed each other's time. She wondered what his Christmas was like with his fiancée. Sometimes guilt punched her but other times she found comfort in being a slight priority to someone. Something which had slowly ebbed with the passing year in her own life outside the hospital beast. Whilst at the start of her newfound place of work it had been like her university days with meeting different people, everyone investing in each other's stories, the bubbles had been created and people slowly settling made her feel like her existence in her flat left her a little too lonely. She definitely didn't fit into the small town vibe and her "come down" mind often reminded her that she was a horrible person which is why people stayed away, beyond her own fetishizing of her sadness she sometimes wondered if it was because she came from up north, or was the truth she wasn't good at being alone with herself, because in all honesty she knew she couldn't complain considering nearly every weekend she did manage to do some sort of activity. She just always felt like it wasn't enough, that she always went home and woke up the next day feeling the same. Her phone beeped again, she looked down at the little preview. She smiled to herself seeing the message was longer than said preview.

"This stocking present made me think of you... we should..."

It caused her comfort to be getting some kind of Christmas text. She staved off her arrogance that saw her as more important than the man texting's fiancée. She just sat in the glow of someone caring. That glow mixed in with tiredness made her float towards her house. Her heart softened. She wondered how long would be appropriate before she replied, she wanted to chat to him on Christmas to further fulfil her need to be wanted, however too early a reply would imply she was rubbish and boring and wasn't doing anything at Christmas.

Entering the house was an interesting challenge that only ever came about after she had done a night shift. She would fight with the lock, the key stick and unsticking, as if to taunt her and leave one final challenge before her bed. The loud uncoupling of the lock jarred in dissonance, a final song as the door smacked the other side of the wall. Stepping in above the slight tangle of shoes left by yesterday's version of her as a trap for today's version of her. She managed to make it into the living room.

No matter how many times she said it would be different, nights always ended the same for her living room. Different things were placed across the floor, from used plates which she swore she would clean up when she got home each morning, followed by wrappers of her snacks, which had slowly become more commonplace with odd shift patterns as well as having money. She needed to put out the recycling which also saw their home in the corner of her living room. The very growing cascade of glass bottles, making her lifestyle look worse than she swore it was. It was cold so she managed to jump past and dodge the obstacles, turning on her heating before retreating to her bedroom with its walk-in **floordrobe**.

Half the clothes that lay on the floor barely fit her anymore. It was her own fault given her knack for tight crop tops which was in complete juxtaposition with the newfound comfort food first-year doctor belly. She swore it was her mature transformation from petite to curvy. As she wore her pyjamas, she slid under the covers looking at the light seeping through her blinds, pre-nights she wished for blackouts post-nights it didn't matter. She looked again at her phone, writing her response before checking again and again at the message sent to her dad, no reply yet, she didn't or at least didn't think she minded. Minding wasn't really in her capacity at the moment as she drifted off to dreams which probably meant something, her brain surfacing all her feelings she pushed down but she never remembered her dreams so how she would ever learn from them.

At least they were always in technicolour.

Christmas Day 12:00

They always went on a family Christmas day boat trip if the weather allowed. It was his favourite moment with his father and brothers. He loved his embroidered sea coat which read his name in capitals, now with an addition of Dr as a Christmas present. He looked down at it with a big smile knowing that it helped him look even better than he normally did, waiting to post the Instagram selfie he added a red circle to really show it off to his many dedicated followers he sometimes called friends.

Dr Richard Twain.

His name was written in maritime gold on top of a deep-sea blue of his coat with lapels and designs to make it look like he was in a military or militia, after all he was a Twain and one of the better-looking ones. That in itself spoke volumes, because the Twain's were an above average looking clan.

The sea was a little rough, it was winter, but the last few Christmas holidays on the coast had been kind to his family, whilst when he was younger snow did fall on this day it now was always sunny. Sometimes it rained, but it was as if the winters had warmed to his sailing ability.

His father, a stern yet laughing man, stood in front loading and tying ropes. Leading and impressing him, he always wondered if he could match his father. He decided to stand next to him and slowly emulate all his movements. Standing with his upper lip as stiff as his father's.

"So, how is it being in Darthington?"

His father's elegant voice cutting through, he imagined weakening the knees of the mermaids around them.

"Well, it's a good laugh ya get me, plus I'm really getting the hang of the doctor thing I think?"

"A Twain never finishes a statement as a question."

"Right father, I'm getting the hang of being a doctor!"

He pushed his anxiety and stresses around the last few working days with that sentence alone, he felt the generations of old wealth and the Twain name pulse through his veins from heart to lungs to head to toes and back. It was almost as if the world favoured them, the sun peeking through the overcast onto the boat as it went further out from the Marina.

*

Lunch was always the same; loud voices, proclaiming achievements, each one claiming to be better than the other one, yet his dad despite his age always managed to one up them all. His mother sat with her glass of Prosecco smiling with the corners of her mouth, a kind of half smile to the man who she ... Loved... or at least he made himself believe it, after all he was a well-functioning adult, so his home had to be well functioning as well.

His mum turned to him, "So are you just going to live your life alone then?"

"Mum, I'm plenty popular with the ladies."

He proclaimed his eyebrows raised like a boy, his chest out, feeling like some kind of animal trying to scare away the predator.

"For one night maybe."

She took a sip as the others had tuned in to the conversation and like a stag do oooooo and burns were shouted throughout the room.

"Look there's a fellow doctor that I'm getting on with, so maybe next Christmas."

His mum took another sip.

"Ooo a doctor."

"What does her dad and mum do?" His dad quickly interjected.

"Why does that matter?"

"Well, it's just smart to marry someone who not only will earn money but has money,

310

especially when you start thinking of continuing the clan like your brothers."

It was a joke, but it felt like it had a kernel of truth. He hadn't asked Izzy about her background but she was a shy well-spoken girl so it couldn't be too *bad*. She probably did horse riding as a kid, if he could prove that then that would keep his dad happy, anything below horse riding was probably not good enough for a Twain, or more so the truth, a girl like that would see through his facade and see the fake bravado as not funny but the indication he probably wasn't a good person.

He always thought that getting into medicine and being a doctor meant he was a good person, but the more he spent time with the doctors he realised this is not mutually exclusive.

There was more laughter as he watched his dad move his glass of wine as he told another story of when he was cheeky in his youth, once again one upping everyone in the room. One day he; Richard Twain would do that, he needed to do that.

Christmas Day 17:37

The tidying up had begun, they usually hosted Christmas as they were the family with no kids. It was always Uncle Abdul's house which the family would visit.

The chorus of the kids saying his name again in thanks for his presents, whilst the extended family got a few drinks in and some free time from the kids. He didn't mind, he enjoyed the novelty, it didn't wear thin when it was actually a novelty. He chuckled at himself and thought he'd share that with the other half who would roll her eyes, their version of laughing with each other.

As the little kids went to play around with their newfound toys, their joy of Christmas was still alive, the oldest being 11 still just about believed in Santa and Father Christmas's stocking present would entertain them all for at least the next 24 hours.

He watched his wife glide with the plates of desert and cheese, like a dancer her elegance mesmerised him. She appeared next to him to deliver a kiss on the cheek as she went towards the kids who gathered around her like she was in her own right, a Father Christmas of treats. Their eyes glistened, salivating for the chocolates and he hoped for the grapes too. Although he would have only had chocolates as a kid, hence the hefty fine from the dentist in his formative years.

The adults all sat around the table, chattering, smiling and even making jokes that shouldn't be said in the vicinity of kids, but then again it was Christmas, and the kids definitely were too busy with their treasures to notice. His Port filled again as more laughter roared, his throat burning with each drink, he let his eyes wander to locate the Gaviscon in the house, before sifting off to the other room only to see the sweetheart with it ready for him.

"Also, I found this on the floor a few days ago."

She handed him a letter with his name on it and big red letters which read confidential. He wondered if that stopped anyone opening it, it's not like other mail wasn't confidential and should be opened. He took a sip of port and then a sip of Gaviscon to mellow out his inner fire, known as reflux. He let himself scan the letter. His heart not only burned but galloped along.

He had visited his GP and then had a scope in his throat, he at the time had refused to have any sedation and fully regretted the decision with his mouth still on fire since then. His eyes and mind not letting him tangent focussed in on the last line which summarised the letter.

"What does it say, dear?" His wife enquired.

He felt a blur and then loud buzzing in his skull. He read it aloud more to himself than her,

"We would like to arrange a follow up appointment to discuss the results, we will see you on 27th of December at the outpatient unit."

"Oh." She paused.

He once again vocalised the obvious,

"They only bring you back if it's bad news."

Chapter 9: Rubba, Lub, Dub & Woosh

She sat as the bubbles engulfed her body, slowly cleaning the mess from the walk they had taken slightly through some boggy marsh together, not as romantic as your usual affair. Her name being called brought her back out of the sensation of the mixed water and lathering bubbles on her legs.

"Hey Rach, I've left a towel outside for once you're done but it's up to you if you wanna cover up."

His voice cheeky and ambient, as if this was normal, it didn't feel normal, but then she was unsure if it was good or bad it was hard to tell with the way her stomach rocked back and forth as if she were out at sea, depending on who you asked being out to sea was either a good or bad thing. To Izzy a bad thing no bet and to Rich a great thing.

She let her head get lost in her post-Christmas blues, she had been slowly noticing her party body wasn't keeping up like it should, her abs being slowly coated by a few layers of fat, her hips childbearing and the pounds had piled on although no one around her would ever tell her. The man outside, or was he a boy, would say she was fit or hot or sexy, especially if it meant they kept doing what they were doing.

*

The ward rounds hadn't changed, the way she juggled all the folders and cursed every time her pen's ink ran out hadn't changed either. All that had changed was it was no longer new and different, she had become cynical and started to speak like her consultant, reg and SHO. Like a child she had been moulded into the image of her forefathers and was doomed to repeat their sins.

She looked at the positives of gaining her Fy1 weight. Her arms definitely carried the folders better and like a camel she could go longer without food and carbs; she had her backup humps. She smiled to herself; she at least had her sense of humour. Other things that had come with her new self was bigger tits and better oral sex according to stereotypes she had learnt about slightly chubbier girls from Dean. They were walking past a few of the curtains, one of them a familiar voice crying out in pain, however they weren't able to help him. She heard her inner monologue which sounded more and more like her colleagues each day. The patient's file got filled with nothing new. Her signature next to the entry but the consultant's name hovered above.

Them having all the responsibility, her merely a ghost in the case.

"Hmm yes, interesting make sure we get an echo for this chap."

The consultant murmured whilst the other two doctors who had gotten more and more in his image stroked there now no longer metaphorical beards. They had joined the rank of medics with beards and glasses. The new revolutionary docs, stylish yet somehow still professional looking, or at least they thought they were, no one had any evidence, no one had surveyed the patients after all.

"You should listen to this Rachel, listen to his heart and tell me about why I'm asking for an echo."

Her consultant turned the grill on, searing her brain and bringing her back to the room. This was going to need more than a stroke of her "metaphorical" facial hair.

She looked around her neck to see the one thing that made the patients not shout at her. The fabled stethoscope, the tool of the doctor, although how useful it was in the hospital could be argued. After all, if there were any signs of trouble in the lungs or heart a scan would be ordered to confirm this, sometimes without any signs it would take someone saying the word wheeze and an X-ray would already be requested before you could think about it.

Slowly, probably looking quite untrained, she removed it from the zone of comfort to look at it before placing it in her ears, double checking it went in the right way around. The cold steel followed her cold hand being placed on the patient, his immediate reaction to pull away followed by the same inane chatter she had had many times. Sorry cold hands and awkward laughter followed by something about warmth. However, the silver lining was it reminded her the patient in front was a person, and most people didn't like the cold.

Initially she heard nothing, not even a heartbeat, quickly checking around to make sure no one had noticed her surprise, is this why the consultant had wanted the Echo, would that show what someone could have instead of a heart. She tried to summon her knowledge of the heart from her years at medical school, which were a blur of comedowns and hangovers. She took a small breath in before placing the cold steel at the other areas of the patient's chest, the areas she remembered from her exams that you had to press on for a passing grade. Still nothing whilst she held his hand feeling his pulse, it was there. She finished in the fourth area, she lifted her stethoscope and at the moment she realised why nothing had come through the tubes. She had not turned the small valve which switched between the bell and the diaphragm. The two sides of her stethoscope. She let her face go slightly red before pointing her chin forward followed by a hmm, using her acting skills she switched the valve over and placing that on the four areas and the high-pitched sounds of wiring and what sounded like a water flume were quietly noticeable through her ears, although to describe it or think of what may be wrong with his heart using her ears seemed archaic and impossible. She wondered if the consultants made it up as well. She thought they probably practised their hmms to sound more convincing, a skill she would need to develop but nowhere did it tell you on the portfolio it was needed for progression as a doctor. The eyes on her now like a game quiz waiting for her to answer their wise old host, who didn't portray much about what he thought of the game show he hosted like a less mean but curter version of Ann Robinson, she wondered if her reference was dated, it probably was and anyone hearing into her monologue would roll their eyes at her unoriginality at naming the only well-known mean game show host. There was also Simon Cowell, take that silly audience.

"Ummm, I guess there's a murmur, yes..."

A few nods from her colleagues urged her slightly on, although the vague statement didn't need her stethoscope she knew and probably the consultant knew that it could be deducted from

A) Him asking to have a listen, no maniac would make you listen to a normal heart, now that would be cruel.
B) He'd asked for an echo; it'd be silly to do so without anything being abnormal.

"True, but what kind of murmur did you hear here?"

She didn't really hear, she wondered if there was something philosophical about it, did they ever really hear their patients, unfortunately this would not fly in this Socrates style of questioning.

The coin flipped in her head; it was literally 50/50. Either aortic stenosis or mitral regurgitation as they were the most likely and the easiest to hear. Although she would never let patients know this, after all a 50-50 is not what 5-6 years of medical school taught, it was also terrible odds when it came to life.

The coin flew in the air and her eyes followed as it landed on the ground.

She blurted her answer.

"Aortic stenosis?"

It was an answer, but her confidence or lack thereof made her voice it like a question. The well-known Fy1 pitch was loud for all to hear. "Of course, Rachel it is a classical sound, like a high whistling pressure, through a tight tube, you see that's how I imagine it and that helps me remember it."

The lecture began and Rachel pushed her mind to listen not to wander, she was sure this man who had been at the game for a long time actually had good knowledge to impart, but once again her brain that she had binged on instant gratification because it did feel oh so good had decided listening wasn't going to be achieved.

"That's how I always remember it."

Missed it again, she cursed internally. However, he seemed impressed at her, was it for guessing or looking like she always listened.

*

The bathwater again was nice, and it was before a night out, weirdly dropping and having water touch your skin really did enhance its effects. She liked the fact it made her skin softer than it was and really hid the mild dermatitis she suffered from. Now that would be a mis-informative piece of information for the public; MDMA cures skin disease or at least your perception of them. She thought the fact it was the mess drinks, a free booze for all affair, would guarantee some fun. Unlike them she was always the fun one, the one people wanted to hang out with on nights out, and maybe during the day too, her slight rubbishness at medicine probably meant they felt good talking to her, she was there for everyone's self-esteem, *well except her own,* she heard her mind speak out of turn.

"Shh, you're meant to be coming up brain, not coming down, however we all know the coming brain is best".

She said in a singsong Liverpudlian accent. Talking to herself, probably a bad sign or the first sign of a good night she giggled, she was hilarious After all. Looking at the time she took a sip from her bath beer. The bubbles on her throat and on her skin mixed in, making her feel like one big sexy bubble, if bubbles could be sexy, she imagined anything was sexy on MDMA or everything was just sexy all the time if you were a guy, she felt woke saying that, down with the kids.

Well not kids but sexy 21-year-olds, she found she was attracted to those girls in those age groups and men in the older age group 30's which means her dating app profile was basically to anyone who wanted some in this small town, well apart from the retires, but then again she hadn't tried golden oldies and she had heard that STIs and sex was on the rise in nursing homes.

*

"You'll never believe what happened!"
"Hmmm."
The audience of other doctors listened intently to Rich who was sitting in front of her swinging and swigging his beer half of it on his shirt and the other in his gullet.
"He then said, but doc that's not even possible, I had my right leg amputated. Like I felt a right twat because I'd been ushered into the wrong bay, to check for a lesion on his right leg. I felt a little smug when I turned to the nurse and replied back with what I thought was a killer joke, saying we've cured it there's no longer anything on his right leg. I thought I'll get a laugh, maybe even a number."
The crowd gave his drunken stand up a quick giggle including Izzy who she watched smile directly at Rich, god she wondered if this was bad for Rich or her or the fallout when they both realised it wasn't ideal the way they thought completely differently about each other.
"Anyway, she then leaves in a huff and I'm in trouble, for bantaaaaa, I just don't get it!"
"Yeah, it is a joke, some people are too sensitive these days," another doctor who

looked exactly like Rich and spoke far too much like him intervened. She thought what are the odds of someone else having the same jaw line, one from years of inbreeding, being a colleague. She then remembered they were in medicine which made the odds pretty high.

"Izzy, what do you think?"

Rich had gotten her involved, like a magician inviting someone on stage. She probably didn't appreciate it but the fact she smiled and was about to reply probably made Rich feel Izzy did. She wondered if she was right about how they felt, although she did notice, Izzy had soft skin and a tight body, making her rather jealous.

"Umm, I guess, maybe, ha, it's not like you would know what to do anyway, lucky he didn't have a right leg."

A few more giggles and laughs, she watched the obviously rehearsed routine of bowing in defeat. It was obvious he had done it before. the truth being everyone had, well at least anyone who had done dating in the 2010's as a young adult. After all, most people wanted a little fire in their partner, but not too much to make them insecure.

"Yeah, let me tell you about what happened to me, like I couldn't believe the consultant said…".

The boy who looked remarkably like Rich smiled as it was his turn to be on the stage. She couldn't remember his name; they probably had talked. Everyone knew each other in this town, especially within the doctor world. They all had mutual friends on social media even if they were from opposite sides of the country, they were worse than SARS or swine flu.

He ended his story with a question this time for her, "then I had to ask Rach to get them proper review from a medic. I trust her more than the orthopod."

It was her turn, "probably trust me more than yourself though!"

He did the same moves Rich had done and everyone else laughed again, the stage act continued.

*

The shots had been done and the same club they had been in all year was playing the same songs, she reminded herself she can't drink anymore now because it was past midnight, and she was at work today rather than tomorrow.

She always forgot its name, people called it the factory, others called it unit. Given it was one big storage unit but then again, she had never been even slightly cognitive during a night, because she was behaving herself, she managed to read the sign above the bar. **Emmental.**

Interesting name. Must be a Swiss owner.

The dancing continued the crowd that had been at the pub, had whittled down, Izzy never staying, never having experienced the factory, Rich trying his best to kiss in the corner with smiles and shouting to try impress the girl more than his jaw line and not too bad body given the on calls he's had to do. She wondered if the "I'm a doctor" did work, due to the fact you spend most of your time with healthcare workers, doctors aren't as impressive as they were on TV. There are no mysteries and people who work with you realise that you are a human quite quickly. Much harder to figure all that out in a cheesy nightclub.

The crowd was filled with students as 1 o'clock hit and most people she knew had left. Only Rich, his clone and the girl Rich had now impressed enough she was clinging on to him remained. Although with her not black out drunk eyes she could tell she wasn't a girl but an older lady. A likely MILF. Not bad for the bucket list.

Once again, the dancing continued. She thought she liked the song and that's why she stood there dancing with the person she now called Rich the 2nd, his hands on her skin felt amazing, she wondered if to him her dermatitis had been cured. His hand explored her lower back and for some reason grabbed her arse and thighs, things that now flopped a little, she took a step back. His grabbing wasn't sensual and therefore she pulled her head back, she laughed as he tried again and pulled back before contorting out. He seemed almost offended, she wondered if he realised she was the one who should be acting offended.

She moved away and whispered in his ear about work before leaving.

She watched as they kept dancing, she wondered why the effects of everything weren't as strong as before and she wondered if the theory of tolerance was becoming a reality for her.

*

In bed, once she was still, she realised her sensations were still enhanced and she was able to give herself a treat before she caught the four hours of sleep that would hopefully keep her going tomorrow. She enjoyed herself much more, the 100% cotton sheets and pillow she used as a companion were presents from her family and she was grateful for the higher quality which became a deluxe sensation to her. A final moan and a rapid set of heartbeats, her fit bit had recorded the slightly fast rate and left a notification on her phone, and then she drifted off to sleep.

*

The morning routine when hungover and coming down had been practised to a tee. She knew everything she wanted and had it all prepped, a flask of coffee to take on the walk in, a couple of paracetamol and ibuprofen, a quick antacid and an anti-sickness in her pocket just in case. She drank her 2l bottle of water as well as grabbed her prepared bacon sarnie from last night, she fried it in the microwave. She brought plenty of the above-mentioned tablets, she felt like a walking pharmacy. She sprayed her perfume all over and not only brushed her teeth but she also used mouthwash as well. If she could rinse her mouth in bleach, she would. Awake or the best acting of being awake, she stepped outside the door, each step onto the concrete felt heavy. Her mind, an anchor, making each step even heavier. It was her come down coming out. Luckily God was forgiving her even if she wasn't forgiving herself, the sun shone down with a crisp air, the perfect weather to keep you refreshed but not miserable, the perfect come down weather.

The walk in the early hours in the sun proved refreshing for her as she walked past those who were doing their morning runs or walking the dogs or keeping their children at bay. She wondered what they had at home and did with their free time. She always wondered if she should join in and become a little more civilised instead of being a hungover mess who lived for the weekend but somehow still ***wasted*** the weekend days. She probably should explore the town and surrounding green countryside. It was near the sea too, the sea used to be fun, and she used to do fun things in the sea. You could impress with surfing as an extracurricular less so doing MDMA and drinking, the boat races she won were not ones with medals.

Each step in her trainers she had were heavy despite the promised featherweight technology of her shoes. She imagined they were made by some kind of magical gnomes or more likely children in sub continental Asia, but why feel guilty about that when she had to focus on working. She had enough personal guilt. The doors of the hospital loomed; its jaws open ready to devour her.

She stepped into her white whale, imagining her name badge calling her Ahab.

She had "volunteered" to hold the fort on the surgical admission unit, despite her limited (meaning no) surgical experience.

She watched the bellyaches on a Saturday come up and walk into the waiting room. she had learned this was a good sign of reasonable overall health. She readied her patter; she would introduce herself as the surgical doctor, and she'd have a boss surgical doctor who himself had a big boss, like some kind of video game last boss who transformed many times, a hydra who once you got rid of one head three more appeared. If the patient navigated all that he would have a prize. What that was, she was unsure.

The first chap had the same story she had heard said a million times throughout the hospital. Pain that had gone on for months which was now getting worse. He wondered what "it" was, as if separate from him, his "tummy" turning against him. He wondered if he'd been afflicted by anything from the outside, including saying his father had gotten kidney stones, which she found funny for something your own body produced. She did the customary placing him on one of the examination couches, drawing the curtain back, the wall of confidentiality that no one could hear past. He made jokes about her cold hands, and she felt his stomach trying to elicit the pain, trying to feel if it was "soft". He whined and whimpered throughout the examination. Certain points she pressed on caused more discomfort although it all fell softly under her hands, there was nothing hard and his body never tensed. The universal sign he was okay, then again, he didn't feel okay and that did mean something despite her mind telling her to dismiss his symptoms as not urgent or important enough for the surgical team in hospital. She wanted to, it would make it easy, and she could sit on the desk awaiting the next belly with her head down taking a big sniff of the cup of coffee. She had gotten good at preparing coffee, her record was 30 seconds to have a fully brewed cup of Joe. If medicine failed, then YouTube virality awaited her. She hedged her bets and wrote and explained the same plan she would no doubt repeat several times over the day.

"I can't find anything that makes me think you should be in hospital, but let's get those bloods and let my boss help out."

With her shaky hands but strong grip, to protect the pen from the hungry vultures who would steal it if left laying anywhere in the hospital, she wrote her plan.

Impression: non-specific abdo pain
not peritonitis
Plan
Await bloods and senior RV

She signed her name once again as Dr Amis; her signature got sloppier throughout her year as an actual doctor.
*
1
2
3
4
5
The cup was out of the cupboard.
6
7
8
9
10
She pounced and pulled her heavy feet, then her hands opened up the second adjacent cupboard.
11
12
13
14
15
Her eyes scanned for any coffee not labelled with someone's name, the guilt too much if she were to be caught pilfering even a few granules of freeze-dried roast.
16
17
18

19
20

One glass container having no one's name, screaming to be used, it was fair game, no ring on its finger! Her spoon scooping, losing only about 10% of the roast, before hitting her mug, the hot water dispenser pressed, flicking boiling water on her arms. She ignored the non-significant burns.

21
22
23
24
25

The milk comes out of the patient fridge despite the warning this fridge was for patient food and drink. It pours and splashes, some coffee escapes over the side of the mug.

The cup is ready, but before it can be picked up.

26
27
28
29
30

A paper towel wraps itself around the mug and removes the stain from the bottom, she trundles back to the main desk waiting for more patients to visit the surgical admission unit. She sips, it burns slightly and tastes awful, but it was the only high allowed at work.

*

The patients she was seeing, had similar problems, all made the same cold hands jokes, like a show on repeat. Once she had seen the last one by closing time of the admission unit she then had the registrar arrive to make decisions about the patients.

The one improvement on the ward job the surgical admission unit had was the size of the patient folder, given the circumstance they had a maximum of three bits of scribbled paper at once. She wondered what happened within the hospital to make people's folders larger and larger, so much so the notes eclipsed the person that you saw. Sometimes on call you'd treat the notes not the person, spending up to ten minutes with the notes but wincing at a minute with the patient lying in front of you.

The *reg* arrived, his easy-going nature coming from his confidence, maybe arrogance in his ability. Much of it was needed, for the reassurance of the patients. So they may hope for some kind of return to the real world beyond the hospital walls. She imagined the wall like a membrane separating heaven from hell, although which side was which changed the further she had gone through this year. He laughed a lot as he approached her, he used to laugh and flirt more, now he probably noted her arm and leg width. She reassured herself her physique was for the more mature man, the man whose porn changed from petite to curvy. The angular jaw of the man named Mo protruded as he finally looked down at her.

"So shall we clean up before we close up shop here?"

He laughed, looking for her laugh, she rolled her eyes which made him pay a little more attention to her.

"Present them then, feisty one..."

She looked at his face, he knew, she knew, that sounded better in his mind.

Six "bellies" had been left.

1. A man whose bloods showed a slight abnormality, in his kidneys mainly, but he was now well, his stomach no longer sore. His groin was now free of pain and his testicles well. Which he reminded her of again and again, that testicle was definitely watching curvy. Mo reassured him that he would shag again and that if he had any more pain to go to his GP and that he probably had a passing stone, saying a scan would be useful in a few days but only if things didn't fully go away, after all it was the weekend. So, reading Mo's subtext; not my problem because you aren't

dying, Mo managed to convince the man his sex drive was safe and to go home and recover. Or wank.

2. The next was a lovely elderly lady who said it had all started when her son had refused to look after her, that she needed help with her pain, nothing was found apart from the abnormalities of age. She knew it would take a lot of talking, mostly about the lady's memories of the fabled husband, as well as listening, something Mo didn't really want to do, he mentioned the word all okay and symptoms to do with stress. It was well known that stress does manifest in the stomach, the butterflies of Aristotle and his old wives or the autonomic fight or flight sympathetic and parasympathetic system. The patient left knowing that Mo was happy and was probably happy to lord over her son that her stomach problems were due to his miscare. Rather than her own psyche.

3. Mo arrived with his wings and halo for the next chap. He had suffered all day due to her inaction over a boil on his back. His fears that one day one of his spots may claim revenge on him for picking at them was coming true. With a swift knife and less talking the content slushed out with some

minor followed by major chord screaming, she noted it was all weirdly diatonic, a musical epitaph not expected from the so-called gym lad. Next, they packed the wound with a strange sterile ribbon which looked a lot like something from her mother's sewing kit. A small dressing and a few massages of Mo's ego later and the deed was done. The patient went home.

4. The next chap's blood tests really made her worry and Mo seemed to poke and prod the stoic specimen in front of him trying to prove he was really sick, but he just didn't wanna play along with the lab results. She noted he remained still, saying he was fine, no matter how many times her *registrar* repeated the words but your numbers are really bad, I wouldn't wanna be home. She wondered if she would be at home with those bloods results and who else has been sitting at home with them that would never know that maybe they needed to be admitted to hospital, or maybe not, it was truly an unknown. He relented to the unknown in the end and she watched him get into the gown, it seemed he transformed when he lay on the bed in the gown, suddenly not only did he look like his blood tests, he became his blood tests.

5. The young lady Layla stood in front of her. The patient was her own age, but with eyes that had seen far more. The abdomen in front of her was thin with scars where the gods of surgery had laid their steel, where they had cut to cure to heal yet here they were again in pain still sore, the blood tests still a little deranged, waiting for yet another scan. She noted from the notes quite a few CT's had irradiated the young lady's body, though the dose of radiation was nothing compared to the anguish complained of. She wondered how one ends up in that situation, what factors and degrees of separation there were between the lady and her. Were there mothers any different, or perhaps their fathers or lack thereof, could it be a little unlucky to have had a doctor guess what was wrong confidently and lead her down a path in which answers were solid, although it couldn't be just that as she had also had her appendix out with a small scar on her belly matching the scar this young lady had, a matching pair. Snap. Was it conceited to think she was better, she was actually healthier, some people who had seen her lifestyle would disagree. She also didn't have the health seeking behaviours this lady did, so was she the one at greater risk. Layla had been gowned before the official plan

"come in for observations and a scan" had come out of her registrar's mouth.

6. With the last patient, a 12-year-old kid called Ross, it felt like she was reading a textbook or a question bank which even at 18 she would get the answer to.

A young man came in with abdominal pain for the last five hours. It had started in the middle and moved to the right side, it was now very tender, and the pain was constant. Worse on moving and coughing.

She could almost hear her *registrar* ask her, was it:

a) Constipation
b) Merkel's Diverticulum
c) A syndrome you definitely didn't know existed named after a probable Nazi or at least racist doctor.
d) Appendicitis
e) All of the above

She had answered quickly "next we have a kid with appendicitis Mo."

He smiled, he liked certainty and answers.

"Sounds like it is Rach! Good catch, it's always fun when it's textbook, but we have to use every case as a teaching point, what would be the other thing we have to make sure it's not."

"I guess constipation, maybe urine infection because in kids these can mimic appendicitis,"
"Even better, yes those are what people forget, for someone from perioperative you're not too bad on surgical knowledge eh!"

He tapped her shoulder with his angular hand and made her feel one of the team as he smiled at her. She smiled back and wondered if he was married or not, after all nothing wrong with having one from the team, she did like how angular and muscular he was, she stopped her thoughts before they got wilder, she didn't need the press of sleeping with two doctors in the hospital, not in this small town, she imagined the kangaroo court of her peers would be hard-line.

With the minimal amount of paperwork done for the last case the unit had then been officially closed as the nurses and staff running it sighed with relief, their day finished a little earlier thanks to the luck of the volume but also hopefully thanks to her efficiency. She didn't get a "well done" but rather she got a "you should keep working like that, because we wished everyone else did."

The problem with helping the admission unit finish and close shop meant the rest of the shift was spent in the noise and overture in the emergency department, a place thanks to friendliness, she had shined in reasonably well despite her fight/flight system always being on during her time in there, like some kind of marathon runner. Although her weight had been within healthy ranges at that time. Probably burn off more running around and letting the chaos behind you act as a personal trainer. The chorus played as she arrived onto the scene, everyone had smelt her like blood on the water, the sharks circled.

"Are you on for surgery, Rach?"

She heard them sing to her in chorus. She wanted to say no but her arrival and the knowledge of her colleagues who were staffing the ED made it impossible to escape the lasso they now had around her.

"Yeah it's me, I got to pay for my sins."

Within an instance she had piles of paper land on her arms, none falling, given the stabilising force of her large arms, the ones she called her steel beams. She had plenty of reviews and referrals and a few "can you please just look at this," she remembered the surgical admission unit acted like a barrier, like a general at war, shielding her from the front lines down in the ED.

Her *reg* had popped down to help her. He had a big smile, as if he was a super soldier waiting, hungry for the battlefield, willing to defend the hospital from the enemy, which she imagined he saw as the patient themselves, as he high fived her for every discharge. The nurses seemed to celebrate each like a goal, with her providing the assist to Ronaldo in front of her who had delivered a precise strike.

Another discharge or "goal" had led her to walk past resus, a glancing Dr Abdul had noticed her walking with paperwork.
"Hey Rach!"
His face gravely serious, there was no raised eyebrow or twinkle, it stopped her in her tracks, she stared at him, seeing a different side than before, the calm of the man replaced by the assertiveness of a serious doctor.
"Hey."
She hadn't even finished the word before he kept going. His words moved her legs towards the situation he was inviting her to.
"I need the surgical team in resus, now!"
Her adrenaline was heavy as she walked into the busy resus room. The bodies piled in, a rugby ruck all pushing against the one entity they were fighting against, death, the grim reaper himself. She looked at the man who was the host for this, a young lad, not a bad body, obviously a regular gym goer. He lay looking pale barely responsive, she wondered if he would remember this battle that took place over his body.

There was a man with an ultrasound machine playing with dials whilst sonic waves were sent out, the high pitch beyond normal pitches, probably about to become a *jazzy* frequency. He looked even more worried at the screen playing with dials further as if to wish the image away.

Abdul looked at Rachel, he must have sensed her nervousness at the war front.

He tried to smile, it wasn't his usual authentic one, but it gave her some hope.

"One breath and check your own pulse first. Is your r*eg* around, can we get him?"

She did as told and found the things slowed a little. Not enough, but maybe just about to squeak one word past her now dry lips, it felt like she had gobbled up the whole Sahara.

"Yeah."

She turned around with her tail between her legs, not a soldier but a messenger perhaps, she justified her role in the war front, although she felt like a deserter.

She looked around the department, every nook and cranny, every little hole, probably went too far by looking at every cubicle peeking behind every corner, but in the moment of need Mo had vanished. She went to look at her phone, to give a call, noticing her hands shaking, the numbers took three times to write, the ring went out.

"Hey, I think they need you at resus."
His curt voice replied,
"I'm already there."
His voice too had transformed from the jokey, potentially shag you in the on-call room tone to a serious military tone. The phone died; he had hung up. It was now her role to go and most likely watch, what could she offer apart from babbled one-word answers, sweat and a dry mouth. All the advice she had was to keep doing what she was doing, is this what they wanted her to keep doing, her stomach began to reject some of her previous coffees. She took another breath to keep it from brimming. She had automatically run to the toilet, hiding in there with the door shut. She spat out some saliva which hadn't been doing its job, leaving her mouth drier. Her mind was running out of similes and metaphors. She looked in the mirror, looking for a speech to keep her going, she managed to speak to her reflection.
"Come on Rach you're there to learn anyway, you won't actually make any difference!"
That was what she needed, with a slightly braver face and a rinse out of her mouth she walked onto the battlefield

There were flashes and loud shouting from everyone, Mo watching at the end of bed pretending to lead whilst Dr. Abdul actually gave the commands.

"So, we need some more blood products please. He's got a bleeding leaking aneurysm and he's not gonna do well unless we get things sorted."

That goes without saying, she wanted to reply, bit ballsy for the doctor who had just vomited, she apologised to herself, nearly vomited in the hospital toilet.

Slowly the tug of war continued with more people piling in getting more and more products through the veins of the man barely alive, the grim reaper looking down below not interested. His power was so vast that it took a whole army to keep him at bay.

*

The monitors stabilised and the man still breathing managed to look around him, the event over people slowly walked out till it was her, Dr. Abdul and Mo.

Three left to look at, everything strewn aside the syringes, the gauzes, the ultrasound machine. The department needed to run and this man whilst still looking horrible seemed to have moments of life in him. He had been "stabilised", the resus had done its part of the fight. Her and Dr Abdul eyes now on Mo.

"Okay Rachel, can you fill out the pre-op paperwork, you've done it before I believe, I think we need a vascular surgeon on site as this guy won't make it over to the royal in time. I can start. I have done a few aneurysm procedures as a junior *reg* back at the royal. I'll leave letting the theatre know to you Rach."

This was all business and Rachel was being asked to join, so much for her speech.

She went onto the computer and proceeded to print off the paperwork for theatre, going into autopilot as this was the day job being a perioperative junior. She started to scrawl in the most illegible, but still identifiable female handwriting. She did wonder why print off to write on a piece of paper, getting the worst of both, the computer and the writing worlds.

There was no need for communication skills that her medical school had bashed into her year by year; the pale husk of a man could barely respond. A series of nods answered the tick boxes she had to fill for the anaesthetist to then check over. One by one she ticked the boxes of the organs in front of her, to her it seemed mute, his age 26, his condition critical and no matter the preoperative paperwork they had to operate surely. She continued to listen to each of his body parts. Checking his pupils, his neck, his chest, lungs and heart, she wondered if she heard a whoosh. It was faint, she continued, a whoosh was probably her hungover head.

The boxes ticked, the paperwork filled and the organs with one swelling and leaking was taken away by the nurses towards the theatre. She had rung theatres, somehow managed to laugh a little with the on-call team as she warned them about what was coming up, a truth known to all those in health care;
Laughter kept them from crying.

*

It was her job to hold the fort as millions of people rushed to the on-call theatre. She saw that her bleep had issued a cardiac arrest call, she wasn't part of the team merely an observer, but she knew there were tummy pains she had to see down in ED who also needed help and the cardiac arrest team would do their bit. She continued downstairs, a soldier on one front, wondering if the man from before had fallen to death or not. Her head still spinning, she thought she definitely needed a drink or few after this shift, she looked at her phone hoping there had been a response from the man, Dean Perez. She shouldn't be seeking a response from him. He was her Suzy and she was desperately seeking him. His last text was mildly flirty, but "the bathtub" was the place to continue it, as his fiancée was asleep at her family home post night shift.
To choose morals or mortality.

She didn't care, she asked for a blood test for yet another abdominal pain, she kept hearing the ED overture in the background. The one she titled, *breach breach baby.*

*

She focused on the bubbles of larger size she would start off with, weirdly helping her spinning head, she wondered if she'd be better served as a professional drinker.

Morals or mortality, or a lovely bath to rub lub dub in maybe even have a whoosh in when he came along. His fiancée was nowhere to be seen, so she and him could give a middle finger to the grim reaper who had hung around floating above her, an unwanted guest for this evening.

Chapter 10: Unknown Unknowns. (Day 1 of the trial)

She looked down at her badge, it was May now as she looked back up at her laptop. The screen jittered with each sparking of the wheels against the rails, the train most likely from the 1950's an old bus on tracks. There had been an outcome placed on her portfolio. Soon enough her badge which read Dr Isabella McCullen Foundation 1 doctor, would read the rather more appealing Foundation 2 doctor. Not that a number made much difference, however it did imply she was fully registered. A lot of good that did, it hadn't helped at the shop which had run out of her favourite lunch. No more marmite sandwiches, no more jam or even worse stale bread. She had to buy lunch today. She wouldn't even know the options at the shops near the court.

She thought about the last few months and about what had unfolded. She was surprised as anyone to see the outcome which meant she had passed her year given she was on her way to a coroner court. Not that she was the main character or the villain on the perch, more just a witness and someone involved in the care or the mis-care of the patient, the mis-care of the now deceased 26-year-old. She had left Darthington and was in the neighbouring "big smoke", the main county city; the court lived there as it served the whole county. The big city lights glaring on the train pulling into the station, a train she had gotten a seat on, because society deemed her a pretty girl and the weird man had given up his seat, although he kept looking back, she wondered if he expected a prize. She stood up; everyone now stood up racing for the double doors. Everyone in a hurry, no one able to wait 2 minutes as they crammed like sardines out of the tin hopefully into the open mouth of the world outside.

The weather had decided to hold a note of dissonance, a juxtaposition, to her situation it was beaming sunlight with the perfect breeze. Not at all mournful for what she or her colleagues had to go through. Each step heavier despite her wearing her best formal dress and shoes, once again the skirt fitting perfectly around her petite figure which had flourished in comparison to the others in the year, her secret of the marmite diet shining through. She knew she had to write a diet book about the next big thing, maybe she could nervously plod through that if her medical career ended today.

The building of the court loomed ahead with its gothic architecture and its placement in the middle of a garden made it seem in a different time zone, in a different world to what she knew. A manor long forgotten in time where punishment and justice must occur. She took a further step and it seemed to loom over her as if it was bending its neck to take a good look at her, the windows being the eyes of this particular monster. Her heart raced a little quicker. The door coming into view which also sat much larger than her, or was it an illusion, the old wood creaked with her hand on it, it shifted slowly like suspense in a horror film, she expected a jump scare.

C
R
E
E
E
E
E
E

Ee "Heya Izzy, looks like the cast is all here, I'll be your knight in shining armour!"

The big bellowing laughter, worse than any jump scare, his face with its perfectly bred jaw line shone at her.

"Hey Rich," she smiled. "Probably could do with a knight in a pinstripe suit, maybe with a law degree!"

He smiled, she giggled back, politely.

"It's not like we're on trial Izzster."

Ughh the new nickname suggesting familiarity hit her bones. She decided to smile it off.

"We're just here for facts. A lot more happened to that guy on our weekend, remember."

He smiled more, she shrugged it off as he offered his arm to link.

"Lady?"

"I'm alright thanks," she whipped back for once letting her guard down, although that seemed to have no effect on Rich's confidence, he smiled.

"Fiery, I like that!"

More bellowing laughter, she went back to giggling to avoid lines like that.

A rock and a hard place commonly crept into her mind around Rich.

*

She had noticed that everyone inside had gathered like they would do in a high school canteen. The nurses involved all sat together laughing away. The doctors in different groups depending on their specialty and level, solemn, as if offended to be seen here. The family of the deceased, who she had never met, all dressed in black like the goth kids, but with a reason to be gothic. She couldn't keep her eyes on them too long before the swelling of guilt which threatened to stick her feet to the ground like some shitty student night club would.

She turned quickly to see her group. She was meant to sit by her two colleagues she had met on day one, Rich and Rachel. She slowly took her place on what she imagined was her stage amongst her colleagues. Letting them chatter as she listened. She wondered if they would get a lunch break.

The old building seemed to both shine and be dusty and dull, an oxymoron, the doors all wooden creaky yet grand and menacing, like a post-modern piece of art invoking conflicting feelings. Her eyes kept looking towards the family, she wondered if they knew who she was, considering she had no idea who they were. However, their dark garments and the shallow look in their eyes told her they weren't medical, wounded; yes, but not wounded healers.

*

They all sat down in the chairs lined up behind a big desk, like school children gathered round for a lesson, she never did like school, it did not lend to her personality, although her dislike wasn't too bad, she did get the grades for a doctor after all.

Each person took their seats next to her on either side, Rich and Rachel, bolstering the middle of the class. Not the *bad kids* who sit in the back; the surgeons involved in the case, but not the geeks or nerds who sit near the front; the attentive anaesthetists but also the family members. Next at the front she noticed another man, he had the eyes of a healer, but wore a fluffy jumper instead, with a frantic haircut or lack thereof one and a beard. She imagined he was what they mocked as GP in the hospital, she wondered of his role as he sat next to the family.

She glanced again at the surgeons all looking down or chatting and grinning, all looking angular as if part of a gang, led by Mothinder, with his grimace and smile towards her, she felt uneasy like the class bully was watching her, she felt nervous and wondered why his face looked gleeful, almost like he still thought he was a hero, she wondered if she would ever be a "confident" doctor like that or maybe "deluded", she paused unsure of which quality it was, she ended up being jealous of both.

She expected a man in a wig, with big black robes, demanding their attention ready to swing a gavel to lock them all away. She felt the guilt of a shoplifter or someone who had brought back 60% booze from abroad. Only one of those situations rings true for her. The doors creaked open again this time more swiftly as if the person using them had done this many times before, she looked back blinded by the light as if this was a talent show reveal. Her brain filled in the reference for her.

Next up; the bringing of doom for doctors, the great leveller. The meek will inherit the earth if he has anything to say about it. The wigged one, Mr Coroner.
Despite all this in her head the light revealed an anti-climax, she was wrong, instead a friendly middle-aged man had walked down the aisles his matchstick legs in dark corduroy trousers with a tweed jacket on his white shirt and a tie which hung low, his large glasses from twenty years ago had cycled through the fashions and now looked trendy even on his very unassuming face. He apologised as he went past every row, making himself known. Sitting at the teacher's desk he looked up, eyeing everyone, she wondered if they all felt the same pang of stomach acid followed by their hearts racing. He looked down at the pieces of paper in front, his glasses naturally

moving to the ridge of his nose as if a connected part of his being. His voice came, no booming, no commanding, just a normal well spoken English voice, enunciating every word, with some slight accent she couldn't pick up the dialect from, it made him sound familiar, like a family member.

"Today all of you here are at Her Majesty's Coroner court. Let me talk through what this court is about. This is not like some kind of TV court case with objections. We are gathered here not to blame, but to reveal and think about the cause of death of Mr Jason Argonaut. There are questions always to be asked especially in those with unnatural elements to their death. Whilst death is natural the cases can be not so. I will ask and be asked and that is my role. First thing's first. I will confirm the details of this case."

"Mr Jason Argonaut. His date of birth was 5th of January,"

she didn't catch the year.

"Making his age 26," at least the maths had been done for her.

"His cause of death, a ruptured thoracic aortic aneurysm. Now we ask the how, who and why. Before this I would like to welcome the mother of the deceased to give us context to this brilliant life."

There was a pause at that, she noted the jumper clad man who sat next to the family as if a translator ready to explain the minutiae of the medical world, a language and a people onto themselves. He seemed to place a hand on the mother who had hung her head. Saying something into her ear as if the puppet master she stood up and walked across.

Now this was the bit she imagined the audience waited for the way they did for a comedian's most famous routine or joke. Like Michael Macintyre and his Scottish legal tender joke. She for once laughed at her use of the word audience. Rich would probably be proud of the act of self-pleasure. She sighed; audience was a glib term she was using to describe everyone there. Something to quell the thoughts and rising guilt levels within her slender frame which shook violently, she'd call herself buckaroo, with all the movement she made.

The lady stood, not tall like in the movies, but silently and hunched, speaking into the microphone which did nothing to tune the voice to a more commanding tone. The whispers being picked up with extra sounds on each p or b, she doubted this mother was microphone trained.

"I agree that everything said today is the truth, the whole truth and nothing but the truth."

A pause and an individual reaction mounted by everyone in the room to the word truth.

"So, Jason was a lovely boy, minded himself, looked after himself and was always caring, maybe even too caring to a fault. Never complained. Never. Complained."

That felt like a jibe to everyone there. It was the moment she saw the mother's eyes, filled with mother's love transformed into a mother's fury, formidable to say the least. After all those who didn't complain seemed to have less fuss created on the wards although she wondered if it actually changed what happened. An answer she really hadn't been in the game long enough to know. The story of Jeremy continued, about his wonderful life, a eulogy of sorts, every word filtered into the room, another life gone, like many before and after, tragic. Whether an avoidable death was to be found, she always wondered if these things really did make difference, she was unsure about her religious affiliations. She sometimes liked the idea of God as a protective factor, the removal of free will held her actions unaccountable, but then it held others who annoyed her unaccountable as well.

The story finished; this man was a saint, described in a heavenly way, even Jesus didn't get this much praise in the bible. Then again this wasn't a story, it was a grieving eulogy, and she felt a little like an awful person thinking like that. She wondered again if she was accountable for her thoughts, depending on the preacher, it was probably the devil visiting, probably had spread because Rich had placed a hand on her shoulder earlier.

The coroner once again stood up letting the mother sit back down and sob as the man with the woolly jumper placed his hand again on her shoulder, she imagined he had cotton comfort compared to aggressive closeness that she had gotten from Rich. She looked over at Rich and for a moment she wondered if he was looking for comfort as his face showed some vulnerability, was there even a glassy look to his eyes. She kept looking almost in awe, he looked back and gave her a smile.

Leaning forward he whispered, "careful, eyes up here," he tried to smile, not as bellowing as the first time they had met. God why did he try so hard to be unlikable. She would forgive him and decided to squeeze his hand for comfort. He squeezed back.

The comfort whilst unwanted was probably needed as the coroner started to speak, his lips opening up between his beard, his glasses on the bridge of the nose shining the light onto their faces.

"Next let's talk through the summary of the case provided. I will then ask people to come to the front to answer any questions I may have about what happened. This is not some kind of legal affair, it's a run through of the facts. So, we will have facts but said clearly in layman's terms so as to not confuse anyone."

A mixed statement she wondered what the tone the man in front was going for. He trotted a fine line of scary and comfort, promising no blame but saying there will be criticism. How one can happen without the other made her wonder, maybe no official blame but the teared family will attribute criticism as an admission of wrong or even worse guilt and guilt was always hard to live with, even time found it hard to heal.

"Jason Argonaut, a 26-year-old male, first presented to the ED department on the 22nd of August. He was seen with a complaint of shoulder pain and was seen by one of the Foundation years 1 doctors, Dr Richard Twain. The summary from the meeting is written here by Dr Richard Twain."

She felt the jerk in his hand muscle, the nervousness of a man who would never admit it.

The essay had been read, and she thought it was a very good summary and very fair of a first interaction with the patient and she wondered if she would do anything different. She may have talked more to the senior but resented doing so because she agreed with what Rich had thought. So, he acted on what they all thought, but did not clarify that was okay, which sounded bad. It sounded arrogant although it was probably sensible. She recalled her feedback in the department, she would have been told not to be so nervous and clarify, although looking here it may have saved face.

There wasn't a break as she saw the glasses shine again as the mouth of the judge moved further calling Rich to the stand, one last squeeze before he walked, his smile ongoing, was it guiltier to look worried or to still be confident, a part of her knew she would find out.

There had been a break called at the end of the "Grilling" of Dr Twain, whilst it was not an extensive one or a high heat one. It was more like a slow roast or a slow cook, not too aggressive to the meat but left it tender and beaten. People took a while to start shifting out, it had been 2 hours and it was now time for coffee. They had a thirty minute break in which to choose one from the building made of instant or indulge in the costa across the road, although she wondered if that was part of the test too. Would they frown upon doctors under scrutiny showing off their riches and excessiveness with whipped cream atop their supposedly bitter drink.

She really wanted it but she held off, she went for the sludge and went to look around the building itself not wanting to confront anyone and also wanting to find something to reduce the adrenaline that was now pumping through her veins. Like an onlooker onto a car crash her senses had made her anxious, nauseas and she could feel her heartbeat. She thought of the tender meat Rich had become. She felt like someone hungry, but without the appetite for food. She took small steps with her paper cup filled with disgusting coffee that she took small sips on, the first time almost spilling it because she had decided to try and walk and sip, a big mistake, a very well-known one to anyone who had ever done the same. She wondered if her inner monologue would be a terrible or mediocre stand-up routine. The next time she sipped she grimaced with no walking and dodging to distract her; it actually tasted worse.

The pillars and chairs in the building led upwards, making the building appear like a castle for the coroner. However, on closer inspection of who inhabited the other floors it looks like the king shared this grand building with solicitors, insurance companies, estate agents, one dentist and one herbalist.

She wondered if they knew the significance of the coroner and did he get the meeting room when he wanted or did he have to book in advance in case there was an herbalist conference already going on. She then decided to check out the toilets, or maybe she just needed the toilets. She didn't need to justify walking to them, she wasn't at some club with someone chatting to her. She walked taking in the columns and marble, the faux Mediterranean architecture different to the normal gothic and post war architecture she was surrounded by in Darthington. She liked the bathroom; it made her feel like she was in Rome. In the bathroom itself the marble glistened further, whoever they employed as the cleaner deserved good feedback and there was a big poster about how the whole building was environmentally friendly thanks to Mr Dyson himself. The Dyson air blade hand dryers hung on the walls, no hand towels here. This officially made them better than everyone else she thought they thought. She walked around and found one of the stalls before sitting down, the cool seat always giving her a small jolt as she did so. Her legs and uncomfortable shining boots showing beneath the stall doors. Reminding her that part of the discomfort was the shoes she was wearing. It was at the moment she let her urine hit the toilet bowl, all in one stream, the noise always drowning out everything else, the time to try and switch off her mind. Before doing so she heard someone walk into the bathroom with a familiar voice.

It was commanding yet weirdly vulnerable; the high heels clipping, and clopping revealed it was her consultant from ED, Dr Bethany Anderson. She seemed almost hurried and not in control.

"I told you I got the job at the Royal, I just got to sit through this absolute muck up at Darthington and then we can talk about it."

Some babbling like a small piccolo or even smaller trumpet came from her obviously fancy phone.

"Yes, I know I didn't chat to you first but you said you'd support me plus you can't hold things against me you've forgiven me for! Look I know this is right, for me and for you and Millie. It's not some honour or loyalty thing. It's the way people live, this is the next step, it's what's right."

The trumpet felt like it played a minor chord.

"I'm sorry honey, let's chat later. It is date night after all."

One last flat note before the dial tone was heard.

She heard Dr Anderson wash her hands, then heard the hand dryer turn on followed by the door being slammed. This allowed some urine to leave her, she was nervous when people were around the door.

11:30 had everyone shuffling back to their seats. The school kids returning from recess chatting away, everyone spilling the gossip from their schoolyard trip. Still chatting as it went from a swell to a lull as the coroner walked in and when he stood he commanded silence.

The case continued this time the bathroom telephon-er/big bad, but still nice to her boss Dr Bethany Anderson was called. She stood in front of everyone as the coroner spoke. She strode with her heels as if arriving to a fanfare, the family looking up as the woollen jumper man translated, they now were looking for answers rather than the blame target sought when Rich had been on the stand, this was an expert and sometimes people still didn't mind listening to experts, despite the current political climate in the country.

"So, we have listened to Dr Richard Twain's initial meeting with Jason and the initial assessment of his symptoms of shoulder pain."

The coroner once again straddled the line.

"This was the consultant on-call during that time. Please if you can in layman's terms answer my questions."

"Yes," she replied professionally.

"So, tell me about the assessment Dr Richard Twain made of Jason's shoulder pain."

"Of course, so, he did everything right."

Despite her saying that there almost seemed like he had done wrong floating in the air which focused the family onto Rich, his hand returned to her shoulder, she let him., she had some empathy. It was hard not to in the current atmosphere.

"Everything right for the shoulder assessment?" The coroner quizzed.

"Of course, the exam was done right, yes. I guess as a first encounter it's at the level expected of a foundation doctor."

"Layman's terms please."

"Oh yes, a Foundation 1 doctor is a doctor who is in the first year after graduating medical school, taught to be thorough and safe, but lacking in experience like a plumber who just finished the apprenticeship."

The family nodded, baring teeth, the blood of Dr Twain in the air. Or was that just her view of things taken from the side of her colleague, the teeth could also be that of grief, the blood deepening their sadness.

"It was the first-time seeing shoulder pain in a patient, where the first management must be addressing what is most common whilst being safe. Sometimes experience teaches you to ask different questions when it comes to people waiting in the Emergency department for something simple."

"So, you are trying to say that there are some extra questions you may have asked in this scenario?"

"Maybe."

There was bustling at the front.

"Maybe?"

A pause as her heels shuffled.

"Well, it was a first encounter, and it depends on the climate we were in, whilst not ideal to admit these factors do play within the health service."

"Climate?"

Another shuffle. Dr Anderson replied to the bearded man.

"Yes, how busy we are, who was asked, when things were done and in the end this is not anything that would have changed the management of the case at that time."

"Ahh okay."

He nodded and let her shuffle one more time before turning like a game show host to say, "the last question; the condition, later described as an aneurysm in Mr Jason case,

could the shoulder pain have been an early symptom?"
"Yes…".
The air filled again, Rich hand holding on, she felt if he let go of her, he would disappear.
"And no."
An eyebrow raised from the coroner's head into his bushy hair. The grey and salt pepper mixing into one shade.
"Because it could have been the aneurysm or some Muscle pain, I don't think there was any overt evidence it was definitely one or the other."
"An unknown," his brow seemed to talk on his behalf.
"An unknown unknown to Dr Twain" she replied, the heels shuffling with each repetition of the word unknown. It felt like she had said the word more than twice.
Each word tightening the grip Rich had on her and subsequently her grip on Rich.
Unknown seemed to repeat in her head.

*

The case progressed and next time she felt her body stiffen was when Dr Abdul was next, heels replaced with the squeak of old loafers, she hadn't seen him for a while. His body greyer than it had been, eyes more tired and the twinkle of his eye replaced with a mild exhaustion. His previous smiles were replaced by winces, there had been rumours around the hospital, how he was ill, not quite right, some nicer than others. Some more respectful than others. Some jokes which allowed people to ignore their own mortality when a colleague was faced with his. She wondered if she had guessed his personality as she was sure Dr Abdul would appreciate that kind of humour."

"I had asked Izzy." There was a pause as she heard her name now enter the room, now being introduced to the story being told.

The eyebrows raised and Dr Abdul coughed before returning to his sentence.

"Sorry Dr Isabella McCullen to discuss and review this chap with the *reg*."

"Why was that?"

A normal question to be asked next although she felt it allowed the spotlight to land on her she wondered if the family didn't like her, they'd never met her but maybe it was her make up or terrible unfashionable boots or her lack of jokes or smiling too much or not smiling enough. She took a breath. Grasping her legs, thinking of her lunch. It slowed her down a little before her tummy rumbled to embarrass her in other ways.

"Well you see," another cough and wince from the grey man whose hair was barely standing and seemed to slowly vanish with each effort he made on the stand.

"I was concerned about a repeated attendance with shoulder pain."

"Concerned about what?"

"That there could be a referred pain pathology."

"Referred?"

"Yes, some parts of your body if there is something going on will cause pain in a different part, like a warning signal. Now this is unlikely but must be thought of for those where the measures for other reasons of the pain have not led to any resolution."

"Naturally, so you mean you've tried to treat the likely stuff now to think of the unlikely stuff?"

"Yes."

"So, continue your report Dr Abdul, you had asked Dr Isabella McCullen to review?"

"Yes, given my tests had been negative I wanted to see if the surgical team thought anything of the referred pain. I mean I had asked her and Dr Twain to discuss with their specialist *registrar* to have a look."

"Of course, given she was a Foundation 1 doctor."

It felt like an insult even though it was accurate, like an internalised bully victim she accepted her weakness as a foundation one doctor. She felt the squeeze of Rich's hand, it was slightly comforting, she imagined more so for him than her. Although the next words out of Dr Abduls mouth seemed to provide greater comfort than closeness and a hand.

"Well, the Foundation doctor has a different role to the specialty doctor. They act as a conduit as well as the purest form of information gathering and allow us to still remember things we had forgotten and keep us up to date far better than without them."

She smiled at the strong defence of her role, it felt like he was standing up for her, the family nodding along listening to him seemed to draw their curiosities away from her, or her name. She saw him for a moment in defence. He looked stronger than he had done even when they had met him, fire in his belly and eyes. His hair growing back colour draining back into his cheeks and nose. Smiling away he looked momentarily happy, and the room loved it.

"Very good Dr Abdul."

Even the coroner left his impartial role for a quick complement. It was momentary as he quickly switched back to the role of the judge.

"So, tell me Dr Abdul exactly what did you ask Dr Isabella McCullen?"

"I asked her as per the report to review the patient and involve the *registrar* in his care. I

hadn't specified exactly what that involvement was and maybe I should have. I was happy as long as her *registrar* was involved and advised."
"Very well. The rest of your report will be read at the upcoming days, and we will ask Dr Isabella McCullen to appear after lunch for this case and then in the following days the *registrar* Dr Mothinder, as well as a reappearance of Dr Richard. All who have more of their reports to read out."
Everyone shuffled, knowing the lunchtime bell was about to ring.
"Let's get our lunch break then, thanks everyone for your brilliant involvement so far."
With a calm demeanour and stepping out of his questioning role everyone was free to eat lunch with a little less pressure, hopefully. She knew one true universal fact, less pressure better tasting food and, in this case, everyone needed some nice tasting food.

The cafe was across the road and lay in the sun on the edge of the park. Rich wolfed down his breakfast sandwich. His carnivorous side coming out, it was unsettling how much he looked like the animal the verb she chose to describe his eating as.
He finally spoke. Luckily without crumbs flying everywhere.

"So, we got the Airbnb. I think it'll be nice having each other around, anyone would feel awful after that!"

Was it sincere or a joke? It was hard to tell anymore.

"Yeah and I'm next ha, I'm sure I'll need your company too, if I'm worth it for you."

She found herself giggling nervously.

He smiled at that.

"Well, you're completely fine, you always do everything right, you're good, I bet he won't even have a question after your report."

It was encouraging. Rich was nice, probably, underneath it all.

Rachel arrived and into view as if to jinx the time that was being spent. Or as punishment to her mind for being nice about the man sitting next to her.

"Oh ah, it's big Rach, everything's gotten bigger, I think in a good way I'd say."

"Ahh Rich, I'd say you have done the opposite, it might all be smaller and maybe in a bad way."

They bellowed at each other, and she watched them bring out the boisterousness in each other.

"Yeah…. small…".

She managed nothing else. Luckily Rachel backed her up, the girl power going full force towards Rich, who loved the attention.

"Ooooooo, I've got two ladies being mean, you didn't have to, I was already keen."

She saw his energy rise with the roll of their eyes.

"So, how's you and the married man?"

Rich interjected, licking his lips ready to feed on the gossip.

"Well, she's his fiancée, not wife! Anyway, it's not my place to question that."

"Yeah, just make him question it."

She watched him grow bigger in stature with the roll of Rachel's eyes.

"But yeah, surely if he spends so much time with you maybe it's only fair he's honest to the both of you."

She decided to interject, trying once again to be in the girl power team.

Rachel looked at her almost in dismay, as if Rachel had heard this many times before.

"Look I don't really think I care in that relationship-y or love way, he's nice but probably just fun and it's not fun once you're actually in a relationship is it, you can't always be drunk or on MDMA!"

A bellow from Rach transmitted to Rich, but seemed to be grounded by her, she was the earth wire, she always found it hard to approve of what Rachel had delved more and more into, something her instincts seemed to be against. Well probably a learnt behaviour from her conservative voting parents. Not that she could complain about her parents' politics; they had given her everything she had ever needed.

"Well just be careful, I mean especially since we're being questioned, I don't think people want to know that you go out and do you know."

"You know you can say the word MDMA." She felt the girl power drain with Rachel's dismissive statement.

"I know but the family probably wouldn't appreciate a doctor admitting that."

"Yeah, because we're not human, we don't do what other people do."

"Yeah, I guess, ummm," She wanted to tell Rachel about professionalism, the role of doctor within society and how being hungover probably does affect decisions. However, it wasn't the place, and she wasn't the person, no matter how much she imagined she was.

The bells rang at the clock tower.

Dong

Dong

It was time. It was her time.

*

"We must resume, and the next statement is from..."

His kind tone transformed to judge with the pronunciation of her name
"Dr Isabella McCullen."
She walked, her stance nervous, she felt like an open book in the way she walked, revealing all to the world, all the eyes were looking at her and she felt them all look through her, naked to all in the room.
"So, tell us about the second encounter in the emergency department in which Dr Abdul spoke about earlier. He had asked you to review or get your team to review Mr Jason Argonaut."
"That is correct."
She stood her posture showing her professionalism, the word **correct** compared to using **right** made her sound wiser than her years.
"So please tell us about it."
She looked down at her paper and decided to read.
"Well me and Dr Richard Twain had been reviewing a different patient in the emergency department."
She took a small pause where she had a really heavily inked full stop.
"I was then asked by Dr Abdul to review this other patient."
"Asked to review."

"Yes, he asked to get a surgical review, he wanted our team to give an opinion on Jason."

"That team being the surgical team." The calm demeanour of the judge urged her on.

She felt like a video game character getting a few extra points every time she spoke, like in guitar hero she imagined she was getting greats or God forbid perfect notes.

"Yes, that is correct."

She looked over to the family, they were content, they looked at her, judging and so far, agreeing just like a computerised crowd.

"Correct," she paused, wondering if that would be a little overkill and overuse. Continuing on, "I then with Dr Richard made a plan which was discussed with the *registrar*. Which ended with him going home for his GP to follow him up."

It was the first time there was a pause in the woolly jumper man before he translated. His kind eyes looking at her, she saw he was the GP. His badge, which she could see from this angle, revealed all.

"The *registrar* for the record on call at the time was Mr Mothinder Fernandez."

She gulped at hearing the name and saw the man simultaneously give a nervous look to the coroner and a somewhat displeased look to her, as if his nervousness was her fault, he

377

probably did blame a lot of nervousness on her.

"So, you and Dr Richard Twain saw the patient together?"

Eye upward arch.

"No, Dr Twain saw the patient. I was just involved in the planning."

"So, he made the assessment, and at what point did Mr Mothinder Fernandez get involved?"

She wanted to shout about how rubbish the involvement was or he was probably telling women they couldn't be doctors or being flirty until they didn't reciprocate, she felt her mind angry, very rarely did it do this, especially when she didn't have marmite and poppy seed withdrawal. She bit her tongue, it hurt to do so. Wincing and with a limp sound to her voice imitating a limp punch penetrating the air.

"We phoned him and told him the story and the plan. Which he was happy with."

"We implied you were both on the phone."

The judge caught her out.

"Well, Dr Richard made the phone call yes. That is the end of my statement…".

Her tongue now freezing up with the pain, but also with uncertainty of what way to address him. He wasn't a highness, nor was he a knight, not a doctor or so he didn't feel like

it, he looked like Santa, that would be the wrong thing to call him.
She opted to knight him (and she did look like a younger queen if she was allowed to blow her own royal trumpet).
"Sir."
He nodded.
"Next I will call Mr Mothinder Fernandez for his first statement to end the first day of the trial."
She gulped as she left, feelings of pressure, as if he would sell her out, through his hatred of her, she worried and closed her eyes.

*

Her eyes seemed to open blurringly with another sip of the wine Rich had brought for the three of them in the Airbnb. She didn't recall much of the last statement, although she was never really mentioned in it, she didn't know if Mr Fernandez was being nice or it was the fact, he considered her insignificant and decided not to mention her, to him she was more like an ant. The truth was she was no one important to him, she probably now didn't even exist in his eyes. Rachel had opted to stick around for a few glasses despite her visitor (one who remained out of sight least they all disapproved) awaiting her to what she called destress after the events of the day. Another gulp helped her focus a little on Rich.

He was explaining the wine and how great it was or was he now talking about how great he was. He seemed to spin both together, failing not to mention himself when mentioning the wine.

"You see, I knew that a Temperillino is what we needed, a full body kick to dull us after that day, like fire with fire. I am pretty good with it all, I mean especially with my wine knowledge I always find a fine wine, like this wine is fine because I found it."

He continued to talk. She missed a little of what he said as her ears filled with the sounds of what she self-consciously noticed were her slurps. No one looked at her, she wondered if she noticed more than what others cared about. Or maybe they were worried about themselves despite never giving the disposition of the type of people who cared how they looked to others.

"Ya ya, well done, I mean it's nice, but you keep mentioning yourself and we'll suffocate on your ego." Rachel said to the elephant in the room.

"I know but you're getting the lesson for free, count your lucky stars, bet you don't get much of that in Liverpool." He was ready with his response.

"Ucch ya posh wank, ya think you know a good wine I bet you just go by price tag, us scouse find a real bargain."
"I know, how is that scouse liver?"
"Probably managing better than yours."
"Yeah probably, however if Izzy drinks any slower then she'll be the one we need liver lobe donation from, Healthiest Liver around I hear." Unfortunately, he had gestured for her to join in.
She giggled a little. The wine soothed her sore tongue. She decided to join in. it flailed like a whip this time with the retort.
"Don't think I'd wanna ration it to you guys, wouldn't learn your lesson. Plus, it's probably a bit too fit for your body Rich."
A few ouch-es followed by more laughter.
She remembered after the wine finishing there was some slightly more serious talk about how they were sad about the patient and how they felt the stress and wondered where they could have all done better. They admitted they had all identified with the words of unknown unknowns. Rachel had stumbled to bed, and she had gone to the other bedroom, with Rich being left on the sofa. Which he reminded them of how chivalrous he was. She decided not to remind him that each mention undermined his appeal to them all. It was a few more moments with blinkered eyes she

381

had noted Rich come in. He seemed tearful. He came closer and hugged her.

He whispered, "I just feel I screwed it up, I should just say I was too cocky."

She squeezed his hands.

"I just can't stay in there, Rachel, too loud and I just feel so alone."

There was no bellow, this was the hand squeezing Rich.

"We can do head to toe." She replied but he kept holding her.

"I just… I screwed up and now you're all involved, someone as amazing and beautiful as you, you know from the first day I met you you've always, to me, been the most beautiful girl in the room."

She gulped a little, flattering yet unwanted. She wasn't in danger, but she wished she hadn't been hearing that from vulnerable Rich, she had been in this situation before with boys, it always ended up wrong, it's why you can't be close to guys and she had been maybe a little too inviting today, a polite distance was what was needed. After all they are programmed like this, she probably gave off a motherly vibe and attracted these guys. She felt the ground roll underneath, she wondered if Freud had been buried under this BnB.

"How much have you drunk; I mean I smell some tequila. Which was for tomorrow you said. For the second day, stress." She questioned.

"Yeah, but she's not you, you're better, and that's without the filters on photos you're so fit, and I feel we just have this amazing chemistry, I'm just saying what sober me thinks. I feel we should be, you know, the way we feel about each other, was more than me and her ever felt"

Confusing, who was he comparing her to?

He squeezed again. It was comfortable, but anyone would be comfortable. It wasn't being uncomfortable that put her off, just her general disinterest in him, although she wondered if the red wine had channelled her mother and father and siblings, like one big Ouija board as she heard *you're far too picky* echo in her head.

"Look Rich I'm just you know a friend not interested in that way and I don't think I've ever let you think that."

"Excuse me."

He seemed to have gathered a little bit more wit as he let go.

"Let me think that?"

"Well, you know I think maybe you're just overthinking things in your mind."

"I think that's a little unfair."

"A little unfair," she felt her tongue now burn with the fire of the Temperillino.
She continued,
"Unfair, that I've had to deal with you being a little forward, putting me in an unwanted situation because I work with you. I thought I'll ignore it, it's just him but if it's all one big thing to get in my pants then I was right to be distant."
"You kissed me that night. When I asked for one, you replied to my texts, you hung out with me and told me that you like me."
"To be polite and I don't remember that kiss being more than friendly and polite!"
"Today you squeezed my hand."
"Because we're good friends, you idiot."
She felt her blood rage, once again her stress levels rose because of a guy. Same story always, was she just too nice.
"Well, what's wrong then, I thought that we had an ounce of chemistry and you didn't, you knew I thought this and instead of being up front you continued to message, to be nice, but also be distanced then nice again. You must know that that's how people play the game. You must know you had me wrapped around your little finger!"
"There's no game, I'm just nice."
"Bullshit…" his breath crescendo-ing to the word.

Both of them standing definitely louder than the "loving couple" next door.

"You can't be this stupid, this naive yeah? You just like the attention, you're like a little manipulator. This is hilarious, innocent Izzy toys and wraps us around her finger."

"I'm not, I was being nice."

"Nice would have drawn a line at some point and even when you backed away, stay backed away or tell me. We're adults."

"Well, you're not an adult like this."

"Because you're acting like a child."

"This is why guys and girls who are single can't be friends."

"No, **that's why** you can't!"

Rich now burning with fire, seriousness something she hadn't seen before. He walked backwards gritting teeth before reaching for the door. He added in a low pitch growl.

"This is why guys and little girls who refuse to acknowledge sex and attraction exist and be upfront about it can't be friends, because they live in a fantasy world where they get attention and know someone might be flirting but instead of being honest and rejecting them, they play a game because it can't hurt because in the end they can say it was all unwanted, well it was wanted."

"How dare you say what I want."

"I agree maybe some of it was unwanted but some of it was wanted because I'm not some kind of deviant. I don't continue if someone tells me it's unwanted…".

There was a pause, she didn't know how to respond, he continued for her.

"Look at your face, you think I'm a bad person, don't you?"

He was almost disappointed as he left the room and there was no slam. Her thoughts left alone she gulped a little and a few tears rolled down her eyes. She felt like she was to blame for all of it, that it was unfair. He was being unfair, especially at this time. She closed her eyes. She heard some moaning from the next door.

"Bet she doesn't do it like this."

"No ughh, she… she doesn't love this as much as you do."

"That's because I'm better, I'm tighter."

"Ughh, so tight, ugh, I'm gonna show you why you always come back for me."

"Ughh yeah, fucccuuuuhhhck" The harmony through the thin walls swelled and with Rachel newfound weight the fat lady did sing. She tried to forget the notes and melody involved in Rachel's man orgasming solo. With Rachel being the support instrument her body the drum.

She put the pillows over her head, this was all unwanted, and she much preferred when Rich's thoughts about her and Rachel's feelings around sex had stayed unknown unknowns.

Chapter 11: Unknown Unknown (Day 2 of the trial)

He awoke and stared at himself in the bathroom, a swell of what was known as hangxiety (hangover anxiety) laid over his body, from head to toe, past his embroidered boxers, which had been given by his now disapproving mother. It read clearly for all to see.

Dr. Richard Twain.

The italics reminded them who they were with and the status he probably didn't deserve. The conversation wasn't fully remembered, and it seemed to be interspersed with pauses of Rachel's moans. Something he had drunkenly helped himself to release his tension and caused him to feel sleepy after the adrenaline involved in talking to Izzy, someone he never expected to end up in a shouting match with, and maybe even lose, he couldn't remember, but he didn't feel like a winner. He'd have to apologise, and in true English manner, suppress his honest feelings. He wondered if things are better in this case as unknown unknowns, and how many times he had lived

with the unknown unknowns without knowing, he paused and chuckled to himself. He slowly brushed his teeth and got his shaver ready, trying to make sure he missed no hairs. He knew that a clean-shaven man came across more professionally. It was all about the stage today as he continued to practice his script, his lyrics like a rap star ready to spit bars. Show his pain and explain. Already rhyming in his head.
One.
Two.
And Wilkinson's third blade brought the hairs right down to his skin.
He was ready, his mirrored reflection giving him confidence, he thanked his parents and his private school teachers for giving him the self-belief he needed when looking in the mirror.

The walk in with the three of them was quiet, the middle act of their trial becoming evident within the burden of their core group, although Rachel seemed a little more pepped than the other two.
"So, I guess my turn isn't till tomorrow, today is pretty short."
"Yeah, it's me and Dr Abdul and I think Mo."
"Yeah, the big one is tomorrow with the surgery." Rach said.

He wondered if he heard some nerves in the unnerved girl.

He noted Izzy had remained silent, she hadn't even glanced or giggled his way. A change. He felt he won the battle of words, but the war of silence he knew he was losing. She looked a little disheartened and no matter the words exchanged, most he barely remembered, he just remembered the tones, maybe the themes or the key they were in, definitely B flat mixolydian, pretentious from him and A sharp pentatonic from her. He realised pretty similar keys, just different scales. A good summary for their "friendship". The quotation marks in his head mimed internally. He tried to include her, a formal white flag.

"Well Dr McCullen here is all finished up, she's a full registered doctor and finished her first coroner's court case, those little students are gonna look up to you yeah? I already am."

He forced a big laugh whilst looking at her, she barely smiled back, but at least her eyes told him she appreciated the comment, and her soft reply, a whispered "Yeah" said he was past silent treatment. Although he now knew not to read too much into her, he had been completely wrong. The truth was deep down he always doubted any girl like her could ever find him funny or charming. He felt the weight of his doubts, this was the time he called the calm before the coming storm, *storm anxiety*.

*

He was stood in his chair with his paper in hand, having been asked by judge and jury to recite his words, his reality of what happened at the second meeting of Jeremy, but only the facts, he did wonder if the facts were also subjective to what he thought of them, was his opinion the facts in his statement. They had received help writing it from their supervisors, the hospital lawyer and their protection agency. This wasn't a trial, but it felt real to him and now he wondered that despite what he thought of as charm was, he was now just being smiled at by the family because they were being polite. He shook himself a little, he noticed the sister of the deceased, who was quite attractive, a slender figure with tied back dirty dark hair, her breasts not large but a perfect size keeping in ratio to her figure. She had perfect teeth and legs highlighted by heels, it was probably not the time to flirt, maybe after, if his statement was well received. A breath in before the performance. Guilt surged for his thoughts about her, he realised, although deep down he already knew, he had a very unhealthy coping mechanism.

"I was asked by Dr Abdul with Dr Isabella McCullen to help provide a surgical review of Mr Jason Argonaut for his shoulder pain. I then went to meet him for a second time. I discussed his pain and if there had been any change to it, we discussed the previous diagnosis and the advice I had given about musculoskeletal shoulder pain including the rest period we had discussed. He did admit he hadn't been completely following it but also that the pain had continued despite time which made me think it needed a follow up. I unfortunately wasn't aware of any other symptoms and therefore believed as it was a chronic problem the GP had the expertise to follow up on this given their experiences with chronic symptoms, especially of pain."

He took a breath, praising the GP had been a smart suggestion by the hospital lawyer, although he felt a little guilty that the words surf and turf had actually been used to describe the handling of the case when he had discussed it with Mo. It never was about a lack of care, it was a coping mechanism, dark humour and nearly every doctor had it and if they didn't, they had to develop. It was an unwritten part of the curriculum. He looked at the man with GP on his badge next to the family, the woolly jumper emitting kindness and caring and hopefully to the family expertise about pain, so they may get the help they needed. He knew he wasn't providing it.

"So, given that I phoned Mr Mothinder Fernandez and I explained the symptoms and the assessment and the plan."

There was a light pause, he felt weird involving his registrar, it was the truth although the conversation provided in his statement was a lot less detailed than the conversation they had, no one needed to know their favourite dish.

"He replied back to me with a plan to follow up with GP for reasons as previously stated."

He let out a big breath before giving a small cough, his own full stop. He looked over at the family, the sister drawing his eye, a few flashes of what could be done if this was a pub and not a corner court flashed across his face and he was glad he was only at half mast, hidden within trousers he used on his dates. He was an easily excitable dog, he looked back over at Izzy and realised dog might be too kind of a word for him. He wondered what she thought of him up there. Probably not much, drunken arguments rarely resolved the next day when anxiety was involved.

The coroner looked down at him and reminded him of a schoolteacher, his eyes asking him to focus.

"So, you didn't get your registrar to see the patient?"

He felt the sting of the question, there was a silent implication that he should have done. The family looked towards, any chances he had with the sister evaporated in the look she gave him. Greif wasn't the aphrodisiac that he had heard it was meant to be.

"Well, I gave the details over the phone and I felt the plan was sufficient. Given the symptoms and other observations and test results."

"Given Dr Abdul asked for a surgical review, was it clear that he wanted a registrar to review it?"

His heart beating for once he didn't have an answer to hand immediately, he looked over at the man who looked a lot more rugged than at the start of the year, he'd aged a century and looked *too weak*.

"Dr Richard Twain?"

The voice of the coroner calm yet demanding the perfect balance re-focused him.

"Umm, to me it was urr…".

The sweat beading down his face made him feel like a guilty man, guilty of what he was unsure, just God damn guilty, his inner voice coming out, reminding him he wasn't exactly a saint, probably even an arsehole, he did know it, did that make him better than people who didn't know that they were twats. He continued to umm and urr. Watching the families' faces turn sourer, their faces resembling a rapidly ageing citrus fruit. He looked over even Izzy not providing him with a smile or much empathy, just a blank look, at least it was a neutral expression, a Switzerland face.

"Urr to me it wasn't obvious. The way I was asked made it unclear."

He sighed out the sentence hoping his humility, an action he rarely did, helped sell his ignorance in the case.

"Very well. Thank you, Dr Richard Twain."

He stayed seated wondering if time had slowed or his legs had given up, as he stood in silence, his head said nothing to him. For one brief moment there was silence.

"You can leave your chair. Thank you, Dr Richard Twain."

He stood up, walked on autopilot and sat in the audience with no one to either side, the pandemic of him causing social distance between him and everyone in the room. Despite this there was no quip coming up. Just silence.

The background noise groaned and roared.
"Next up Dr Abdul Assem."

He sat down isolated, wondering about what his future held, did the others feel he was guilty too. He thought back to that encounter with Jason, how it had been fun, he had genuinely felt like he was doing the right thing, but now he felt his chest being crushed, he wondered if it was his heart. Did guilt and a heart attack feel the same? That was a terrifying thought.

He looked up as he saw the old mentor shuffling his gait, much less stride-full than in his emergency department, the rumours had been fruitful and been true, he had retired and, in that instance, he imagined everyone saw him as a geriatric patient. He transformed from doctor to retiree, from god to vulnerable. A cross-like transformation, he buried the thought, he realised he had compared himself to Judas. No one wanted to be Judas. He could never remember what happened to him, although he remembered it wasn't good.

The shuffling stopped as Abdul stood next to the coroner, two aged men, he watched Dr. Abdul put on half-moon glasses and looked down at the statement on the pretty expensive paper. Dr. Abdul's voice started weak.

However, at the first mention of the emergency department the fire returned, the lion in Dr. Abdul's eyes surged forward. He watched the room be commanded by the now God-like consultant.

"In The emergency department I had reviewed this patient re-attending, for shoulder pain, so I took the history and was in agreement that statistically shoulder pain is most likely to be musculoskeletal."

"So, you were in agreement with Dr Richard Twain's assessment. If so, why ask for the surgical opinion?"

"Well, you sit there and act as if that means it was certain it had to be that."

"I guess in science we look for the answer, do we not?" The first time the coroner had become part of the narrative.

"Because in medicine often its subjective truth that goes on, science isn't certain but probabilities that are close enough to truth that we can live with it. Unfortunately, medicine is also an art which tends to kick and buck like a raging horse when the saddle of "scientific objective truth" is placed upon it."

The last line Dr Abdul had said in a roar, it was a duel between the two and a duel between what he imagined everyone else's preconceived thoughts about medicine were as well. This is what he'd call the airy-fairy bit of medicine, but the family seem to lap it up, his cynical side choosing the word lap to describe their adornment their eyes showed. He watched the eyes of the professor, the sage, twinkle like a wizard duelling. The ending of some harry potter knock off novel. Words being their wands. Dr. Abduls statement might have proved pen is mightier than sword, but he did wonder if he had a sword, he probably could take on the consultant, it'd be the only way he could take him on.

"So platitudes and philosophies aside," there was silence as the coroner lifted his metaphorical sword to come down on the professor.

"When asking for a surgical opinion, were you explicit in wanting a registrar to review"

He waited for the parry from his mentor, the one that would send the strike towards him, to say of course I wanted a *registrar* why else would I ask for a surgical opinion. The steel clash would be the final sounds he'd hear, before he was completely enthralled by guilt, a twain too far. He wouldn't even be remembered, and he wondered how "ex-doctor" would sound on his tombstone. No one really fancied a Shipman. Well apart from his elderly ladies, maybe cougars would have to be his type.

The steel on steel never sounded, instead he imagined blood dripping from the professor's neck, glistening, the lion whimpered, returning from God to vulnerable, it had taken one hit, metaphorically that is. Dr Abdul's eyes gazed down, the now geriatric patient's words came out in what he described as a stage whisper, "No, I was not explicit to my junior colleagues."

"Should you have been?"

He watched, this was unfair, the steel dug deeper, the coroner was going for the jugular or worse the carotid.

"Yes, communication is where the errors are made."

It was as if Dr Abdul had not only allowed the steel to pierce, to cut but had held the handle and helped it along. He was saved on the sacrifice of another. He saw that the sister had snuck a look at him, he hoped for an exonerating look, but his filthy mind saw it for something else.

"So you should have been clearer?"

"Correct."

The metaphorical head rolled, and blood spurted. The blade finished its swing, still sharp, not even blunted by the battle.

*

He sat his head finally catching up to him, banging, the flat white (every single medic's drink) getting cooler by the second, the baristas love heart hadn't even evoked a dirty thought, but he had made the joke to Rachel anyway, the only person to accept his invitation of lunch, the only one mingling with the infected patient.

"Yeah, so you and Izzy last night didn't seem like great friends."

"Hmm what do you mean?" His acting was not on point due to his hangover.

"Well, we heard you."

"I'm surprised you did."

"Oi, what do you fucking mean by that?"

Never had he heard her be so scouse.

"Let's just say we didn't really need to know how tight things were for you down there." He wanted to bellow with laughter, but his headache acted like a censor.

She smirked, sniffing his weakness, "you're not feeling too tight yourself now, are you?"

Her laugh cackled in his head, she definitely wasn't helping, he sipped his coffee and took a bite out of the unhealthiest saturated fat thing he could find, breaking his rules put in place to get him ready for non-jumper wearing weather. His Fy1 reduced his body and mind now to a much weaker strength and after last night his very ego was on a wuthering height. He got why people got fat. He looked over at Rachel and wondered due to her many liaisons with sexual partners, drugs and alcohol whether that was the reason for the recent transformation from thin university student to curvy professional doctor. Or was that knowing you're gonna get fucked anyway so why bother missing out on things like delicious bacon sarnies. He decided to ask after another bite, the crumbs flying in Rachel's face, he didn't wince despite this, she was unavailable, nothing would impress. He was shallow, he knew he was lucky he didn't believe in God, because what waited for him in that case was as described by the bible itself: *__Unimaginable hellfire__*.

"Do you ever," another chomp, a gulp, "get scared he'll get bored and move on to his wife. I'd be worried, I'd be jealous too, but I'm probably too traditional and not as liberal as I heard you are."

He managed a half bellow, boy did it hurt his face to do it.

She looked back at him playfully, "well you've not found out how liberal I am."

He did like the *__hellfire__*.

Rachel paused, vulnerability in her voice as she spoke to him.

"But I don't know, sometimes I want to be like this is it, the last time, you have to choose,

I am falling a little. I feel there's always a time frame or a number of shags you can have before someone develops feelings, unfortunately it's human nature."

"Wow insightful, I don't think I have any more sex jokes in response." He tried humility again.

She smirked back at him, "wow the great Richard is full of bacon but not able to spit any out."

She bellowed; he noted that she was a good bellower.

He was now a little intrigued, "so what do you do when you get to that number of shags?"

"Two options, be mature, explain and walk away, or self-destruct."

There was a small pause before she continued, "I'm from Liverpool so being mature is probably not an option."

"You can say that again, you northern birds."

"Oi, I'm allowed to say it, you're not, you posh twat."

The fire filled the room, his flat white heating up a little, his bacon sarnie tasted better being warmed in his mouth by her fire.

"I'm sorry madam, I won't do it again, how immature of me." He joked and she smiled back.

"It's hard falling for someone isn't it." He let his sincere side slip.

"Yeah, I know," she nodded.
"Especially when you think you've got a chance, but you never did and suddenly everything is in question."
"Not easy, we all meet those ends."
"Yeah, I just thought, the way she acted."
"People are difficult, we are all doing what we think is the right thing, that's based on our upbringing, our parents and how much we like or resent them."
"Maybe my right thing and her right thing clashed."
"Maybe" Rachel looked at him and he felt supported, she was pretty good at listening. Good at saying the right thing or now what he thought was the right thing.
He looked back up, a gulp to stop the bread pieces escaping his mouth, after all he wanted as much of the sandwich his overbite would allow to be in his throat and not on the floor or shot at Rachel's face. Another gulp to finish. A sip.
"Maybe indeed. It's not like we'll ever know what she was thinking." he pondered.
"We rarely ever get to see another's inner monologue." Rachel smiled back.

*

He sat down on the sofa, this time Izzy began moving towards him and Rachel in the next room. He felt forgiveness start to surround him. The half day had been the treat he needed, tomorrow would be the last day which focussed on the third encounter of Jason. Neither him or Izzy were involved, initially they both had thought of not going along but that would be disrespectful and given the light shone on him yesterday he'd rather he get as many good boy points as possible. Like a snivelling cockroach he wanted to keep himself alive. Although cockroaches would likely outlive the human species so it can't be too much of an insult to compare himself to one, more a compliment about his ability to adapt and survive, which is really all that mattered.

"So, how's your head?" Izzy moving forward, her words edging closer but her body still far apart.

"Better now that the sun isn't out to annoy me."

She gave a half giggle, obviously afraid to laugh at what he said, a wise move he'd only misinterpret it. He knew, he already was.

"It's funny how a hangover makes us miss the day, the drink giving us the ultimate choice: day or the night."

She said with a sympathetic look at him. The worst look a girl can give you. Well, the worst one if you fancy them. Probably okay if you were a genuine human-being looking for a connection, which he rarely ever was. At least he acknowledged that about himself. Insight was the only thing that probably made him sane.

"Or you can burn the candle at both ends, keep going before the candle can't take it anymore." He replied.

"Hmm I guess you could, some people might call that unhealthy." A raised eyebrow from her to him, the conversation was maybe actually flowing, he resisted the urge to compare his penis to healthy or make an innuendo. Their words got closer,

But bodies were still very far apart.

"I don't know, is it now the time to do this, we finally have money, we're still young, relatively protected, no dependents, isn't now the time to gather experiences to see more, to do more, so we don't regret just sitting around doing nothing when we're older?"

"I think saying doing nothing is wrong, it's unwinding letting the mind rest, watching TV which in itself gives you a viewpoint of the world. Just because adrenaline isn't pumping through your body doesn't mean you're not living life; doesn't mean you have to regret."

He looked up at her, her eyes genuine. He felt their "right things" clash at that very moment.

"Don't you worry about sitting still?" He inquired.

"Why would I worry," the genuineness coming through again, something he couldn't comprehend.

"Well, I mean it could pass you by, you could miss out."

"But then again maybe you're missing out when you have that headache or sleep in or not feeling what I feel when I relax."

"Am I? What did you do during all those times I slept in or had a headache then?"

"Well, I enjoyed really nice breakfasts, brunch dates, and went for a run or cycle."

"Really?"

"Well, I tried to," she smiled, looking happy with it.

"Is that good enough?"

"For me it is, we are free to do what we want and to make our happiness and being content is the only real happiness in my book." She stood a beacon of truth.

"So deep down you are that word." He spat. "Content."

"Yeah, I guess that's what I'm asking?"

She smiled back at him, it was pity again, he knew he was going nowhere near her pants. Well unless it was a pity fuck, but something told him Dr Izzy McCullen wasn't a pity fuck kind of girl.

"Well, it's nice to know who I am and what I like, I don't do anything more than that."

"Lucky that," he said for the first time with no joking intent and actual resentment towards this belle of the ball.

"Why is it lucky?" Intrigued her words closed in on him.

Despite this he noted their bodies were still distant.

"You get to be content, feel good about yourself, not seek things to validate your being. My mind doesn't let me do that, it's constantly running, constantly trying to prove I'm better than what I really think I am."

He let the words vomit out, his inner self, his essence coming before their joint existence in the room. His *bad faith* fully on show, God he had to stop listening to philosophy podcasts.

"For someone who is so confident, you sure are insecure."

There was a pause as he felt her words act as a scalpel cutting into his insides. His rib cage cracked, his heart beating and lungs taking small gasping breaths. Naked, he was the patient to her surgeon at that moment. Vulnerability, an odd style on him and one he didn't enjoy.

"Yeah, I guess so, it's not that uncommon, especially amongst us guys." He spoke with sincerity.

"Because I'm meant to be vulnerable and insecure and shy, it gives me mystery. It's probably why you like me; you like the idea of finding out more about me." She said, peering further into his open being in front of her.

"Then if you know that, why do you continue to hang out and chat to me?"

"Maybe I like the flattery, maybe you force that out of me, maybe it's the medical world we live in that my loudness can't be heard because the assumption has already been made about me by seniors, nurses, patients and you. That I'm the little quiet kid, I need the attention and that's even before I've opened my mouth."

A little insight into her thinking went a long way, his heart attack or guilt was back. He took a sip of the clear guava drink in front of him, helping neither feeling, just exacerbating both.

He imagined his medical file.

An alcohol exacerbation of guilt
Differential of gastroesophageal reflux disease

Luckily written in terrible barely legible writing. So, no one would ever fully know, they'd just make their assumptions depending on what they saw on the outside. Jumble words together to fit with what they think is

going on, whoever "they" were, probably some collegiate council of nosy doctors. So nosy the plague doctor masks wouldn't fit.
"It's weird to be the one leading and talking in a conversation with Dr Richard Twain."
This time it was her turn to bellow, she must have been practising, he had noticed, it was giggling bellow a "gebellow". He wondered if he could patent the word, he was sure it'd get a laugh on a date.
"I guess so, I just didn't expect to hear this, I'm used to you just laughing at what I say."
"Well maybe it's okay to actually listen." She smiled.
"Yeah probably, it's not too bad is it?" He managed a smile as well.
They both genuinely smiled for what he realised was the first time in each other's company. Their words bonded showing a conversation was happening.

So close with words.

Yet.
Their.
Bodies.

Antagonising.
Too far for him.

However.
Best.

Distance for her.

"So how do you feel about this whole case?" He asked ready to listen.
"Well," she sipped her red wine which coloured her lips perfectly melding with her lipstick, her nice pale facial features more lit with the light of her rosy cheeks.
He liked to listen, especially when they were this pretty. Although he probably should listen to the words. He focused in, trying his hardest to forget his shallow side, he was trying to bury it deep.
"I just think it was really difficult to do anything right, it was just so unexpected, like it was so unlikely. A man with shoulder pain, has an aneurysm, a guy who hits the gym and then gets shoulder pain, I mean it's not something you could have spotted."
He nodded along, she was giving him the alibi, he could grasp move their bodies closer in pity, he chose not to, because you can't have sex whilst having a heart attack, his chest pain flaring up with every one of her words.

"But Dr Abdul asked for a surgical review."
"We did that, technically."
"A lawyer technically, not a medical technically."
"Is there a difference anymore?"
"Hmm?" He was thrown back at her insight.
"Well people are always so scared of medico legal, and now we'll probably become very lawyer-y, I can already feel it will become a part of me." She admitted
"Like some kind of PTSD," he inquired.
"Yeah, a defence mechanism of our bodies, whether it helps us, or the patient is another question."
"It'll just be won't it." He gave in.
"Yeah, hang around like a bad smell. It'll be part of the answer to the question of who we are."
"But what we are is in flux. We can always change," he pleaded.
"Surely it compounds and dilutes," she added.
"Yeah true, but still, it doesn't have to define us, just contribute."
"You know when you listen you can be comforting. I can see why patients like you." She admitted.
He stopped for a moment; he swore he felt their bodies closer.

However, she had noted his movement and on one wiggle of her derriere now they were further
Apart.
"Patients, not people?" He asked not wanting the answer.
"You were listening, not just seeing this as flirting or some kind of conversation revolving around you." She said and then looked sad with her next sip.
"I'm going to bed." She gulped it down and floated all dream-like towards the room.
"You don't mind the couch again?"
"You're not really asking, are you?"
"Not really…".

The pause stung.
"Look I don't think we could have seen it coming, and I guess we have to thank Dr Abdul. It'd be wrong to let us be defined, he would not allow it." He added trying to fill the silence.
She smiled back, "you will definitely be a good doctor."
Izzy continued to float. Her body finally disappeared from his eyes. The next placement he wasn't with Izzy they were moving on, she'd be in general practice and him in psychiatry. In a way this was her

showing she was disappearing from his social life.
Patients would like him.
A good doctor.
He understood that she was implying he was a good doctor but maybe not a good person. Or at least that was her subjective truth about him. Her facts about him were not definitive, but at this moment, it was her way of saying I'm not interested. It was her saying I tolerate you because you are fun at work and work alone.
Speaking of which he looked up at his drink, took the rest as a shot, let his heartburn settle and started getting the couch ready for sleeping. Wrapping in the throw he thought again of her smell that was left over. At least she'd placate him at work, work **alone**, the words ringing in his head.
Ow well, he was good at being alone.
At least this "good doctor" was preserved. A sacrifice bore him to continue the one thing that made him tolerable to others, maybe he did care what others thought of him. He wasn't sure yet, probably he would never be 100% certain, but at least a little surer as his life went on.
He was uncertain and alone, what a sensation. He smirked as there were so many unknowns,

at least now some were known unknowns rather unknown unknowns.

Chapter 12: Unknown Unknowns (The trial: The final day)

Waking up after some good sex always put a smile on her face, but that was to be expected, Dr Rachel Amis was not that original, she likes movies and long walks on the beach. She, like every other person on the planet, liked sex. In times of uncertainty, the certainty of a partner who can make you orgasm was invaluable, like gold. During the first day of the trial, it had been relaxing, but the second a little scarier, the coroner slowly transforming from calming to questioning. She had seen the effects on cock sure Rich. He'd even been sombre and actually had a conversation at the cafe. She saw into his true self. She was still wrapped in the covers waiting for the other man in the room to finish using the shower, the heating was on and the steam from the bathroom was enticing her, she got warmer and warmer which made her feel good, God why did Britain never truly get warm. She fondly remembered warm holidays especially to Malaga and Ibiza, destinations where you can wear nothing and still be too warm. She

missed that feeling and knew this summer it wasn't possible to visit. She was an adult now; it was hard getting one week of let alone two weeks on the rota of a foundation doctor.
"So, last day, eh?"
She heard the voice come from the shower.
"Well, I thought it doesn't have to be our last day here." She made sure she sounded extra playful. Like the puppet he was after their session he replied eagerly.
"Ooooo I like the sound of that."
He paused before continuing.
"But..."
"But ugh, that doesn't sound like the good kind of but... Why don't you just come back to this but" She had replied quickly:
a) To make a good joke, plus always good to mention your but to a lover about to make an escape.
b) To slow the inevitable bad news, she was about to hear, like a child who didn't want to be told off.
"You know I've got that teaching seminar thing."
She walked to have a closer look and get warmer in the steam, although soon regretting not being in the duvet.
"Well, you barely mention it. I thought it was the excuse to get out of here."

"What makes you think I need excuses, anyway, you know me I do what I want."

"Yeah yeah sure sure, no one who does what they want, keeps mentioning that's what they're doing."

He grabbed her and gave her a deep kiss. It was a good tactic to shut her up, he was a little- scratch that- very vain and didn't like to be answered back to.

"Anyway, I better let you shower, you've got your trial as well."

"I feel you're avoiding the question…"

"What question," his voice acting surprised. Although she wasn't particularly convinced by it, her review of the acting skills would be quite critical.

"The one where I asked if you wanna stay here or do a few days in the city together, you seemed to enjoy that idea last night."

"Yeah but that was after I came, you know I'll say anything after that."

"Very common denominator humour there. I'm sure every guy has made that joke at one time in their unoriginal lives."

"Probably, clichés are cliché because they are common. I am a horse not a zebra."

Rolling her eyes only seemed to make his smile bigger. He continued to deflect, "So go get ready for your trial and I'm sure we'll work it out after okay."

"Yeah, sounds good," It didn't sound good to her, she'd much rather have something to look forward to, now there was going to be uncertainty all day.

She had dressed in a smart dress, one that was tighter on her compared to her university days. Nothing she owned fit to her now curvy appeal. Hopefully the outfit still maintained professionality. She hoped she had a "I swear I know what I'm talking about" look.

She looked again at herself in the mirror unsure she took off the dress and looked again at her underwear. She had been hopeful that the ones worn were enticing yet subtle as to show she didn't care, but she could still be sexy. God, she needed to write for cosmos she'd be fucking fantastic at it. The adjectives and expletives would add to her appeal as a writer, salt of the earth after all. Well as salt of the earth as a middle-class doctor could be. At least she was Liverpudlian, adding some credentials. She watched him on his way out as he made the obvious joke.

"I wouldn't wear that, might not work on the coroner, although on the other hand that's one way to make me jealous."

"Ha-ha, well done, weren't you fucking off?"

"Probably yeah."

He smirked as he ran out, she swore she saw a half chub, he definitely was a secret sub, well a not-so-secret sub...

*

The walk to the court was a little different as it was her turn, like a video game it was level 3 for player 3 and the way she walked felt as if the planet's gravity was given all to her, she watched as the two ,no longer involved but there to "show respect" which roughly translated to "saving face", glide, and bounce along, like gazelles on the moon, or man on the moon, whoever came of as the one easier to move, mixed metaphors aside she had to remember what her statement involved. She was going before the registrar and the expert opinion of Dr Bethany Anderson. So, she'd probably be forgotten as long as the questions from the bearded man didn't chew her out.

One step at a time the building loomed and like a dance floor of a rancid club, each time she lifted her foot she had to fight with the ground. More so because her foot decided to disagree with her hips and do the opposite of what her brain was asking. Yet none of her colleagues looked back.

She kept up, just about, the effort of her moving body completely exhausting.

She looked up at the doors of the grand old building which hosted more than the coroner's office. A myriad of businesses all shared the building. It was probably a money saver, but it did help her calm a little, there was always a law office upstairs. She could escape quickly to get her defence attorney, although it did make her wonder if that's why they had set up here, was it to prey on those doctors as they left the trial?

C
R
E
E
K

The doors opened with Rich and Izzy in front of her, almost like an air hostess allowing her into the flight, or perhaps something less appealing like the shepherds to the gates of hell.

Stop being so dramatic,

she heard her come down brain say to her, for once a supportive thought from the come down brain which over the last couple of months had become a separate identity in her.

*

She had pre-emptively taken the hot seat, which in reality felt quite cold on her now slightly bigger probably, well, definitely more attractive behind. She was sure it would warm up, one way or another.

Everyone stood with the coroner, she recognized the man sat with the family as the GP she had met before, the one who had made her think they could maybe help people, although that may be his bias inferring onto her bias. Also, it did depend on your definition of help.

"This is the last day where we will discuss the last hours of the life of Jason Argonaut, as you can understand this will be very highly emotional for all involved here. So, if at any moment proceedings need to be stopped, we can do so, we are here to support and ask the right questions, not to distress and blame."

The silence surprisingly echoed agreement between all the parties.

"Now we begin the third day and we have Dr Rachel Amis to tell us about her encounter with Jason. This will be followed by a few others; this is the encounter on 15th of March when he was admitted to resus as an emergency. Please proceed Dr Rachel Amis."

He looked over at her, his glance passing on the baton.

"Hello, um yes."

Breathe in you fool. God why had she done a little MDMA last night. It was only a smidge.

Can't even say your name right!

Even with a smidge the come down mind was out, in full force it seemed. The gates of hell open in her cerebral cortex. On a positive note, she remembered some neuroanatomy, something she knew she wasn't particularly good at, maybe come down Rachel was a certified genius. A dangerous thought some might say.

Well, I am much better than you anyway.

What an arrogant self-conscious she had.

"So, tell us about your involvement with the case of Jason Argonaut on his third attendance."

Coughing and clearing her throat like a singer before the stage.

You wish I'm sure it'll come out very flat.

She breathed in, "So I had been doing a locum shift, a shit where you fill in for a space within the rota."

Tell them about the rates you charged.

"And we had finished seeing the patients in our surgical assessment unit where we assessed those well enough to come and sit down before being seen."

A pause to look up at the family, she saw the GP with the kind face explaining everything she was saying. She tried to use less jargon but even less than a year into being a doctor you really adopt the language, one of the easiest second languages to learn the jargon of the modern techno doc. It was based on an ancient language like many others, the jargon of the self-assured arrogant pretentious old school doc. There was now jargon to explain how you were speaking too much jargon.

"After that the job of the foundation doctor is to go down to the emergency department and start seeing patients who may be for the surgical team or even need surgery and report back to the registrar who would be, with help of a consultant when needed, leading the management of the cases including performing surgery."

Yeah, and tell them how you thought you should be managed by him, or maybe how I was with you the whole time because you hadn't been all clear headed by that time in the afternoon, that far into the hangover; come down combined.

She resisted the urge to say the last bit aloud.

"Then Dr Abdul asked for my assistance with a patient who would likely need surgery."

"Likely?"

"Well, I guess definitely, the patient."

She was cut off by the coroner who stopped her continue the depersonalisation, "Jason Argonaut"

Tell him he's a bastard, only I get to make you feel bad.

"Yes, Jason Argonaut was very ill. We thought there must be a bleed of some sort."

"Bleed of some sort?"

"Well bleeding, yes he was behaving like a patient who was bleeding."

"Was this visible?"

"No, I guess internal bleeding from one of his vessels, primarily the main one in the chest and abdomen called the aorta."

"So, your involvement in such an acute case, from my understanding and from your description it sounded like you needed senior input."

"Yes, correct."

"Did you get this?"

"Yes."

Did you? Didn't he already know!

"So, you informed your senior and were involved then in the effort."

By involved you mean standing there, listening to the heart once, which was already done.

"Hey! I wrote stuff down." Accidently airing her dirty laundry.

A silence, the stress getting to everyone she was forgiven by the faces she saw all around her.

"Yes, we scanned him with ultrasound and my *registrar* Mr Mothinder Fernandez asked us to contact the vascular team and get the theatre ready. He needed a quick operation, or he was going to die."

How convenient, life or death.

"Was there anything else you were involved in?"

Go on, tell them you did the preop, you were the pre-op doctor, you did fill in that paperwork.

Whilst it was true that wasn't in her prepared statement and in reality, the anaesthetist would have to check it anyway, the hospital lawyer had said it was irrelevant.

Was it, did you check that the work you had done had been checked?

It wasn't her job.

But everything is part of your job, isn't that what they taught us.

She wasn't in the right mood to check.

What, your excuse is I was hanging, so someone else had to pick up my slack.

It was meant to be someone else who did it anyway, it was the one time she was allowed to be wrong; she was learning.

A pause before she spoke, she let the word escape her mouth,

"no."

LIAR!

She wondered if she had seen everyone have a disappointing look on them, from Mothinder down to the coroner down to the sister of the patient. As if they all knew she was the perioperative doctor, she was waiting for the objection. It didn't come. However, no matter the justification, to be called out would be the nicer punishment, instead she had to deal with it internally.

Oh, it'll be tough, think how much you drink and use now, you'll always have me hanging around. I ain't feeling sorry for you or us, whatever you want to call this Gollum like interaction. Even this isn't your own original work.

No one ever felt sorry for her whether it was her action as a doctor or a person. At least she'd feel good and continue her job. She distracted herself thinking about what exciting and adventurous things her and Dean would do tonight. She had a few things prepared for it, including what was underneath the smart and lovely looking dress she had worn.

"Thank you very much Dr Amis. Next it will be Dr Abdul who will tell us about the emergency management in the case."

She stood up and walked past the family and the GP, he smiled at her, she mustered a smile back before turning away, her tired eyes leading her to sit next to the group of other doctors potentially spared by these days, spared because they didn't know, and they weren't expected to know.

It was bad form but she did nap during the next bit, she was brought back when the words coffee was muttered, well more likely because Izzy jabbed her so hard in her love handle she felt electricity through her whole body, god that girl was bony, bony wasn't as sexy as she thought it would be.

Jealousy is the highest form of flattery.

She thought imitation was.

Well, you just being mean is because you wish you were bony again.

Coffee would shut herself up, come down on her always hated coffee. She'd need a strong one, a cortado.

Not a cortado, can't we compromise on latte or maybe decaf.

"No compromise today." She walked, speaking a little louder than she should have, but it was already too late to save face.

*

Awake and come down suppressed the trial was able to continue objectively for her. She watched Mr Mothinder Fernandez take the stage. He strutted and entered stage left for the final song of this play.

"Now let us begin with our last session, once again I reiterate that this is an emotional time, and we can pause, and we can excuse people as needed."

No one stirred apart from a small pant from each member of the family, she wondered if it reflected badly that no one from the medical world made any effort to move. Although maybe the internal grief in a way is more respectful. The ability to stay solemn and carry this for what she imagined would be most of her medical care, Jason Argonaut would live forever in her medical practice.

"So, Mr Mothinder Fernandez you were previously involved in giving advice about Jason's case but you were also the surgeon on call when he re-attended the third time?"

"Yes."

"Please tell us about Jason and your involvement."

Jason is the only person who the coroner didn't use full title and name for, it was a smart move she thought, humanising him, whilst leaving them as perched angels or devils involved in the sacred life of an innocent lamb.

"So, in the first instance I was asked to provide advice over the telephone about Jason."

Not charismatic like normal, the angular man was curt and official, efficient, almost cold. He had also emphasised the word telephone. She could feel Rich stir despite the two seat and one-person buffer.

"In which the probability, given the story I was told, was that it was a chronic muscular problem or a problem which could be followed up by Jason's doctor."

The coroner didn't interrupt, she expected him to but even he was caught in the flow of words. The angular man clasped the paper as if it were a dumbbell and continued to look down and read.

"As we all know there were other nuances in the case that over the telephone, I wasn't aware of, however the doctor had made a decent assessment and a conclusion that is to be expected of a foundation doctor."

There was no way to read that apart from derogatory, although she had watched the registrar try his best to remain neutral, well apart from his word choice.

"Unfortunately, as everyone is aware Jason then re-presented due to the development of his pain and symptoms and on triage it was noted he was a lot more ill and qualified for immediate attention in resus. I was then informed of the case and made my way down to be involved immediately."

"Given that you thought the case was chronic and muscular, why the hurry?"

The first intervention to test the angular man, who with his quick edges was able to reply. Luckily everyone had ignored the "who had actually called him", no one had noticed the inconsistency between hers and Mo's stories. For a moment part of her wished they did, she was feeling guiltier by the second.

You should do, say you object, go on.

She knew she wouldn't and what was the voice doing back. Damn it wasn't a properly made cortado, probably only one and half shots of coffee. That barista did look confused at the order!

"Well, his observation had changed, and they were signs of bleeding, so the very unlikely had obviously occurred and me having done a vascular surgery job within my registrar training knew that action and theatre was needed immediately."

"Very well and you organised the effort."

"Well involving the emergency and anaesthetic consultant we got things ready."

He had gone with her lie, although she hadn't seen the anaesthetist at resus, and she now wondered more than ever if he had checked her work.

"Very well, was this what was expected in this case?"

It was the very first time he looked up, looking straight at the family, his edges, his angles, they softened. He went from an acute aggressive drawing to soft blurs of colours before her very eyes as he spoke.

"I knew that we didn't perform acute vascular surgery in the unit, and he was meant for a tertiary centre but there was a very real case he wouldn't make it. I immediately informed the vascular consultant on call who happened to live nearby and took him to the theatre to begin the case as I had skills which could

Save

his

life!"

She noticed it was like one of the first episodes in the television show ER. However, she doubted Mo knew about that and probably meant every bit of the generic arrogant statement, this wasn't an act it was his true belief, which was why he was able to be the senior *registrar* on call and is why he had made it that far in his training.
"So, you acted in the best interest and by the sounds of it had a contingency plan." The coroner replied, completely drawn into the soft circular man's story.
"Yes, that is correct. However."
A pause at the word however, it was the fancy way of saying but after all.
"However?"
The family now looked enthralled, they would read a novel written by Mothinder, it was direct and to the point, no neurotic faffing around. It also had gory details and a hero character.

No wanted a story about multiple people who all screwed up a little who didn't particularly give off a hero's journey vibe.

"Well, the case was pretty far advanced and when starting it was an uphill battle."

She watched the family now eating up the words and they were enjoying the meal, lapping it up eagerly, they'd leave a good trip advisor review.

"Can we have details rather than metaphors?" The coroner asked, the one critic in the room.

At least someone said it.

Both of her identities could agree this time.

"Well, there had been a lot of blood loss and it was an almost complete rupture of the vessel running through the chest which supplied the body. We clamped it and tried to sew it but the blood loss was already too much, by the time the vascular surgeon arrived there wasn't much else to do unfortunately and that was the hardest thing to accept. We of course continued and spent hours in theatre. Trying to save life, trying to fight Death!"

The nodding heads from the family were like a standing ovation for Mo.

"Very well."

Even the critic enthralled, universally loved this story would be. Mr Mothinder Fernandez's story would be the only one remembered here, for the rest of them involved nothing will be remembered except by them. They would carry it and life would roll on and roll over. It would continue. She would probably drink and maybe do a little less drugs. Rich would make jokes and Izzy would be wiser than her words but no one will notice because she'll always be the quiet one.

*

They all stood there; the curtain called the coroner stood to read his final statement. The family sat down solemnly, but maybe more understanding, no one angry, no one pointing blaming fingers at them, in a way no one cared about their involvement really. It seemed there was something bigger at fault whether that be God, the system, the collective or culture, it just wasn't one of the individuals who had started with her in the emergency department at the start of the year, although all of them were quiet. She swore she saw the wounds and dirt around their faces in their expression as if they were returning soldiers, the war had been declared by the government, they were inconsequential, the government was to blame here.

"So, in summary and with a little advice as was written by a senior clinician reviewing the case Dr Bethany Anderson, who could not attend due to other comments within the trauma network."

She wondered if Dr Anderson had asked for that much detail to be given away, it was a strong move after all.

"Jason Argonaut attended the emergency department three times, where the case was managed by different clinicians in different ways, every time given the evidence in front of them nothing would be done differently in 99% of those reviews. The biggest issue on the third attendance was his mode of arrival through triage and into a centre without vascular expertise. This is something that may have changed the outcome, but something which was not controllable given the circumstances and Dr Bethany Anderson is in agreement to this.

This was a failure of systems; a **Swiss Cheese Model** in which mistakes or missed opportunity all coincided and the holes matched up in this disaster, the avoidable loss of Jason's life.

This investigation will be forwarded onto the trust and the emergency department board to think about and learn from.

I thank everyone involved, especially the family who have been an undeniable important facet to this process. Apart from my mixed metaphors everyone has done their bit today and may you all live and learn from this. Thank you, please sit and then leave in an orderly fashion."

She wondered at that moment was the justice delivered enough for the doctors and more importantly was it enough for the family. Their faces said for today it was. She tried to match it, learning what face to hold whenever asked about these last three days.

*

She watched as Izzy and Rich boarded the train, they had everything they needed, and each carried their baggage.

"So, I guess I'll see ya guys back at Darthington."

"Yeah, we'll get something organised, a game night or something," Izzy smiled.

She smiled back; it was an attempt at normality.

"Yeah, I can beat all of you." Rich bellowed.

Normal felt different, but it was as close to normal as she would get. She tried her best bellow to join in.

A redundant and meaningless noise.

Yeah, she thought, a meaningless noise, how punk.

Returning to the Airbnb, her empty room left too much space for her thoughts to disperse and gather in front of her eyes. She waited as the clock ticked, any moment he would come, she could be distracted, she could feel good.

*

Being an hour late was a little unfair, so she finally gave in to playing the game and went for the telephone.
It rang.
Once
Twice.
Three times.
Still no answer.
About to give up, finally his voice, in a hushed tone came though.
"Hey, what's up?"
She was meant to be cool and chill, but the day had made her reach her limit, she now knew where the line for her was.
Never go to a coroner's court and then wait an hour for a shag, you might be cranky if you're Rachel!
She whispered to herself. She felt the sarcasm didn't help her anger levels.
"What's up, come on you know what's up you twat!"
Her Liverpudlian accent shone through. Her liberal use of certain words was also there.
"Alright Cilia." He Responded with a certain I am the wittiest tone. However, she thought it was a terrible reference, cilia never swore, at least not on the telly.

"So, I guess what's up was we had the Airbnb for one more night."
"Oh yeah, I forgot sorry the fiancée called. We didn't finalise our plans anyway."
"I assumed the fact you didn't reply meant go ahead."
She wasn't very happy at all and her gut recoiled, mixing sadness and anger, *sanger*. Ooo, she could do with some sangria.
"No replying meant no answer, it's like someone not replying to your time and date. You wouldn't then turn up to where they haven't said yes to."
"But they said yes days before deciding on the time and date."
She was definitely needing sangria after this.
"Yeah, I guess, but you're assuming, you can't assume." He was wriggling.
She tried to reel him back in.
"I think it's unfair."
However, he snapped or tangled her line in the next sentence.
"Well, I don't think you get to choose what's unfair, she is my fiancée, you're someone I shag."
"Umm well."
"And we'll shag again anyway, maybe it doesn't matter, it matters for me that I stay with my future wife."
"Ohhh..."

She spoke to herself internally, wishing for her Liverpudlian fire.

"You… you."

"I thought we were clear on the expectations here."

They had been via their words, the actions and Dean's behaviour had not.

I mean it is a little what you deserve. Come down her screamed into her mind with glee.

"Anyway, just enjoy some alone time. I gotta go, I don't want her thinking anything."

"Oh yeah I guess we don't want people to know what they probably already know. Or even worse, know the **truth**."

"I don't think you get to ride the high horse, if I'm in the dirt so are you."

"A little mud wrestling?" She relented

"I'm sure that can be arranged back at Darthington."

She didn't respond, that was the strongest she managed, not able to say no, but she wasn't going to say yes.

A small silence and she hit hang up.

The room was cold, no heating on, she reached the last bottle of red in the guest house and hunted for anything citrus, a makeshift sangria was made, she didn't know she could make sangria so tasty as she sipped it. It was an unknown unknown about her sangria skills.

At least she learnt one thing today and that was to accept she knew little else.
She sighed.
He was a bastard anyway.
Least he got some flak from her come down mind, small steps after all. She was a bitch yes, but he definitely was a bastard. Or some other horrible word that most people down south wouldn't tolerate if they could read her mind.
She shouted it out after her next sip, "what a cu…"

The End

A Gathering of appendixes:

Appendix 1: Dr Abdul 1 month later

He had read the letter to himself again.

Dear Doctor,

Re: Dr Abdul
31 Amcourt way
DT5 6ER

I met this lovely gentleman who is an established professor in emergency medicine who had ongoing symptoms of gastric irritation as well as ulceration. He had been losing weight and appetite and had put this down to the stressful job and his age, whilst this was understandable, we elected to investigate further with an endoscope and further CT scan as you are very well aware.

Given that at our last clinic appointment we talked about the results and unfortunately, we found gastric cancer staged at t3n2m1.

As you can understand this is quite an advanced stage and whilst there are no surgical options and limited chemotherapy options, we had a long discussion about outcomes, and we have elected for palliative supportive care in which Dr. Abdul is happy to fully engage in and we appreciate your ongoing care and support for this patient.

Many Thanks,
Dr Phillip Throne
MRCP FRCP Diploma of gastroenterological oncology, BSC MBCHC MRES PHD.

He had resigned months ago when he had found out. Now the trial was long gone, and he watched his wife packing for the Indian subcontinent, to try and tick off the bucket lists. At least he'd be allowed lots of morphine, it was weird she looked more beautiful as she loaded the taxi. She dressed beautifully for the plane and for once it was for him as well as the outside world.

"Alright get moving you're not dead yet." She smiled back and he let his eyes relax and smiled back at her. He felt happy, content and ready. They let the taxi drive them towards the ending. They rode together towards the beautiful sunset.

Appendix 2: Dr Bethany Anderson 21 months later

She stood having just had another meeting with the new registrars joining the unit at the Royal. They had a good trauma background and knew how to talk the talk, although she could see no twinkle in their eye. They were competent and that's what the royal looked for, it needed more doctors given the increased pressure with the reduced hours and further reduced services at Darthingtons emergency department. Basically, her old work place covered nothing acute after the investigation last year. Even the place and office where she had been a junior to Dr Abdul had disappeared.

She walked and got into her car, the Tesla. It now had a few more scratches and was a little more worn down now she commuted a larger distance as she worked in the city. The small village had kept it pristine, now it was a little more ragged and harder worked but got to be shown to more people, she wondered if it was a good trade off. She looked at her phone. She saw that for once she had time to spare. She picked up the phone and rang James.

"Hey"

"Hey"

"So, you're picking up Millie then for this week?" She inquired.

"Yeah, we said 7 pm, I'm surprised you're ringing this early to delay."

"No, I was ringing to say I'm happy for any time after 6."

"Very well that sounds brilliant." His voice was happy yet hurting her due to how really happy it did sound.

"She's very excited for you as always, don't treat her too much. You know it's unfair if I'm the bad guy." She pleaded.

"Yeah, I can be mean." He was distant.

"So, are you happy with that?" She tried to grab his attention.

"Cool well I'll see ya after 6, bye." A cold tone from both James and her phone.

The cold hang up tone continued, she wanted to say love you but had missed her chance. As always.

She drove the Tesla to the Darthingtons' cemetery. She arrived and grabbed the now slightly drying flowers as she walked to a tomb stone etched with the plaque, she had looked up to for all those years. She had been a little driven and not seen the signs that would have told her she didn't have much time with him and the last conversation with him whilst nice left so many things unsaid, so many apologies forgotten, so many moments never spoken about, and thus it would always be.

She looked up at the winter sunset before placing the coronations on the slab. Moments in silence passed before she knew it, she had to leave to be on time.

She read the plaque one last time,

Mr. Abdul AbuRahman Assem, FRCEM, MRCP, PHD, MRCS, Directorate of Education and simulation at Darthington River District General Hospital.

She left and she looked at the time, she smiled and imagined that the old dog would ***genuinely*** laugh that for once she managed to be on time.

Appendix 3: Izzy, Rich and Rach four and half years later

He had stood in the queue of the busy pub for quite a few minutes now, all three of them invited to his event. He read the program he had prepared. He read it aloud, almost proud of his name on the flyer.
Dr Ebbidah - views around the uses of local community hospitals and the services it successfully provided for its people. He watched the three doctors he had seen at the trial in front and was intrigued about them accepting his invitation. They also hadn't noticed their conversation being too loud not to be heard by eavesdroppers. The scene unfolded in front of him like an unrehearsed play.

Int Jarlsberg pub
Sunny afternoon, summertime.

Izzy
It's so nice to see you guys. Been ages since we caught up
Rachel
Yeah, we all look a little too old now, probably finally old enough to try and actually get a games night organised!

Rich
Well after all we did get promised another one.
Izzy
I would do it but the husband is picking me up after this.
Rich
Wow, husband, I see that probably explains why you have something small and shiny on your finger.
Izzy
Well small is mean! I think it's lovely.
Rich
I definitely could have gotten you something bigger.
Rachel
Or your dad could have.

Laughter in the group echoed through the pub like a studio audience.

Izzy
What are you up to these days Rach, still sticking around here?
Rach
Yeah, I'm a northern girl but kind of found my place here in GP. Plus, I'm a junior partner now! I'm a big boss.
Rich
Lucky for some

Izzy
What have you been doing Rich?
Rich
"Well just locum-ing, making the big bucks, hence why I could have gotten a much larger engagement rock Izzy.
Izzy
Of course, but maybe there's something else which is bigger and rock like with the hubby.
Rich
You don't have a reference point to compare and define big I feel.
Rach
But she can definitely tell your overcompensating

Again, the laughter continued as they moved closer to the bar with their camera man (what he chose to describe himself as), too enthralled in their story which provided some easy listening and lowest common denominator humour. He thought and hoped the play he eavesdropped on was enjoyable. It was probably an average sitcom at best.

Rach
So, Izzy apart from avoiding board games with us and being a wife to this husband, anything you're doing these days?
Izzy

Well, I'm doing anaesthetic training, which is fun, I learnt all sorts of stuff and do get to be a little bossier, now I'm a registrar.

Rich

Oh, wow you're a hero then now, you can't tell me that and flaunt your ring, breaking my heart aren't you!

Izzy

Well, I guess you're breaking your own heart with jealousy.

Rich

Ha, I'm ruined again, I bet you are married to a meddling kid, and I bet he has a pesky dog?"

A terrible reference but one that got the group mutually laughing, it sounded polite, but it was still laughter, and he was sure he could see the energy emitting from them infected the room. They finally arrived at the bar and the bartender joined their play.

Izzy

I'll get this

Rich

Ooo big spender, I feel like the locum I can treat ya all

Rach

I'm just going to sit back and enjoy whoever wants to treat me, although I've changed a little, I'll only give so much away for a drink, not all of it, leave some mystery eh.

Izzy

You see it should be me, I'm the dink, you guys are sinks.

Rach

Wow you're confident. There really has been a big change for you! There's been no umms, but a sink might be an old Izzy insult.

Rich

Old Izzy doesn't insult

Izzy

No guys, it's an anagram. As in I have double income no kids, a sink, compared to single income no kids, a sink.

Rach

Well, done you've managed to shag and use condoms and you were good enough at it that you convinced a man to stick around. I don't see why that makes you the drink buyer.

Izzy

It's quite the talent, don't you think? Don't be too jealous, I'd say green isn't your colour Rach. It was more Rich's if I remember.

Rich

Ow wow, too much for me there, I'm really going to go home and cry tonight. But if you're that happy go ahead, but I warn you my drinks aren't cheap.

Izzy

You know it's the Jarlsberg, it's well cheap.

The bartender looked at them, also having eavesdropped. He proceeded to ask Izzy about the order.

Izzy
Well, I'll have a medium glass of Pinot please.
Rich
Ooft fancy I'm proud Izzy, Rach as they say ladies first.
Rach
Well, I'll just have a Diet Coke.
Rich
Woah you have changed, no alcohol, mental.
Rach
It's only noon.
Izzy
Goodness, I have to agree with Rich.
Rach
Well, agree away the both of yease. I'll be having fuckin' diet coke, *please.*
Rich
Fine, fine you terrible Scouse. I'll have a pint of Jarlsberg ale.
Bartender
Very well all coming up. Any food? We have a Swiss cheese platter on offer today.

They all nodded. He watched them take their order number. He watched the three walk around the pub, it was an old church after all and sat down in a pew style booth. It was almost holy. After years of being in the town he smiled to himself as he finally got the pub's name. He looked up at the old painted sign hanging above the bar.

Welcome to The Jarlsberg.
An old church, now a public house.
However, Christians don't fret.
After all there's nothing holier than Swiss cheese.

A shit pun, but one that brought a smile to his face.

The Actual End.

Dr Ziyad Elgaid Bsc, MBchB and MRCGP

Raised in Glasgow and having graduated from the universities of St Andrews and Manchester in 2016. He has worked as a junior doctor in London prior to completing GP training in Devon in 2021.

He has always had a keen interest in people's stories and hence why he chose general practice to base his career in. Based in Exeter a city with many tales and using his experience having studied, lived and worked from north to south of the Great British Isles, he is now using his interest in writing and the stories around him to set foot into the world of books.

If all goes well hopefully more stories to come………

Printed in Great Britain
by Amazon